What People [Are Saying About]
Sharon Ewell [Foster's]

Ain't No [River]

"Foster's prose is often evocative and eloquent.... A rewarding read from an author to watch."

PUBLISHERS WEEKLY

"An entertaining story about family and relationships that incorporates the wisdom of Bible verses throughout...a well-written story."

BOOKLIST

"Ms. Foster has exceptional talent in creating a wonderful book. And in preaching the Word without being preachy. I eagerly look forward to more of her work."

SCRIBES WORLD REVIEWS

"*Ain't No River* is beautifully written and reaffirms Ms. Foster's place among the literary elite."

PAMELA WALKER-WILLIAMS, PageTurner.net

"A must-read, inspirational, and spirit-filled account of human struggle that transcends generations, gender, economic status, and cultural differences."

RHONDA K. SUTTLE, National Director, NAACP ACT-SO

"Like a tune that sticks in your mind, *Ain't No River* will stay with you long after you've finished reading the last page."

CANDY DAVISON,
Women's Ministries Coordinator, Sandy Cove Ministries

"*Ain't No River* will capture your heart and soul."

VANESSA WOODWARD, founder and CEO, Journey's End

"Ain't no other book like *Ain't No River*! Foster unveils her flawed characters layer by layer and then dresses them up in redemption."

NETA JACKSON, Trailblazer Books and Hero Tales

A truly unforgettable story—a story that touches the emotions deeply and reminds us that there is always hope."

ALICE GRAY, creator and compiler of the bestselling
Stories for the Heart series

"A rhapsody in prose. It is an intriguing look back that also speaks loudly to the times we live in. For a religious novel to simmer in the African American religious tradition yet carry a universal message is a rarity. Readers will be thankful for this rare and splendid work of love, faith, and art."

> BARBARA A. REYNOLDS, president, Reynolds News Service;
> author, radio talk show/television news commentator,
> syndicated columnist

"*Passing by Samaria* takes a sensitive and thoughtful look at a revolutionary time in American history. Foster's characters are unforgettable; full of life and unhesitatingly charming, they drive this powerful book."

> KWEISI MFUME, president and CEO, NAACP

"A stirring novel.... Searches the depths of purpose, reconciliation, and the high calling of God's love."

> FRANCINE RIVERS, bestselling author of *Redeeming Love*

"Sharon Foster introduces a vibrant new voice to inspirational fiction, offering wisdom and insights that are deep, rich, and honest. With uncanny accuracy, she climbs into the minds and hearts of her characters—young and old, male and female, black and white, rich and poor. *Passing by Samaria* is about much more than race; it's about grace, pure and simple. A glorious, life-changing read!"

> LIZ CURTIS HIGGS, bestselling author of
> *Bad Girls of the Bible* and *Bookends*

This stunning first book by a gifted author sings from the first page to the last. A literary masterpiece!"

> DIANE NOBLE, award-winning author of *Come, My Little Angel*

"The world has a fine new storyteller in Sharon Foster. *Passing by Samaria* is a gift of characters and story and faith."

> ROBERT BENSON, author of *Living Prayer* and
> *Between the Dreaming and the Coming True*

"This unique addition to the Christian fiction genre is highly recommended for all collections."

> *LIBRARY JOURNAL*

Sharon Ewell Foster

Riding Through Shadows

Multnomah®Publishers *Sisters, Oregon*

This book is a work of fiction. The characters, incidents, and dialogues are products of the author's imagination and are not to be construed as real. Any resemblance to actual events or persons, living or dead, is entirely coincidental.

RIDING THROUGH SHADOWS
published by Multnomah Publishers, Inc.
© 2001 by Sharon Ewell Foster

Published in association with the literary agency of Sara A. Fortenberry

International Standard Book Number: 1-57673-807-8

Cover image by Mike McGovern/Index Stock Imagery
Background cover image by Image Bank
Cover design by Chris Gilbert/Uttley DouPonce DesignWorks

Scripture quotations from *The Holy Bible,* King James Version

The Holy Bible, New International Version (NIV) © 1973, 1984 by International
Bible Society, used by permission of Zondervan Publishing House

Multnomah is a trademark of Multnomah Publishers, Inc.,
and is registered in the U.S. Patent and Trademark Office.
The colophon is a trademark of Multnomah Publishers, Inc.

Printed in the United States of America

For information:
MULTNOMAH PUBLISHERS, INC.•Post Office Box 1720•Sisters, Oregon 97759

Library of Congress Cataloging-in-Publication Data:
Foster, Sharon Ewell.
   Riding through shadows / by Sharon Ewell Foster.
      p. cm.   ISBN 1-57673-807-8 (pbk.)
   1. African American girls—fiction. I. Title
PS3556.O7724 R5 2001   813'.54—dc21   2001003174

01 02 03 04 05 06 07 08—10 9 8 7 6 5 4 3 2 1 0

For Ervin McIntyre
Thank you.

Acknowledgments

*M*y writing is only a reflection of the rest of my life—my spiritual, physical, mental, and emotional growth and health. So, I am honored to thank all of the people who nurture me and bless me.

Thank you to Minister Darlene Gray and the Morning Glory Intercessors at New Psalmist Baptist Church.

Thank you to Minister Allan Gray and the Tuesday morning "God Chasers" discipleship class. I love you all.

Thank you to Minister Allan Gray, my sister Sandra Foster Heard (thank you for your God-ordained deeds when I was in Chicago), and the most honorable Reverend James T. Meeks, pastor of Salem Baptist Church of Chicago. In one weekend, in three different locations, each of you unknowingly ministered to me about the effects of prayer on unseen realms and breathed life into this book. Thank you for being God's good servants.

Thank you to Andrew Attaway and the entire Guideposts family, which has enfolded and encouraged me.

Thank you to NAACP President Kweisi Mfume, the NAACP, and other guardians of freedom for fighting the good fight and for opening doors.

Thank you to Multnomah editorial VP Bill Jensen, my editor Karen Ball, and my agent Sara Fortenberry for leading me to the ring.

Thank you to Robin Green of Sibanye, Inc.; Clara Villarosa of The Hue-man Experience; Emma Rogers of Black Images; Black Writers Alliance founder Tia Shabazz; African American Literature Book Club founder Troy Johnson; Black Images Book Review editor Mondella Jones; Pat G'Orge Walker and Angela Benson for showing me the ropes.

Thank you to my lovely mother, my handsome father, and my beloved brothers and their families—all my nephews, nieces, and cousins. Love is worth fighting for.

Thank you to my adopted Starks family members—Daddy Steve, Mama Marian, Coach Steve, Vanyanee, Janee, Thai, Lexie, Lynn, Matthew, CJ, Candy, Baby Julius, Clarence, and my bestest buddy Portia, who is always listening, praying, and laughing with me.

Thank you to the little girl from Living Word Bookstore in Chicago and the Elkton High School honors English classes and Youth Outreach for Christ. Thank you, Ms. Jury, Ms. Thomas, and Ms. Black.

Thank you to Karen Walker, marketing whiz, for being a friend and for all your support. May your love and marriage be exceedingly and abundantly beyond anything you could think or imagine. Thank you to Joel Kneedler, publicist and friend.

Thank you to Mother Johnson and Sister Doretha Brown.

Thank you to Liz Higgs, Diane Noble, and Francine Rivers for your sisterly love and encouragement.

Thank you to Mrs. Helen Canady, Mrs. Helen Wachter, and Mrs. Ledora Allen Williams.

Thank you to U.S. Army Master Sargent MSG Tony Epps for reminding me that fitness is a lifestyle change. Thank you to U.S. Army Sargent Major Freddie Davis for a frank conversation and much inspiration. And thank you to the Lord for satisfying my mouth with good things so that my youth is renewed as the eagle's.

Thank you to those who minister into my life—Bishop T. D. Jakes, Joyce Meyer, Evangelist Jackie McCullough, Reverend Valerie Wells, and Minister Terry Hawkins. Thank you to the visionary pastor of the New Psalmist Baptist Church of

Baltimore, Reverend Dr. Walter Scott Thomas, First Lady Thomas, and the New Psalmist Family. Thank you to my spiritual father and mother, Bishop Howard Oby and Mother Portia Oby.

Thank you to my cousin LaJuana for always loving me and for bringing Tyler, Texas, to life.

Thank you to all my East St. Louis and St. Louis friends and relatives, especially Lena (Sydney's mommy), Debbie, Jaye, Angela, Stephanie, Tye Taylor, Chuck Spearman, Jerome Heavens, and Ervin.

With great love, I thank my children, Lanea and Chase, who lifted my wings as I flew into my brand-new life.

Finally, God, I thank You for Your faithfulness and for keeping Your promises. I thank You for restoring ALL, for loving me first, and for being all that You are in my life. Be alive in this book, and may it be pleasing in Your sight.

*For our light and momentary troubles are achieving for us
an eternal glory that far outweighs them all.
So we fix our eyes not on what is seen, but on what is unseen.
For what is seen is temporary, but what is unseen is eternal.*

2 CORINTHIANS 4:17–18, NIV

*For our struggle is not against flesh and blood, but against
the rulers, against the authorities, against the powers of this
dark world and against the spiritual forces of evil
in the heavenly realms.
Therefore put on the full armor of God,
so that when the day of evil comes, you may be able to stand your
ground, and after you have done everything, to stand.*

EPHESIANS 6:12–13, NIV

*Lift up your heads, O ye gates, and be ye lift up,
ye everlasting doors; and the King of glory shall come in.
Who is the King of glory?
The LORD strong and mighty, the LORD might in battle.*

PSALM 24:7–9

*Yea, though I walk through the valley of the shadow of death,
I will fear no evil.*

PSALM 23:4

PROLOGUE

If I could see Sheri again, I would tell her. I would tell her that what happened at her mother's house had very little, if anything, to do with her. I would tell her that her mother probably didn't even know. That she probably didn't do it on purpose. That her mother probably had other things that tormented her. I would tell Sheri how they did not believe me—did not believe me about her. We would laugh and talk about how they poked and prodded me. How they did not believe me. How sometimes even I wondered. I would tell her that despite everything, I made it—I did shine.

I would rub her shoulder, if I saw her again, and tell Sheri to rest.

PART 1

ONE

❧

Huntsville, Alabama, 1986

ommy. Mommy!" Shirley's youngest child's voice startled her. "Mika won't leave me alone. She keeps looking at me. And making faces."

"What is it, Lexington? What is she doing, exactly?" Shirley looked toward the door and heard Lex's feet scuffing on the floor. She imagined that he was shifting his body weight—what there was of it—from foot to foot. Shirley made sure she did not raise her voice. "Can't the two of you just get along?"

"You know how she is, Mommy. Mika is irritating me. She's *trying* to make me fight her." His six-year-old fingers played with the doorknob. "On *purpose*," he added.

Shirley fought to keep the smile out of her voice. "Mika, are you annoying your brother on purpose?" It was hard to find time for some good, old-fashioned self-pity with the two of them around.

Another set of feet flew down the hall, more fingers on the

door. "Mommy, you know how *Lexington* is." Mika, her eldest, cleared her throat. A bomb was coming. "Besides, he *knows* you told us not to tattletale."

Shirley shifted where she sat on the bed, reached for her book of daily devotionals, and stuck it into her overnight bag. It helped her convince herself that she was making headway packing, getting ready. "You are right, Mika. We're not tattletales. But you know what? It's not nice to pick on people smaller than you. You know that. I know you don't want to start off the trip already in trouble. So stop irritating your brother."

Silence. Then, "Mommy, Lexington is gloating!" Mika always called her younger brother by his full name when she was angry with him.

"No gloating, Lex. Gloating is just as bad as irritating." Shirley leaned and picked her powder blue nightcap up off the floor. Sometime ago, someplace she couldn't remember, someone told her that blue was a powerful color. Sounded good to her. She was trying to grab hold of every little piece of power she could find right now. "I hope with all this going on that the two of you are ready: teeth brushed, socks and shoes on… We have to be out of here in a few hours."

Shirley lifted her head and stared into the dresser mirror across from her. She had it all together and knew exactly where she was going.

Right.

She rubbed her hand over her self-done, homemade haircut. It suited her mood, but something about it reminded her of a bad toupee. Reminded her of a man she had seen on the city bus when she was much younger—the first time she realized some black men also wore those bad wigs. The thing on his head had looked rough, had looked alien, had looked obvious. "Why bother?" she had wanted to yell to the back of his head, to the black scouring pad on top of his head.

There were still whispers outside the door.

"Are you all ready?" Shirley didn't expect an answer, not really.

Fingers left the doorknob, feet flew in the opposite direction, down the carpeted hallway. "Almost." Mika's word sounded like it was following her toward the room she and Lex shared.

Shirley strained to hear their muted voices. "Here, *Lex-ing-ton,* take your toothbrush. Hurry, before we get in trouble."

She stood, walked to the door, and opened it to hear better.

"Do you love me, Mika?"

"Yeah, Lex, I love you. Now, hurry up before we get in trouble."

Shirley exhaled the breath she'd been holding—didn't realize she'd been holding until the air went out of her—and relaxed a little. "That's what I like to hear, you all. Take care of each other." They were busy; it was quiet. She could look out the window and cry, just let the feelings worm their way through her bones.

She walked to the dresser, laid one of her hands on the brown legal-size envelope, leaned her weight forward onto her hands, and bowed her head. It was way too hard to pray, so she cried and ached, opened her mouth and screamed—but not out loud. Not anything that would distress or worry the kids. She pressed down harder. In their little apartment, there was no room for a wailing wall. The dresser could take it; Mika and Lex couldn't.

Across the room rain fell outside the window. The green

grass, the gray color of the sky, the way the water collected on the glass pane making tiny streams—it reminded her of home. Of one of her homes. There hadn't been so much tension then. She didn't have to remind herself then to relax her shoulders, to mentally press them back into place.

It reminded her of the days just before she met Sheri.

"Mommy?"

Shirley turned her head, wiped away the evidence, and composed herself. "Yes, Lex?" She was good at keeping it out of her voice.

"I was thinking…"

"Don't worry. We're going to be okay." She smiled at him. "Even better, we're going to be great."

"How will Daddy find us?"

"Don't worry about that. We don't have to worry about that." She actually sounded chipper. He was too young to understand, too young for an explanation.

"What if he comes here looking for us?"

A six-year-old question, but it was a question good enough to break her up in the middle of the night, good enough to make her hug her knees to her chest. "He won't come here looking, honey. We don't have to worry about him coming here." The sound of cars coming and going in water came through the window. "You just finish getting ready, Lex. Okay? Everything's under control."

Lex tilted his head, then leaned to scratch one of his knobby knees while he watched her. His Afro was out of control. "Okay." He turned and left the room.

The map lay spread out on the dresser, next to the envelope. California, someplace between San Francisco and Sacramento—maybe the Napa Valley—was circled in red.

Their stake money was in the envelope. Eighteen hundred bucks, all they had. And their course was plotted, give or take a hundred miles or so. She traced the line on the map with her finger. There might be work in San Francisco, or maybe she could get into nursing school at UC Davis—there were always jobs for nurses. She had to focus on looking ahead, for all of them. There was nothing to look back for. They were California bound—the new world—except for a side trip she had to make to see Mother Johnson. But that wouldn't take long.

"Mommy?" Lex stood in the doorway in a pair of Underoos and a really ugly plaid jacket, his comedian jacket. "Can I tell you a joke?"

She sat down on the bed. "Shoot your best shot."

"What did the penguin say when he fell down the steps?"

"I don't know."

"Help, I've fallen and I can't get up!"

Shirley laughed. Mika came and sat beside her on the bed while Lex retold the joke. Mika snorted, and Shirley laughed again—just two chuckles short of hysteria.

She looked at the envelope, the map, and her children as she laughed.

This story has to have a happy ending.

TWO

⟨⁂⟩

East St. Louis, Illinois, 1967

hirley rode her bicycle two blocks from her home, down Trina's street, Sixty-First Street. Trina was an older girl who everybody said was a niece, or cousin, or something to Tina Turner. Her famous relationship made her stand out among the few Negro kids in the newly, begrudgingly integrated neighborhood. And Trina was always dancing, shaking, and singing to prove it was so.

Shirley tried to blow a hard gust of air from her mouth. She hoped to repel the braid that kept trying to snake its way into the corner of her mouth, an event that threatened to distract her from her riding.

Her bike was shiny and new—a color like candy-apple blue, if there was such a thing—with training wheels, almost as new as the fresh tar on the street, but newer than the freshly laid chat. Tiny rocks spat out from behind the rotating treads, the big ones and the small ones.

The late summer sun baked Shirley, and sweat trickled

from her hairline down her slender throat and into the collar of her white-and-pink-flowered cotton shirt. But because she was only eight, Shirley was not bothered by insinuations sung on commercials or by the perspiration and stickiness. Instead she concentrated on pedaling through the muck on the road—muck that, particularly in sunny spots, was almost like hard, stale peanuts ground into black-strap molasses.

Green grass, almost like a crew cut, marched from the front porch steps of ranch-style houses right up to the curb—no sidewalks. The street was lined with pear trees, and Shirley steeled herself to as likely meet bees as flies. The housing subdivision where she lived had once been a pear orchard—the fruit's sweetness was heavy in the air—and she had learned quickly after moving to the Centerville section of East St. Louis not to swat at the bees. Instead it was best to summon courage and bravely ignore the enemy insects that buzzed her as she rode.

As she pedaled, "Summer in the City" drifted through the screen door from someone's radio. It was one of her favorite songs, and if she had not been on her bike, she would have been dancing. On the curb doing the Philly Dog that Big Uncle had taught her or the Mashed Potatoes that Daddy had taught her. She might not be able to ride, but she sure could dance. Her mama said so. And she liked hearing music on the street from cars, or maybe from someone's handheld AM radio, especially the hours on the weekend when they played Negro music and she could hear Major Lance or Martha and the Vandellas singing songs like "Hitch Hike." From another window she heard little Stevie Wonder singing, "I was made to love her…"

Shirley gripped the handlebars, her fingers wet with sweat, and pedaled on. With each pump the shiny blue bike with white trim tilted from side to side. The blue, white, and silver handlebar streamers flailed and flapped.

Shirley turned toward her cousin. "Rosie, we got to get off this street. It's too hard to pedal."

A veteran cyclist, Rosie looked cool, calm, and collected. "It's easy," she said, then fairly caused her bike to do figure eights and pirouettes. "I can't believe you're *eight* and just learning how to ride a bicycle. Everybody where I'm from knows how to ride. I guess they wait late to teach little children from East St. Louis how to ride."

Rosie was too snotty, but Shirley didn't think she could tell her cousin to go *back* to Cleveland *where she came from* and keep her own new bike upright at the same time, so she kept silent and kept pedaling. They were almost at the corner. Besides that, if she wasn't with Rosie it was pretty sure Mama would not have let Shirley ride her bike so far from home. She was out of voice range—too far to hear her mother's voice if she hollered.

Anyway, Rosie was always showing off; telling her off wasn't going to change that. Shirley stood up so she could pump harder.

Rosie laughed. "Girl, you are sweating!" Rosie cackled while she swooped along on her bicycle, looking more like a witch than a ballet dancer. All she needed was a witch's hat—or maybe a trail of green smoke. "Look at you. You look nasty. And it looks like you gonna fall off that bike any minute now."

That was it. Shirley had had enough of Rosie. Even if she *was* out-of-town company. Even if Shirley was able to ride on Trina's street because Rosie was with her. Even if Shirley didn't have any other Negro children to play with on her street… none of that was worth putting up with her sassy-mouth cousin. Enough was enough.

Shirley turned her head toward Rosie, but before she could speak she heard the two dogs barking. The same two dogs—two bullies—that had killed Sparky not more than a month ago.

The lady on the corner had told her about Sparky, how hard he fought, especially for a little dog, but how the two big dogs double-teamed him. Tore him to pieces, she said. The big dogs didn't like Sparky—and the big dogs didn't like kids.

"You better look where you going, Shirley!"

It happened so fast, she didn't remember much.

Her ankle caught in the chain—there would be bicycle grease on her white socks and Mama might get mad. Shirley thought about Evel Knievel; then she was in the street and there were little rocks sticking in her hands, and her palms were bleeding. Shirley closed her eyes. If you didn't look, it didn't hurt as much. She didn't want to cry. Somebody might see. She was on her stomach and couldn't breathe, but she knew it was just the wind knocked out of her—Big Uncle had told her about that. But the rocks on her knees hurt, and she didn't believe she could walk or get up.

"You okay, Shirley? I told you you were gone crash that bike. Can't ride worth nothing." Rosie's voice sounded miles away. "Girl, you bleeding! Look at your ankle."

Shirley could only grunt.

"I'm going to get Big Uncle since your daddy's not at home. Don't move. You might be close to death! Your back might be broke, girl." Shirley heard Rosie's bike rolling away over the chat. "I hope don't no car come. They won't even see you lay-ing down there! Run right over you."

Her mother's voice came to Shirley while she lay in the street.

"People can think fast when they're in danger," Mama always said.

"You know that's the truth," Little Uncle had agreed. *"They can do the impossible. Get strength from nowhere. I even heard of a woman lifting up a car by herself when her son got run over."*

It hurt, but Shirley crawled to the side of the road onto somebody's grass. *Please, God, don't let anybody smash my bike flat as a pancake.*

Shirley turned her face into the grass and cried.

"There she is!" Rosie was back. "Somebody must have runned her over and threw her body up on the grass."

"Hush, Rosie!" It was Big Uncle. Without another word, he lifted Shirley, cradling her in one arm while he grabbed the bike with his free hand. It was okay to cry in front of Big Uncle; Mama said he had a tender heart. Shirley buried her face in his neck and wept while he told her it would be all right.

Back at home, Big Uncle took giant steps up the length of the driveway, dropping the bike outside the white picket fence that surrounded the house. Shirley knew she was an emergency case because Big Uncle didn't bother to unlatch the fence—he just stepped right over it, though he was careful not to step on any of Mama's flowers.

By the time they stepped through the door, Rosie had already alarmed the house. She was running back and forth yelling, "She got run over! Her body was on the side of the rode, bleeding and everything!"

"Oh, Lord. I wish your daddy was home. He knows I hate blood. I don't think I can take any more. He's going to have to find a new job—the military never leaves him home when I need him! What am I—"

Big Uncle told Rosie to sit down somewhere and hush

telling stories before he gave her a real story to tell. Shirley was hurt, but she could still see her mama and Mama's first cousin, Gale, who was Rosie's mother. Cousin Gale swelled up like she was going to bust. She started yelling to Big Uncle that he didn't have any business yelling at sweet little Rosie.

"Hush now, Gale," Big Uncle told her. "We ain't got time to fight now." Then he looked at Mama. "I got it, Geneva. Calm down. She's skinned up, but she's okay."

"I just hate it when he's gone. A woman needs her husband. A child needs her father around. I know there aren't a lot of Negro pilots and he needs to stand up for the race, but he's not Reverend King. How much proving does a man have to do? He's got to stand up, I know, but when do Shirley and I—"

"What's going on?" Little Uncle walked in from the TV room and squeezed in between Mama and Big Uncle. "That ankle looks pretty bad," he said.

"Think so?" He and Big Uncle were twins. Mama said no one would ever think it. Big Uncle was big and dark. Big hands, big feet, big belly, big smile. He was the heart of the two, Mama said. Little Uncle was light skinned, with wavy hair. Little mustache, little behind, little eyes. Just had a big head, Mama said. He was the brains of the two, Mama said. Big Uncle had a whole lot of common sense, but Little Uncle was the bookish one. He watched all the news shows, read all the papers, and provided all the pontification the family could use. Little Uncle was deep, Big Uncle said.

"I think so, Big. I don't think it's broken, but she's going to have to stay off of that for at least two weeks."

Mama said school was starting on Monday. Can't help that, Little Uncle said.

"You cry if you want to," Big Uncle said, while he cleaned

out the wound on Shirley's ankle. "Grab hold to my shirt if you need to."

"Make sure you clean it out good. We don't want any infection." Little Uncle pointed to a place in the swollen flesh where there was a lot of gravel and dirt.

"I can't watch. I just can't watch. I wish your daddy was home." Mama shook her head and fanned herself as though she was about to faint.

Cousin Gale and Rosie whispered in the corner. "I was ready to go anyway," Shirley heard Cousin Gale say while she threw their clothes into their suitcase. Big Uncle was trying to be gentle, but it hurt anyway. Shirley tried not to cry so she wouldn't worry Mama—and knowing Rosie was leaving somehow lessened the pain.

Little Uncle shook his head, then headed back to the TV room. Daddy said Little Uncle's job was to know more and better what the newsmen said than they did themselves. If he didn't have all that information, no telling what might go wrong with the world, Daddy said.

Big Uncle didn't have that kind of job; he had courage. So he was there to fix Shirley's ankle and to shake his head when everyone else accused her of faking.

Big Uncle raised his hand. "Now, now. The child is hurt." Big Uncle didn't say a lot. But when he did, that was that.

Mama knelt down and took Shirley's hand. "I'm sorry, Shirley. You know Mama hates the sight of blood." Then she began to sing.

"All night, all day,
Angels watching over me, my Lord.
All night, all day,
Angels watching over me."

"Sing with me, Shirley." She held Shirley's hand, and the two sang together.

All night, all day,
Angels watching over me, my Lord.
All night, all day,
Angels watching over me."

"My goodness, I just wish your daddy was home."

Sheri sat on the concrete blocks that rimmed the front yard of the house where she lived. She leaned forward and made white scratches with a nickel on the concrete steps that were to the right of her. One, two, three steps that led to the sidewalk that led to the front door of the house she lived in. She was quiet—she was always quiet at home.

She closed her eyes and imagined she was far away, adrift on a sea that would lead to China. The seas were dark and tossing. The sky was threatening. Sheri imagined that when she finally arrived and disembarked, the people cheered. Under gray skies, they rushed to the boat to greet her, to extend their hands, and to ask her why she had been away so long. Some of them cried because they were so happy to see her. "We've been waiting for you," they said. "How could you have stayed so long in a foreign land?" Then Sheri, dressed in finery—dazzling white, embroidered with the finest gold—began to cry while they held her safe in their arms. She told them of all that she had been through—all the sadness, all the nightmares.

In her imagination, Sheri cried tears, just like the real tears that now slid down her face. The people held her, and she cried until she heard the words they always shouted in her daydreams: "Hallelujah! Trouble's over!" Then the sky turned blue and the sun shone bright.

Sheri held the daydream as long as she could. But when it faded, she looked back over her shoulder at the house where she lived and lifted her hand to shade her eyes.

THREE

Shirley limped along behind the other children, trying to keep up. Sometimes it was hard, especially
when they started running. But they always stopped
and waited, never leaving her too far behind. They had to stick
together. Everybody knew the rules: Don't talk to strangers;
don't get in their cars. But they knew something more. Watch
out for carloads of white teenagers—sometimes they threw
more than epithets. They threw french fries with ketchup on
them, or cups of soda. Clad in their letterman jackets, they
would yell at the elementary school children, "We don't want
you here!"

If not the teenagers, some of the grown-ups might get us. They
don't want us here. Call us niggers. We got to stay together or we
might be plucked off, grabbed and taken to the viaduct. Might drive
you past the manicured lawns, the pear trees, the park.

Might grab the children of Negro teachers, doctors, nurses,
clerks, government workers, and mailmen and call them trash.

Might snatch you and take you to the viaduct.

"What they do to you at the viaduct?" someone might ask.

"Hang you or tar and feather you, maybe drown you," someone might answer.

"For real?"

"Yep, just like Emmit Till," someone would say. "They got mean people and KKK around here—they don't want us here."

There was just a handful of them in an angry, resentful white world. And if there were those who were not resentful, they were not making themselves known.

So the children watched for bad people hidden behind manicured lawns and neat houses, driving Fords and Pontiacs. The children stuck together—even if one girl did have snot running out of her nose every day, even if one boy was too fat and prissy. All the parents were at work, and there was no point in worrying them—nothing they could do about it. Maybe Reverend Dr. Martin Luther King would rescue them, make things better like their parents said. But that wouldn't be anytime soon. So they had to stick together, no matter what. There was safety in numbers. Chances were at least someone could stay alive, someone could live to tell the tale. The group never let Shirley fall too far behind.

Trina stopped and threw down her books. "Come *on*, girl. We going to leave you." She took the opportunity to shake her hips and show off her bright red stretch pants with a piece of black elastic that stretched from her cuff, down her ankle, and into her shoe. Trina had to be related to Tina Turner—there was no other way her mother would let her wear her pants so tight. There was no other way she could do the hitchhike so good, no other way she wouldn't be ashamed to dance so wild while they walked down the street on the way home from school.

"Some white man gone grab you, girl," one of the kids would say to Trina. But she didn't care. She just shook it and shook it until one time a white man driving a yellow VW Beetle slowed down, laughed, and blew his horn while "Shotgun, Shoot Him 'fore He Run Now" blared from his window.

"See, we *told* you, Trina!" All the children pointed and ran.

But here she was again, on the way to school, still dancing. She had to be related to Tina Turner.

"Come on, Shirley," Trina yelled back over her shoulder while she danced the Watusi.

Shirley tried not to limp. Her ankle still hurt, and Little Uncle wasn't sure she was ready for school. But she didn't think she could stand being home from school one more day. "Please, Mama. It doesn't hurt anymore. See?" Shirley kept her face from registering pain while she forced herself to walk. Mama shook her head, not sure.

"Let her go," Big Uncle said. And that was that.

Shirley caught up with Trina and walked beside her. "You might flunk, you know that?" Trina said. "You smart, but you been out so long, you just might get left back. Even if your mama is a teacher."

That was impossible. Even if the reading groups had been picked—even if there were Redbirds and Bluebirds and Yellowbirds—school was what Shirley did best. She could not wait to take her rightful place in the first reading group. "I'm not going to flunk."

"We'll see. This is Centerville." Trina stopped talking and went back to shaking her tailfeather.

Shirley's family had moved to Centerville a month or so earlier—the first negro family on the street. The house her family moved into was like the other dollhouses—some longer, some shorter, all ranch style. In Centerville, the men and boys mowed their lawns and pulled weeds every Saturday, except for when they were raking leaves or shoveling snow. They were careful to follow the safety announcements not to pull their mowers backward—or in any direction that would cut off their toes.

The women in Centerville rarely came outside. Shirley saw them only when they took their children to school. The women were silent and faceless and did not seem to Shirley to work. The Centerville mothers emerged like clockwork from their homes and got quickly in their cars. They looked frightened, and Shirley thought that something must be wrong with them, that they must be what her mother called *sickly.*

Shirley's family had a cat that had kittens. One of the kittens was scrawny and looked confused. Shirley's mother, who knew everything her family needed to know, said the cat was sickly. He was very thin. He was white and his hair was so short and thin you could see his pinkness and blue veins underneath. Her mother did not tell her not to touch him, but somehow Shirley knew he didn't have the strength to endure petting. The kitten looked confused and frightened, and she did not think he would survive in the box in the garage that held him and the rest of the litter.

The Centerville moms did not have voices—not words, anyway—they did not have jobs, and she could not remember their faces. But Shirley was sure they existed, was sure they were not ghosts, because she had heard that sometimes the mothers came to school with cupcakes and murmurings. Sometimes she saw them in the IGA grocery store—but only briefly because they were sickly.

Shirley felt sorry for the moms, but she had soon learned that the moms did not feel sorry for her. In her neighborhood, in her school, she knew the moms did not like her. They did not always say so, but she saw it in their fear and she saw it in their children.

The only thing the moms did was their children. And the children in Centerville were beautiful. They smiled, jumped, and flitted. In the summer sun, their hair glistened and was golden. They were indeed beautiful. Shirley knew that the moms thought their children were more beautiful than she.

But her mother, who knew everything Shirley's family needed to know, said it was not so. Her mother said she was pretty, and Shirley believed her. And all the warm arms and kisses at church—all the soft, brown, warm voices and the hands that patted her and touched Shirley's hair—they all said she was good, and it was so.

Her mama and daddy loved her and said it was so. Her mother, who knew everything Shirley's family needed to know, said that Shirley came from smart people and could not help herself. Her father graduated from high school early because he was so smart. Her mother said he was cocky, but he could back up what he said.

"Not only is he good-looking, but he is funny. And smart, that man is just *too* smart." Her mother would shake her head. "Don't waste your time if a man's not smart." Shirley and her family were smart people, and they had *it,* her mother said. They could not help having *it,* and they could not hide *it* anymore than the sun could help shining. That's how it was with people that have *it,* Shirley's mother told her. Heads would turn when they were around. Shirley's mother's mother before her had told her about *it.*

Shirley could see it for herself. She had something special, and it made the Centerville moms' dislike a bit easier to live with. Shirley's father was cocky, her mother had a voice and a job, and they were all blessed. Her mother said it, and it was so.

Shirley was not surprised, then, that she soon came to be

the center of much attention on the playground at Jefferson Elementary School.

But she was surprised how.

Sheri looked back at the house; it was quiet. She was probably asleep. And anyway, the sun was too high in the sky for Sheri to go inside—her father was not home. Sheri's brothers were all gone. They were all old enough to stay away. They wouldn't come back home until dinnertime.

She daydreamed about a tea party and what it would be like to have friends over. Maybe, like the other kids talked about at recess at school, she could invite a friend over. She smiled and imagined someone from her class coming to visit. She hugged the imaginary friend and even kissed her on the cheek. Then they walked toward the door. When Sheri turned the knob, a cold heaviness rushed out of the door and hit them. The visiting friend looked at Sheri strangely, waiting for a response. Sheri closed the door, unimagined the friend, and moved the tea party to someplace far, far away…

Then it became a large tea party—a party with all her friends. A party where all the attendees came to see her, to focus on her. All the invitees told her how much they loved her. "*This* much," some of them said, while stretching their arms out as wide as they could. They told her that they had heard of her fear and of her suffering. They had heard about her nightmares, about the monster that chased her every night. But she was safe, they said, and they welcomed her back home.

When she heard car tires crunching on the driveway gravel, Sheri jumped to her feet. She must have been daydreaming for a long time. She had to have been thinking for a long time, because the smells of a finished dinner were seeping from the windows. Sheri smiled at her father and positioned herself to walk into the house after him.

The smell of roast beef and mashed potatoes soothed them when they walked through the door. Sheri's mom was smiling. Her teeth, her face, her hair were all beautiful. Her mom laughed and waved her glass at Sheri's father. There was no ice in the glass; the liquid was dark brown and sparkling like her eyes. "Hello, honey," she said.

Sheri's father moved to kiss his wife. Her mom's voice made different sounds than it made when she kissed Sheri. Mom poured him a drink, and he took it in his hand and carried it to the table.

Everything was perfect. Perfect tablecloth, perfect place settings, perfect glasses. All the food groups were present, including the perfect dessert. The meat was on a serving platter with the perfect amount of gravy; vegetables were in serving bowls filled to the perfect depth.

Almost as if on cue, Sheri's two brothers came in the door, smiling and breathless, as though they had been running for miles. "Hello, Mom," they said. Soon they were all sitting at the dinner table, passing peas, passing roast, passing mashed potatoes. And Sheri passed and tried not to listen to the conversation. Not to the words, anyway, just to the tones. All the forks and the voices were making happy sounds.

The truth was in the tones.

There were lots of manic smiles and lots of digging in around the table, and some "and then what happened was..." until one of Sheri's brothers said "No, thank you" to the peas. "I don't like them," he said.

The tones changed suddenly. The room temperature

dropped, and the air got heavy.

Sheri wished that she were older and had a game, a dance, a paper due.

Mom's tone was edgy, threatened, wounded. "What do you mean, you don't like them?" She said how she would never have said anything like that to *her* mom. She looked at Sheri's father. She said she didn't know why her son always had to spoil things, why he was always trying to hurt her.

The offending brother said nothing, just looked down and forked a little at his roast.

The tone was now angry. "Don't play with your food," she said. "I said, what do you mean you don't like them? What are you trying to say to me when you say you don't like them? You don't appreciate what I'm doing?" All the forks stopped clicking, and the breathing stopped. Dad said nothing; his face looked like Sheri's felt when she tried not to look afraid. Mom's voice got louder and louder. Dad's face looked more and more like he was trying not to be afraid.

"My parents would have knocked me down if I said I didn't want to eat something," Mom said. "Isn't that right, Dad?"

Dad's face still looked like he was trying not to look afraid. "That's right," he said.

The offending brother's head stayed down, as though he was trying to will himself back to the junior high school cafeteria. The other brother looked as though he was searching for a moment, a break, a high-school prom, any opportunity for a getaway. Exit stage right.

Sheri began to feel sick. Her stomach ached, so she tried to put her fork in her mouth in just the right way to make mashed potatoes land on the spot that hurt.

The tone was worse. "You don't like what I'm saying to

you?" Mom gestured at the offending brother, then slapped her hand down on the table. "I said, you don't like what I'm saying to you? Well, you can pack your things and go with your other brother. He thought he was so smart—well, now we'll see just how smart he is. If you don't like what I'm saying, you can pack your things tonight!" She slapped the table again. "He thinks I care about where he is. Well, I don't. I'm not going to have any snotty-nose children that I gave birth to disrespecting me."

Mom was crying now. She was crying on the day when she sent Sheri's other brother away—packed his bags and sent him away. The one they didn't talk about. Sheri was quiet. She was afraid of being sent away…but her stomach hurt, so she dropped more mashed potatoes down her throat.

Mom was crying harder and she jumped up from the table. She looked at Dad. "See how you let them treat me? You don't care what they do or what they say to me. You're always taking their side. Always defending them."

"I haven't said a word, honey," Dad said.

"That's what I mean! Why don't you say something? They think it's just me, and you get to come off smelling like a rose. I'm the one who has to be here raising them," she said. "I will leave here," she said. "I don't have to put up with this."

Dad turned his trying-not-to-look-scared face to a stern one and focused on the son who didn't like peas. "I've told you time and time again not to upset your mother. Here she has made this beautiful meal for us, and now you've ruined it. If she wasn't here, I don't know who would raise you. She is doing everything by herself; she does everything she can to make sure you children are happy. Now look how you repay her. Apologize to your mother."

The tone got worse. Mom was crying harder. "Is that all you're going to do?" she said.

The stern look was gone, and Dad's face looked confused and pleading. "Well, honey…what do you want me to do?"

"*Nothing*. I knew that's what you were going to do. *Nothing*. You're always taking their side." Mom stormed away from the table.

The nonoffending brother, who also secretly hated peas, suddenly remembered he had to get to the library right away. "I've got a group project due," he said. "I have to go. I'll be late." And he was out the door.

Dad's face grew stern again, and he leaned in the direction of the nonpea-eater. "I want you to go apologize to your mother."

Sheri tried to be as quiet as she could while she kept trying to get mashed potatoes on the achy spot. She reached for another helping.

The offending brother raised his head. "But Dad, I didn't do anything. I just said I didn't want any peas. And last time she yelled at me not to put stuff on my plate that I wasn't going to eat."

Dad's face softened just the slightest bit. "I know. But you know how your mother is. You know how sensitive she is. She works so hard to make us happy. Why can't you just avoid hurting her? She just wants you to appreciate what she does."

"I do appreciate it, Dad. I just don't like peas."

Dad's face hardened again. "Well, you can pretend like you like them. That's what I do. Now, go do what I said and apologize to her."

The offending brother, the nonpea-eater, dragged himself from the kitchen and down the hall to Sheri's parents' bedroom. Pretty soon her mom's screaming voice reached the kitchen. Sheri was glad she was not the one who had made the mistake. She would make sure she ate everything on her plate.

Dad rose from the table. "You and your brother make sure you clean up this kitchen. Your mother is probably going to have one of her nervous spells tonight because of this."

"Yes, sir." Shirley was still trying to get mashed potatoes on the spot. Dad walked down the hall, shaking his head, toward the bedroom. Sheri could hear her mom's high-pitched wailing. Her father's murmuring was much lower in pitch. She heard her parents' bedroom door close. Then the offending brother, the nonpea-eater, stormed back into the kitchen. His face was flushed.

"Aren't you through eating yet?" he yelled. He began to snatch silverware from the table, and he slammed the plates he grabbed into the sink. The offender started crying. "I hate it here!" He kicked a chair. "Why does it always have to be like this? How am I supposed to figure out what's going to make her happy?" The nonpea-eater put his hands up to his eyes, his normally yellow skin now scarlet. "I can't wait until I get grown. You can stay here if you want to, but if you're smart, you'll get out of here too. I'm getting out of here, and I'm never coming back."

Sheri got up from her place and began to scrape the dishes. "It's going to be all right," she whispered to her brother. She was afraid for her mother or father to overhear. She was still thinking of what food she might put on the achy spot.

When Sheri and her offending brother had finished the dishes, their parents still had not come out of the bedroom, though the screaming and the murmuring had stopped. Sheri and the nonpea-eater took the evening's garbage outside to be burned. He dumped the leftovers and trash into the barrel their family used to burn away what was unwanted. He stuck matchsticks into the ground, forming a circle around the flaming metal trash can. He struck a match and tossed it into the barrel, then walked around the barrel setting the matches at its base on fire. The glow from the fire lit his face, like someone in a Boris Karloff movie.

First the offender smiled. Then he began to laugh.

The next night at dinner, when the asparagus—which the nonpea-eater also hated—was passed, the nonpea-eater took a big helping. And silently, with no expression, he gulped each stalk down whole. Sheri's mother, her eyes sparkling and her face glowing, looked around the table at the perfect settings, the perfect platter, at the perfect children—then at her husband—and smiled.

FOUR

rs. Canada's classroom was almost mint green, with six rows of six wooden desks with chairs bolted together by heavy iron bands and secured to the floor by equally strong bolts. Each desk and chair was covered by at least twenty years of shellac. Each seat was filled, and students flipped up desktops, scrounging for books and papers. Six more modern desks, with separate chairs, had been added—one at the end of each row. The modern desks were lighter in color with gray metal bottoms and tops that only appeared to be wood.

When Mrs. Canada called out "Redbirds" or "Bluebirds" or "Yellowbirds," rows or partial rows of children moved to join her at the large, circular reading table up front. Clearly, the reading groups already had been picked.

Shirley didn't know any of the children; none of them was from her neighborhood. A large clock ticked on the wall over Mrs. Canada's head, and to her right the large windows along one wall were open at top and bottom. Black chalkboards covered the other three walls. Above the chalkboards were What-I-Did-This-Summer drawings done by the students in the class.

"Bluebirds!" Miss Canada yelled. The students picked to be Bluebirds, the best readers, had already distinguished themselves, had already made names for themselves. Shirley sat at the only desk in the classroom that was unoccupied as the Bluebirds flew to the table of honor and gathered around Miss Canada. Shirley tried not to scratch the polish on the dark wood floor when she scooted her chair into place and sat down. She picked at a hangnail. This was nothing like her old school.

You gonna flunk…even if your mama is a teacher.

Maybe Trina was right.

"Honey?"

Shirley lifted her head. Mrs. Canada was pointing at her. "Come here, honey." The silver-haired woman crooked her finger.

"Yes, ma'am?"

"Come here, honey. What's your name?" Mrs. Canada looked as though she could have been St. Nick's wife, down to the little, round spectacles. Mrs. Canada put her arm around Shirley's waist.

"My name's Shirley." She still had not gotten over being startled by genuine affection from white people. Mrs. Canada hugged her as though she was a regular girl.

"You're the little girl that's been out for two weeks. How's your ankle?" Shirley nodded and shrugged. "Well, we're already in reading groups, so you're going to have to read for me now so I'll know what group to put you in. Did they give you your books?"

Shirley nodded. Mrs. Canada withdrew her arm. "Run back to your desk and get your reader." She waved her hand. "Hurry now." Shirley went to pull her book from her desk, then returned to stand next to Mrs. Canada. "All right then. Start with the first page. Don't be shy. Take your time." The old woman's face settled into an encouraging smile.

Little fingers fumbled with the pages, almost dropped the book—then Shirley began to read. *With expression,* she reminded herself. She was on the third page before Mrs. Canada stopped her. "Can you flip to the last page and read for me?"

Shirley turned to the last page of the primer and read to the end. When she finished, she lifted her eyes to meet Mrs. Canada's.

"Well," Mrs. Canada said. "Well." She took the book from Shirley's hands. "Well," she repeated, shaking her head. Mrs. Canada patted the chair next to her. "You sit right here for right now. I'll put you in your group when we finish the Bluebird lesson." Mrs. Canada smiled at the children around the table, and they began to take turns reading aloud.

You gonna flunk...even if your mama is a teacher.

How would she tell her mother and father that she was not in the Bluebirds? How would she explain it to Little Uncle? Shirley bit her lip and tried to concentrate on the pictures posted around the room so that she would not cry. Her ankle throbbed. She kept her head down but listened while the others read.

The recess bell rang. "All of you outside, except for Shirley." All the other children stared at Shirley as they walked out the door. "Come with me."

Mrs. Canada led Shirley to the back of the room and pulled up two chairs. "Shirley, you've missed two weeks of school, and now that I've heard you read, I can't put you in any of the reading groups."

Shirley's head dropped. *You gonna flunk…even if your mama is a teacher.*

Mrs. Canada cleared her throat. "I have myself a bit of a dilemma here. What am I going to do with you?" She looked at the clock, then looked around the room, leaned forward, and pressed her hands on the top of her knees. "And I just don't have too many options here." She sighed. "I tell you what we're going to do, Shirley. I'm not going to put you in one of the reading groups I have. I'm going to give you your own reading group to teach. Do you think you could do that?"

Shirley raised her head and stared at Mrs. Canada.

"If you don't think you can do it, Shirley, we won't try. But I think you can. You'd get bored reading with the Bluebirds. The reader we're using is no challenge for you. You'd just be sitting with the group, wasting your time. But it would help me if you would work with a few of the students that are having trouble learning to read. They're not getting the attention they need in the Yellowbirds because it's such a large group. But I could take them out and put them in a separate group—the Greenbirds! That's what we'll call you. How does that sound? The Greenbirds!"

Shirley just stared.

"If you don't want to do it, Shirley, just tell me. I will understand completely."

"No, ma'am."

"All right then, Shirley. I'll just let you join the Bluebirds—"

"No, ma'am. I mean, I *want* to teach the group. I want to teach the Greenbirds."

"The Greenbirds it is then, Shirley." Mrs. Canada stood,

took Shirley's hand, and began to show her around the room. The bookshelves, the reading primers the group would use, the phonics charts and easels. "You'll just go through the drills with them again, just like we do the rest of the class. Only you will bring them back here." Mrs. Canada led Shirley back to the cloakroom.

"It will be quiet back here, and you'll be able to work with them without the other reading groups disturbing you." Her teacher pointed to the shelves and the coat hooks. "People's lunches will be in here, on the shelves, but it will be two to three months before there will be many coats in here taking up your room."

Mrs. Canada pointed at the deep brown wood on the walls and floors. "I know there's not a lot of light in here, but you do have this one light source." She reached for the window, raised, and then lowered it. "And I can open and shut this window as you need. When you get ready to start your lessons in the mornings, you'll just have your students drag their chairs back here, and this will be just fine."

Outside the children laughed, screamed, and shouted. Their voices rose up to the second-floor window. "Yes, ma'am." Shirley nodded and smiled. She could see it. Her own classroom, her own students...she would be a teacher just like Mama!

You gonna flunk...even if your mama is a teacher.

Just wait until she told Trina. And Mama, and Daddy, and the Uncles.

"I'll tell your students this afternoon, and you will start tomorrow morning. We will all say the Pledge of Allegiance and sing 'My Country 'Tis of Thee' together, just like always. We'll go through the morning announcements; then when I call the first reading group up, you'll call your group back here."

Mrs. Canada just glowed, as if she had found the cure for polio or a way to feed all the starving children in Africa. "It will work out just fine." She stooped to give Shirley a hug. "Just fine."

Cars whizzed past the sidewalk where the children walked, skipped, laughed, and argued their way home.

"No, you not."

"Yes, I am."

"No, you *not!*"

"Yes, I *am!*"

Trina stopped walking and put one hand on her hip. "You too little to be a teacher. You ain't teaching nobody. You just making it up, and you fixing to get a whupping if you don't stop telling lies."

Shirley stopped and stood her ground. "I am not lying—"

"Oo-oo-oo! You said *lying!* I'm gone tell your mama!" The other kids hopped around while they watched Trina and Shirley.

Shirley pointed at Trina. "*She* said it first. How come you didn't say anything to her?"

Trina interrupted. "Don't worry about them. You just worry about what your mama is gone say when she finds out you be telling stories. And when she finds out you flunking."

Shirley started walking again, increasing the distance between herself and the pack. She stopped before she was a full block ahead—even if she was teaching, even if the other kids did make her mad, someone still might grab her if she was alone.

"Go on, Miss Smarty Pants. Miss Teacher. You don't need us." Trina chided Shirley as the group overtook her.

"Never mind, Trina. Just forget about it. You'll see."

Shirley pulled her knees up to her chest, wrapped her arms around them, and rested her chin as she gazed out the window. The branches and leaves, the moonlight shining on them and the wind blowing them about, made different shapes and figures. On bad nights, the shadows looked like trolls or witches. On good nights, like tonight, they were queens, kings, and even unicorns.

Mama had called Daddy to tell him the good news. "Your baby's going to be teaching. Ain't that something? Eight years old and teaching, ain't that *something*? And we're supposed to be dumb. Well, we all know that's not the truth. If you give us half a chance, we'll succeed. You know part of the problem is they're afraid if they give us a chance we *will* succeed."

"My buttons are about to pop off my chest, baby girl. You keep doing good and make your daddy proud." Shirley and her father had exchanged kisses over the telephone before she went to bed.

Teacher.

Tomorrow would be the first day.

FIVE

⁓

The Greenbirds were all Cooties.

The Cooties lived on the other side of the railroad tracks; they were the last bus stop. "Cootie Town!" the other children crowed when the bus stopped to pick them up in the morning. "Cootie Town!" they cried again when the bus stopped to drop them off.

The Cooties lived in unpainted wooden shacks. They were poor and their skin was gray, as though they did not bathe regularly. The other white kids made fun of them at school, and the teachers did not intervene. "Yuck, Cooties!" The kids refused to sit next to the Cooties in the lunchroom, and the lunch monitors said nothing. During recess and PE, no one wanted to play with them or hold their hands. So they were left out of the activities, and the teachers did not invite them in.

The teachers—except for the one Negro teacher, Mrs. Butter—ignored the Cooties with a sort of angry, practiced disdain. The Cooties responded by being angrily, passive-aggressively invisible. Until lice day. Lice day was the day, every few months or so, when the Cooties were in the spotlight. On lice day, the teachers, using Popsicle sticks like medical instruments, checked each Cootie for head lice. It was the likelihood that vermin would be found that was most probably the source of their group moniker.

Popsicle sticks probed through dirty-blond hair, red hair, brown hair, looking for wiggling nits and white eggs.

"You won't be able to come back until they're gone." The teacher's faces would look pinched and disgusted.

When the moms brought cookies and cupcakes to school on treat days, they avoided the Cooties. The moms' faces looked drained, and they seemed to not breathe when the Cootie children walked past.

The Cooties' clothes were dirty and torn. They did not carry lunch boxes or book bags. They did not smile. They did not frolic. And they could not read.

They were white children, and they could not read.

The Cooties, the only three in Shirley's classroom, followed her back to the cloakroom. Barbara, Misty, and Ken. Barbara was twelve, Ken was eleven, and Misty was nine.

Barbara was hard. She was tall and thick, had dirty-blond matted hair, wore lipstick, smelled of cigarette smoke, and it was rumored that she had been known to run away with grown men from time to time.

Ken's fingers were stained brown from tobacco, which must have stunted his growth because he was short for eleven years. His hair was almost white, with a permanent coating of what looked to be soot. While Barbara was known for fighting then smiling down at her victims if she had to, Ken was known for being plain mean. Anger crawled up his back, over the top of his head, and settled on his mouth and in his eyes—icy blue eyes. He wore a perpetual snarl. He was not interested in reading or in school games, only in the canned meat sandwich, which he pulled unwrapped from his pocket on the Greenbirds' first morning in the cloak room.

Misty was skinny, and she always looked scared. She looked the least like the other Cooties. She wore clean clothes and ribbons in her hair. It appeared that her mother might have been trying to help Misty avoid the community stigma. To some extent, she was successful. During PE, the other white girls would hold Misty's hands for games of Red Rover. During recess, however, she was shunned, for while the children would play with Shirley and other Negro children, they refused Misty's company. After all, ribbons or not, Misty was Barbara and Ken's cousin, and she lived in Cootie Town.

What Shirley did that first day, she did throughout the rest of her school year.

She dragged the phonics and vowel charts, on wooden easels, to her makeshift classroom. Using a pointer, she indicated pictures on the chart and attempted to teach Barbara, Misty, and Ken the reading songs.

Shirley pointed to a pig with a large letter *p* next to it.

"'Baby wants a pig, p-p-p. Baby wants a pig, p-p-p. Baby wants a pig, p-p-p. But Mother says, 'Uh, uh, uh.'" She would smile at them, just like Mrs. Canada. "Now sing it with me!"

The Cooties were expected to sing along. And after letter *p*, there was *d*, and *f*, and *g* through *z*. There were even compound sounds like *st* and *sh*.

Barbara looked amused by the little colored kid in front of her. Misty looked confused. Ken was silent, but surly. It was clear he hated being in the cloakroom. He never looked anyone in the eye—anyone except Shirley—when they were assembled as the Greenbirds. What Shirley saw in Ken's eyes said that he knew his position. He knew the rules and was willing to abide by them. He was a Cootie and he was willing to be shunned, to be angry, to be invisible. But he seethed openly at the breaching of the social contract. Teachers might poke through his hair and humiliate him, but he was not to be humiliated by a little colored girl. He was better than that. He was too good to be banished to the cloakroom with someone like Shirley.

Cooties were less than worthy of being in the presence of regular white people, but the unspoken rule said that they were better than Negroes, and they did not hesitate to call them *niggers*. Ken's position clearly was above Shirley's, his eyes and his mouth said. No uppity little *black* child was going to lord over him or teach him anything. He was inferior to regular whites—he didn't like it, but he accepted the order. But Shirley was inferior to him. Anything that broke that order was wrong. Unfair.

Ken didn't break the rules. He didn't swear or shout. His protest was to ignore Shirley and refuse to absorb any of the lessons she tried to teach him. Barbara and Misty sang, but Ken would not participate.

Every day, with Ken glaring at her, Shirley went through the routine. They drilled the songs and then attempted to sound out words. "C-a-t, cat. Cat!" Each new day, Barbara and Misty learned a new word. Each new day, Barbara and Misty forgot the word they had learned the day before, as though the alphabet were made of foreign, unrecognizable symbols.

Shirley was outwardly patient, but every day she grew more frustrated that her charges could not remember or recognize the words *ball, did,* or *dog.* Frustrated that they could not remember that *p* had the *p* sound and was the first letter in *pig.*

She was frustrated because, at eight years old, she could not understand why they could not understand. Because at eight years old, she could not figure out what was wrong. So they crossed the same ground day after day, with the same results.

Shirley was frustrated because a truth too big and too old for her kept tapping on her shoulder, then running away before she could see it clearly.

But what she did know at eight years old was that their—Barbara, Misty, Ken, and the other Cooties—being poor had something to do with their failure. What she did know was that their being Cooties—being rejected—had something to do with it. She knew their being hungry had something to do with it. They could not concentrate and they could not remember. It was as if a haze, a wall of confusion, separated the Cooties from the other children.

She was not sure what it was. But sometimes Shirley was sure she almost saw it.

In that cloakroom and in Mrs. Canada's class, Shirley learned that what she had learned up until then was a lie. What she had heard discussed by intellectuals, by scientists, by pastors, by politicians, and by common folk was not true. The sentence that hung over her head was not fair. She learned that what the moms thought was not true.

Shirley learned that race did not equal superiority—a strange lesson for 1968. What Shirley learned at eight years old was that all white people were not smart. Most were average, and some could not learn according to normal rules. That was a truth far from the one she had been taught all her life. She learned that what made Barbara, Misty, and Ken unable to learn was probably the same thing that made other children, those she had heard called dumb and genetically inferior, unable to learn. Every day as she taught, she learned the lesson again and again.

And she carried the lesson with her when she walked down the sidewalk with her friends past store owners and restaurant managers, who thought people like her did not belong. She carried it past the crossing guard, who only served the white children and ignored the Negro children as they waited to cross the busy street. She carried the lesson on the quiet, green streets in her neighborhood—streets where the smell of sweet fruit and raw onions mingled in the air. She carried the lesson past neat, groomed dollhouses, where she was not welcome inside.

At the end of her first week, Shirley carried her secret past Trina's house on Sixty-First Street and around the bend to her own street. She carried it while she ran—papers in hand, lunchbox jiggling—the last of the way to her own house, to her family.

Almost home, she stopped. Stared at her driveway—at the car parked there.

"Daddy!" Shirley dropped her papers. "Daddy!" She scrambled to pick them up. "Daddy!" She ran for home, ran for the arms of the father who loved her.

Sheri was daydreaming again. She had her T-shirt pulled over her head, wearing it as hair, wearing it as braids—thick, red braids.

Her mom had told her that when she was born, the nurse tried to bring Sheri to her. "This is not my baby," Mom had said.

"Why not?" the nurse asked.

"This baby is a girl, and I only have boys. Besides, this baby is too dark."

Sheri and her mother were the same color, but her mother would close her eyes and recount the description of the perfect daughter: thick, red braids; light skin; freckles—light skin and freckles like Sheri's dad and like her mom's mother. Her mother said the nurse got angry and said this had to be her baby because there were only two babies in the nursery and the other baby was there before Sheri's mother arrived. Sheri *had* to be her baby; she was the only other baby in the nursery.

"I still don't know why she got mad," Shirley's mother would say each time she told the story.

Sheri sighed and pulled the shirt back down over her head and put her arms through the sleeves. She stood up and looked up at the sun, then back at her house. Sheri danced from foot to foot. She would have to be brave; she didn't think she could hold it.

On tiptoe, Sheri crept up to the door of the house where she lived. It was still early in the afternoon, too early for Dad to be home. Too early to go safely inside, but it was hot, and she was thirsty, and—she continued dancing—there was no other bathroom available to her. She would have to take a chance. She would have to be brave.

Sheri turned the doorknob slowly, eased the door open, and held her breath.

When she opened the door, she knew that things were not right. She could not have explained how, but she knew. Sheri could always tell, her brothers could always tell, right at the door before they saw the evidence they could tell.

Maybe it was the heaviness in the air, maybe it was the way the hair at the nape of Sheri's neck stood on end, maybe it was the temperature…or maybe it was the tangible presence of evil.

Not her mom's evil—but something wicked that walked with her.

However it was that she knew. Sheri's mouth got even drier. Her breathing stopped and she felt as though she were frozen—as though she wanted to run to save her life but could not move. *Help me!* she yelled in her mind, to no one in particular.

There was no one to help her.

Sheri wanted to run back out the door, but something, someone, willed her forward. And as though she had no control over her own body, her feet jerked, started, and stopped until she stood in the living room doorway.

She had seen it before.

Her mom sat in a rocking chair in semidarkness, holding a photo album on her lap. The animation that was normally hers when her husband came home from work was gone. Her head hung. Sometimes she wept, sometimes she shook her head, sometimes she looked angry. Mom was gray and lifeless looking, except for the way her lips moved and the way her fingers drifted back and forth over the photos.

Her mom's face looked small and angry, as though the skin had been pulled back tight. And Sheri could sense, almost see, something…several somethings, like shadows, wrapping themselves—itself—around her mother, writhing in through her ears, through her eyes, and sliding out of her mouth.

She wondered if Dad knew about this thing. If it was this thing that made him try to not look afraid. If it was this thing that made him not protect his children and rescue his wife. If it was fear of this thing that made him go on long business trips that refreshed him but left his children defenseless.

Sheri stood still, just watching and hoping she would

become unfrozen before she was noticed, before the thing that held her mom came for her. Before the thing that chased her each night in her nightmares saw her, trapped her, killed her. *Please*…she begged no one in particular, the one inside of her. Her legs unfroze, and she moved like light toward and out the door. Sheri was no longer thirsty and her bladder had dried. She ran for the concrete blocks at the bottom of the steps.

The dark angels from the Second Heaven looked down on the woman sitting in the rocking chair. They had known her for a long time. They had known her people before her. They had been invited. Dark thoughts, unforgiving thoughts, memories of slights and sins, angry thoughts…they all invited the dark angels down to sit with her. The woman held on to her hurts, and the dark angels held on to her.

Of course, they did more than hold her. They whispered to her that she was in danger, that no one loved her, that she could trust no one. They made their voices sound like her own. They called her poor darling and told her she had been so very, very good and that all others were very, very bad. They reminded her of all she had suffered and told her that God had abandoned her. They taught the woman to trust her own anger and encouraged her to harden her heart, just as they had taught her family before her. They told her that God was a liar, that forgiveness brought no peace, that the meek would be slaughtered. They told her that the strong would inherit the earth, that extending mercy would get her hurt.

The dark angels told her how to make sure she got her way—how to be self-serving—so that she would be safe, they said. They told her she had to use intimidation to control her children, otherwise they would overtake her. They encouraged her to use fear and anger to cause strife and to control those around her. They taught her to use bondage to control others—the same lessons of bondage that other dark angels, principalities, and wicked powers taught to nations and kings.

They did not tell her, of course, that the same bondage would also hold her captive. And they did not tell her that their master used the very actions they had taught her to accuse her to God.

The dark angels snickered and cackled where she could not hear them, and all the while they ate what was left of her spirit and her light. But she was not enough. They were hungry and they had been banished to darkness for a long time, so their eyes roamed the family, the house, seeking whom else they could devour.

SIX

"Is that my baby?"

Shirley's father met her at the door and swung her up into his arms. "Don't you look cute in your little miniskirt and go-go boots!" He kissed her face and then hugged her close. Lunch box and papers forgotten, Shirley wrapped her arms tightly around his neck. He squeezed her back. "No matter how far I am, sugar, you are never out of touch with my heart."

Shirley could not hug her father tight enough. "Oh, Daddy." There was too much to tell—her ankle, school, the lesson—and she did not know how, so she just closed her eyes and hugged.

"Look how big you're getting." Shirley's feet dangled near her father's thighs. He used one of his hands to draw a line across his midsection. "I remember when I would hold you, and all of you stopped right here."

"Okay, you two. Come out of the doorway and close the door. Somebody looking would think you hadn't seen each other in years. You would think no one else was in the room."

Mama laughed. It was not until Shirley was older, until she remembered the looks, that she realized her mother's pleasure had very little to do with her or her behavior. Though Shirley was blessed by—or suffered through, depending on her mother's mood—her mother's looks, it was not until she was older that Shirley realized she had little or nothing to do with what was in her mother's eyes. The source of her mother's pleasure or displeasure lay elsewhere. Shirley was just caught in the ripples.

Tonight, the ripples were very good.

Shirley raised her head, blushed, and smiled at her mother. "I'm sorry, Mama. I—"

Her mother walked over and the three became one. "I'm just teasing, baby. I went just as crazy when I got home and he was here." She kissed Shirley on the cheek, then gave her husband a lingering kiss. "God knows we missed you. God knows we did."

Half in half out of father's arms, Shirley leaned to kiss her mother. Her eyes surveyed the kitchen where they stood. "Mama! You're cooking apples!"

"Yes. And there's pork chops and corn and cabbage. Cornbread is in the oven, and I whipped up a little something for dessert. We're celebrating." She nuzzled her husband's cheek with her nose. "Daddy's home." She kissed Shirley. "Now hop down, put your things away, and then wash your hands. We're just about ready to eat."

Shirley gave her father a peck, and he lowered her until she was able to stand. She grabbed her bag and papers and started for her room.

"Wait, baby." Daddy started alternately twisting his feet while he bobbed his head. "Let me see you do those Mashed Potatoes."

Shirley laughed and started to dance with her father. Mama watched and laughed, then Daddy grabbed her hand to join them. He smiled at Shirley. "You're getting pretty good there, girl."

"Yes, sir."

He stopped dancing and stooped to hug her. "Now run on and do what your mama said."

Shirley ran for the door that separated the kitchen and the laundry room on her way to her bedroom. At the door, she stopped and turned. "I love you all." Then she ran to do as she was told.

When Shirley stepped from the living room into the dining room, the table was full and so were all of the chairs, except for hers.

"Come on in here, girl. We waiting on you. I was about to go ahead without you." Big Uncle lifted his hand as though he was going to grab the fork that lay on the plate of pork chops. "Your daddy had to stop me."

Her father smiled and motioned her to the table.

Her mother came in from the kitchen with a steaming bowl of apples. "Did you wash your hands, Shirley?"

"Yes, ma'am."

"Well, come on then, girl. The news is about to start." Little Uncle pointed at the long, wooden television console, then at his brother. "And your uncle here is going to waste away if he doesn't get some food in him soon."

Shirley's mother shook her head. "You two just cut up so much. You know what? I'm glad the two of you don't live here—at least you don't sleep here."

"Geneva, you saying you don't want us here?" Little Uncle began to raise himself from his seat.

Daddy put his hand out. "Wait, Little, don't take offense. You know Geneva's just talking, just playing. We don't know what we would do if you and Big weren't here to take care of things when I'm gone. I—we—hope you're always here." He smiled. "Besides, who's going to eat all these chops, man?"

Little Uncle sat back down.

Mama sat the dish on the table. "Shirley, before you get settled in, run in the kitchen and turn the radio off for me." She laid her hand on her brother's shoulder. "Little, you know I rely on you and Big. You know that. Don't be so sensitive." Mama leaned and kissed Little Uncle's cheek.

Shirley walked into the kitchen and listened to the conversation coming from the dining room.

"That's why, Geneva. You baby him too much. Always did," Big Uncle said.

"Big, don't you pick up that meat fork. You know you have to wait for grace…Shirley, hurry up before I have to tie Big Uncle up in here."

Shirley laughed and then tiptoed to reach the dial on the large, eggshell-colored plastic radio. "Love Is Here, and Now You're Gone!" the Supremes chirped from the radio. She turned the dial and Petula Clark sang, "Don't Sleep in the Subway…"

For what had to be the fiftieth time, Shirley wondered what AM meant as she turned the radio off. "Here I come, Mama."

"Yeah, come on, Shirley. The news is about to start." When Shirley walked back through the door, Little Uncle was adjusting the rabbit-ear antennae on the TV to fix the picture.

"You need to fix the horizontal hold," Big Uncle said. And

Little Uncle knelt to fine-tune the black-and-white picture.

"How about that?"

Mama put her napkin on her lap. "That's good, Little. Now come on before the food gets cold."

Daddy lowered his head and said grace. "Father, we thank You for this food You have provided, for the one who prepared it, and for those who might serve. Bless this food that it might nourish us as Your word nourishes our spirits. We thank You for sparing the lives of those gathered around this table. We thank You for this moment and for all present. We do not take it for granted. Amen."

Shirley looked around the table at Little Uncle, Big Uncle, her mother, and her father. "Amen."

Little Uncle dipped into the bowl of cabbage. "Look at that, man." He nodded at the TV. "Just about every day there's another riot. People are fed up and tired of singing peace songs and waiting." He shook his head while he held the spoon in midair. "Look. Buildings burning, police beating people—it's crazy."

"Give me that spoon, will you?" Big Uncle reached for the cabbage. "Yeah, people are tired of waiting, Little. But I'm just not sure that's the way to do it. How can we win? They're bound to outgun us. And anyway, like Malcolm said, 'He that lives by the sword, dies by the sword.'"

Mama put the biggest pork chop on Daddy's plate. "I just get tired of it. So much confusion. Why does it have to be this way? Why does it have to be so hard?"

"Thank you, Geneva." Daddy accepted the plate from Mama's hand. "We're living with the legacy of people that took the easy road."

Big Uncle looked up from his plate. "What you mean?"

"Look at the situation, Big. Slave traders wanted easy money, fast money, right? It was hard work to plant or build something, but they knew people that needed labor. People that were willing to pay, so the slave traders took the easy way, even if it was wrong."

Little Uncle turned from the TV. "But they weren't the only ones."

Daddy reached for a piece of cornbread. "You're right, Little. Some of them got help from some people in Africa who wanted easy money, even if it did mean selling other people. And right here, people bought other people because it was easy. It was easier to buy somebody than to have to work themselves or to pay somebody a fair wage. People took the easy road—even tried to blame it on God, and we know the church was right in the middle of it—and now we're paying for it."

Little Uncle nodded. "But they're still arguing over it. Here it is the 1960s and they still want to make us slaves. Man, they still want to say that we're not human, not smart. They still want to say that we're animals, and that if they didn't keep us in control we'd return to our natural state—to being savages. They even use the Bible to try to justify it."

Big Uncle's voice sounded rough. "Makes me sick—sick to my stomach."

Little Uncle jabbed his finger on the table. "*Sick* is right. I hear them saying stuff like 'the Bible condones slavery' and that 'God is silent on the issue.' Makes me want to vomit."

"Little!" Mama slapped her napkin up to her mouth.

"I mean it."

Daddy shook his head. "Anyone who says something like that must be intentionally stupid."

"Honey, not in front of the baby. I'm trying to teach her not to say *stupid*—"

"I know, honey. But our daughter needs to know the truth. This stuff affects us every day. Every day we have to fight to remember who we are, to overcome the junk that people hang around our necks to cover up their own sins, their own wrong. And she's going to have to fight that same fight or die—in her heart, in her mind, and in her spirit.

"I hear people say—we *all* hear it because it's in the news and everywhere we go—that black folks aren't smart because we're the descendants of Africans. We can't read, we can't write, we can't learn calculus. If you hear it enough, you start to believe it. And you know what the funny thing is? When I went to college, some of the smartest students were from Africa. Now, how could that be? How can they be smart and we're not? What happened to us between the time we left Africa, up to this day? Tell me how you explain that?"

Little Uncle shook his head. "Man, you ain't doing nothing but telling the truth."

"That's why it burns me up to hear people hiding behind God, behind the Lord, behind the Bible, to cover up what they did. God was *silent* on slavery? I guess that's not why He sent Moses to free the Israelite slaves? And why He punished the Egyptians. I guess it's not clear when Jesus says to 'do unto others as you would have them do unto you' to 'treat your neighbor as yourself'? I guess it's *not clear* when the Lord says that even the Samaritan was considered the Jew's brother."

Shirley wiggled in her chair; the green vinyl was sticking to the back of her legs. Daddy took a drink of Kool-Aid, then set his cup down. "God is not silent. People hear—they just don't want to listen."

Little Uncle laughed. "Ain't that right. Do unto others...how many people you know would say they want to be slaves? That they want to *not* be able to live where they want to? That they want to *not* be able to get decent jobs? Man, it's crazy."

Big Uncle sighed and shook his head. He picked at his food like he was thinking about something deep and hard. "Nobody can say that God likes slavery if they read the book of Amos in the Bible. That book is all about slavery and oppression. Ain't that where Dr. King got that line about justice?"

Little Uncle nodded. "'But let judgment run down as waters, and righteousness as a mighty stream.' That's what the Word says. Man, they even quote Philemon to try to justify slavery and segregation. Any person with a living heart can read that book and know that Paul was telling the slave owner that the slave was his brother—Paul said he could command the slave owner to do what was right and free Onesimus. But for the good of their future relations, Paul gave the slave owner the freedom to choose to do the righteous thing. For a man to read that passage and say it is not clear—man, I think that's blasphemy."

Mama left the table and went to the kitchen for a pitcher of water. Shirley could hear her mother pounding the metal ice tray, dumping the cubes in a stainless steel pitcher. Then she heard her mother turn on the water full force.

Big Uncle poured himself another drink from the Kool-Aid pitcher while he nodded. "Ain't no doubt about it, Little. Just like when preachers and other people that's supposed to be Christians try to say Paul and Peter supported slavery."

Little Uncle jabbed at the table again with his finger. "You got that right. Paul named slave traders as ungodly and not in accordance with sound doctrine, just like he named perverts, liars, adulterers, and perjurers—I think that's pretty clear. Paul and Peter didn't say slavery was right; they asked the slaves to submit to their masters in order to serve God's purposes, so that their masters might see God through the meekness He put in the slaves. All throughout the Bible, slavery is spoken of in negative terms."

Mama walked back in from the kitchen, placed the pitcher in the center of the table, and sat down.

Big Uncle looked disgusted. "Well, then, why don't men change and do what's right? Why aren't all Christians—Negro, white, Chinese—why ain't everybody standing up and saying that what's happening here is wrong? Some of the people that give Dr. King and the other freedom fighters the hardest time are supposed to be Christians. The folks that say 'just be quiet, this doesn't have anything to do with us.'"

"Because they just don't want to. Because they make excuses why it's not their problem. And you know what, Big? That's one of the first reasons that atheists give me why they don't believe in the church and why they don't believe in God. 'What about slavery?' they say."

"I don't know what it's going to take, Big. When Dr. King and others were walking around begging for freedom—praying, singing, asking Christian folks for help—it fell on deaf ears. It seems like nothing started happening until some of the young brothers—Stokely Carmichael, H. Rap Brown—started talking about an eye for an eye. It shouldn't take that for Christian people to wake up. It shouldn't take a prophet preaching on a hill; it shouldn't take the country coming to ruin for them to wake up."

Little Uncle leaned across the table toward Daddy. "Ain't no doubt about it, Calvin. What gets me, though, is the argument about slavery being okay because the slaves were heathens.

Man, that stuff is truly crazy—just a filthy lie. Who are they kidding? Like they were stopping people and asking them if they were Christians before they loaded them on the boats. All Africans weren't fetish worshipers. All of them weren't Moslem; some were already Christian. There were Christians as early as the third century in Africa. And we are definitely Christians now, and they still treating us bad. Explain that! Slavery been over for years, and people are still getting lynched. Look at that boy from Chicago, that Emmett Till. They beat him with baseball bats and threw him in the river. Look at Medgar Evers. Look at those three college boys in 1964—Schwerner, Chaney, and Goodman. The way we're going, people will still be getting lynched in the year 2000—if we haven't blown up the planet by then."

Little Uncle sucked his teeth. "And you know how it was—lynching was like a festival. They even sold tickets and took body parts for souvenirs—not just in the 1800s, but in this century too. And man, I keep thinking that some of those people that participated and watched, they got to be alive. They got to even be in the church. They got to be going to church and still carrying that around. Yet, and still, they hate Dr. King—the one man that would pray for their forgiveness. Man, I know racism has got to be rooted in the sin of pride. And the Bible said people would know we are Christians by the love that we have for one another. No wonder they don't recognize us."

Mama set the pitcher on the table and shook her head. "I just wish it was over. I don't want to talk about it or think about it. It just makes my blood run cold." Then she sat down.

Daddy shook his head. "I know how you feel, Geneva. But that's still the easy way out. We have to talk about it. That's why this has lasted so long. People don't want to go through anything hard. They want to fix it if there's a way to do it that doesn't put them out or make them uncomfortable in any way. We want to fix the problem, but only if there's an easy way to fix it—a way that doesn't cause us any discomfort. We don't even want to talk about it, but we *have* to talk together, reason together, if we want to kill this cancer. We're going to have to stop dancing and singing around it; we're going to have to stop accepting it—we're going to have to be radical like Christ. And we're going to have to realize that when we leave them ignorant to how their behavior flies in the face of who God is, that we're allowing them to stay stuck in sin and bondage. It's bad for everybody concerned."

Big Uncle nodded. "I've been thinking about marching. I've been thinking I should do something besides watch what's happening on TV. I don't feel right about doing nothing."

"Man, what are you talking about?" Little Uncle pointed at the console. "Look at those people getting knocked upside the head. How will getting knocked upside the head make you feel better?"

"I don't know, Little. I just don't feel good about it."

"Man, you better sit here in this fine house with that big plate of food and be satisfied. You got to be crazy. I'm talking about speaking up, but you going too far the other way. You thinking too hard—let me do that for you." Little Uncle dodged when Big Uncle swiped at him with his napkin.

Little Uncle patted his brother on the back. "I'm joking, Big. But you know in a way I'm really serious. Things are getting more and more violent. People are frustrated. They're tired of waiting for folks' hearts to change. Look at Stokely Carmichael. He was right with King, believing in nonviolence and the goodness of the Christian soul. I guess he got knocked in the head one too many times by those good Christians, 'cause now he's one of the main ones out there shouting Black Power." Little patted Big's back again. "Wonder what would have happened, where we would be now, if folks had responded the way King and Carmichael pleaded with them to right up front?"

He shook his head. "Makes no difference now. Things are like they are. Watch and see if they don't hunt Stokely and the rest of those young brothers like they were dogs. Big, a man like you would just be a target in a mess like what's going on now."

Mama held a forkful of apples poised at her mouth. "Well, I tell you what, Big. I don't even want to hear you talk about doing anything crazy. I don't believe I can take much more. They killed Kennedy, and we're supposed to believe some crazy man did it. They killed Medgar and Malcolm. King is all we got left. And look at how they did those people marching in Selma—men, women, and children—it was supposed to be nonviolent, peaceful. And they beating them, trampling them, dogs biting them. What kind of people that call themselves Christian would *do* something like that? If they did it to them, they would do it to you, Big. And I'm telling you, I just can't take it."

Little looked at the screen and shook his head. "They don't want things to change. And right now, I think they'd kill anybody. No disrespect, but I think they'd kill Jesus if He spoke up for civil rights…and if King knows what's good for *him*, he'll watch himself."

Big Uncle threw his fork down. "Now why would you say something like that, Little? Nobody's going to kill Reverend King." Big Uncle looked at Mama. "Sorry, Geneva." He picked up his fork. "I can't believe you would say something like that."

"Big, you know people are angry. People don't like change, and just like Frederick Douglas said, nobody gives up power willingly. People are going to fight, kill, cheat, steal—whatever they have to do to hold on to power."

Daddy shook his head. "I hate to agree with you, Little, but it sure looks that way. King has been doing this nonviolent thing, hoping people's good hearts would make them do the right thing. Hoping that the love of Jesus would cause men to do right. Funny thing is, it looks like they hate him for it— what they don't know is that King is standing between them and a whole lot of angry young brothers that don't have nothing to lose."

Mama pointed at Little Uncle. "I know what you're saying, but I still have to believe that white people are going to do the right thing. I just have to. I don't think I could take it otherwise. I have to believe that one day they are going to listen to Dr. King. We've been through so much. Maybe I count on him too much, but I believe in what Dr. King is doing and I believe it's going to turn around. I have to believe that." She wiped her mouth and then opened it again to speak.

"Wait a minute, Geneva." Little Uncle grinned at the TV. "My favorite commercial is on. I love that little fella." Little Uncle started to sing. "'Plop-plop, fizz-fizz!'"

"'Oh, what a relief it is!'" Shirley finished the jingle.

"No singing at the table, Shirley."

"Sorry, Mama."

Mama rolled her eyes at Little Uncle and started talking again when the Alka-Seltzer commercial switched to one for Bryl Cream. "Like I was saying, I just hate all of this. It doesn't look like what Johnson is trying to do is working. They still don't want to let us vote. We can't get jobs, can't live where we want to. Look at us. Here we are in this neighborhood, but you know they don't want us here." She sighed while in the background voices on TV sang, *"A little dab'll do ya!"*

"When is it ever going to end? People can't take much more. It makes me sick that my baby has to grow up afraid, that she has to live through all this hatred—has to watch grown people being…being…*stupid!* I tell you, much more and I will go crazy."

Big Uncle shrugged. "I don't know, Geneva. That's why I feel bad about not doing anything. People need help."

"Big, I'm telling you, I don't want to *hear* about you doing anything. I just can't take anymore."

Little Uncle smirked. "Don't worry about him, Geneva. What are you going to do, man? You don't live in Watts, Big. You don't live in Mississippi—"

Mama interrupted. "No, we don't. But we are from Texas, and I *do* want to go there soon. Grandmama Lucy and Grandaddy Demo are getting older. All the old people— Mother Johnson—everybody. And I don't want to wait until they pass before we get back down there, no matter how bad things are. Shirley needs to see her people and—"

Little Uncle held up his hand. "Wait a minute. They're talking about Vietnam."

The newscaster voiced over casualty totals while on-screen images flashed of body bags being dragged through the jungle by helmeted soldiers.

Little Uncle shook his head. "They don't even have the decency to show us dead. You know how many Negroes there are in Vietnam, especially compared to the number of white boys? But they hardly ever show us serving—not even dying."

Big Uncle shook his head while Mama talked. "What kind of thing is this to show on TV when they know people are eating dinner and they know children are watching?

"What kind of world is this?" Mama wiped her mouth and looked away from the television toward Daddy. "At least I have one consolation. With all that's going on, and with you having to be away from home all the time, at least I don't have to worry about you being in Vietnam. And thank God for that, because I tell you, I just could not take it. I think it would kill me."

Daddy looked down at his plate and then looked away.

Little Uncle shook his head at the TV. "That Vietnam is a bad situation. People getting picked off like flies."

Big Uncle looked at Daddy. "Be quiet, Little."

Mama started to cry. "I pray all the time, 'Lord, let all the craziness be over.' I tell you, the only thing that's keeping me is knowing that my family is safe and intact. Jesus knows I couldn't take it."

Daddy laid his hand on top of Mama's hand. "Don't cry now, Geneva. Everything's all right. Things aren't so bad—it's not even really a war."

Little Uncle set his glass of Kool-Aid down on the table. "What are you *talking* about, Calvin? All they're doing is tagging them and bagging them. Bagging them and tagging them."

Big Uncle punched Little Uncle in the arm.

"What you do that for, man?"

Big Uncle nodded in Daddy's direction.

"I tell you, I just couldn't take it. Thank God you're not in Vietnam."

Daddy smiled at Mama. "Not this week anyway."

Mama jerked her hand away. "What kind of a joke is that,

Calvin? You see I'm upset and you want to make jokes."

He shook his head. "I'm not joking, Geneva. That's why I'm home. They gave me leave so I could come home and tell you…I'm on my way. They're sending me to Vietnam."

SEVEN

"hy did you even come home? Am I supposed to be happy you're letting them send you away to die? Leaving me to raise a child by myself?"

Lying in her bed, Shirley listened to her father's voice. "Geneva, be reasonable. What am I supposed to do?"

"You're supposed to think about us."

"I'm in the army, Geneva. I take orders—that's what I signed up for. There are more troops in the field, that means more casualties, that means they need more rescue helicopters. That's what I do, I have to be there. Don't make this harder than it is."

"Don't give me that 'be brave' speech, Calvin. I'm not ready to be brave yet. You can't expect me to say everything is okay when you just come in here like nothing's happening and then drop this on me."

"Geneva, be reasonable. Don't make this any harder on me. I'm the only Negro in my unit. I can't fail. I can't even think about quitting. You know we don't have the luxury of even considering something like that—"

First one pillow, then another—facedown, Shirley piled the pillows on top of herself. She drew her knees up to her chest. Then she pulled the covers over her head. Humming didn't work, either. There was enough between her—walls, pillows, blankets—and her parents' voices that came from the other room that she could not make out the words, but nothing could block the screaming, the wailing, the intonations that always said more than words.

She peeked from beneath the pillows and looked out of her window at the full, round moon. Then she covered her head and drew her knees up toward her chest again.

Rock me, baby Jesus,
Hold me, baby Jesus,
Love me, baby Jesus,
So I won't be afraid.

Her lips formed the words to the song she had made up to protect her when she was afraid. She whispered the song that kept the darkness and loneliness at bay, the song that put her to sleep when the lights were out. And sometimes when she cried, she was sure that He sat on the edge of her bed while the angels drifted around her. Shirley was certain that sometimes He touched her hair and told her to sleep, that everything was all right.

Rock me, baby Jesus,
Hold me, baby Jesus,
Keep me, baby Jesus,
So I won't be afraid.

Shirley pulled her knees up tighter and squeezed her eyes shut.

It wasn't until morning that Shirley knew that at some point she had finally slept.

The covers pulled back, and the pillows lifted from her head. She felt a hand touch her hair. "Wake up, Shirley. Wake up, baby." Then a shake—"Wake up, Shirley." Then a kiss—"Come on, precious." It was Daddy. "Look at you all balled up like a roly-poly."

Shirley flopped over on her side, then slowly opened her eyes. "Daddy?"

"It's all right, baby. Don't worry. Everything is going to be all right."

"You promise?"

His kiss on her forehead was warm and firm. "I promise." Daddy smelled of Old Spice. "Come on now, sugar. Get up. Don't you want to fix your bike so you can get back on and ride?"

"I don't think I want to ride, Daddy."

"Sure you do, Shirley." He pulled the covers back farther. "Let me see that ankle." She held it out and he took it in his hand. "Look at that! It looks good as new. And your mama and your uncles told me how brave you were."

Shirley looked at her ankle and sighed.

"You know why you feel that way, baby?"

She laid her head back on one of the pillows. One of her braids moved as she shook her head from side to side.

Daddy smiled. "It's because the last memory you have of your bike is a bad one—the accident. You just have to make a new memory. We'll do it together."

"Can't ride worth nothing." Shirley could still hear her cousin Rosie's voice. *"Girl, you bleeding! Look at your ankle."* She sighed again.

Daddy pulled her onto his lap. "Come on, Shirley. Listen to Daddy." He hugged her. "I want you to always remember this: When you fall down, you have to get back up. That's just how life is. If you lay down, the bad memory wins. If you lay down, you'll just be scared and unhappy all the time. We fall down, but we have to get back up and try again. Then try again, if we have to. Okay?"

Inside she felt more like a no, but she said, "Yes, sir."

"All right then. We're in business. Now get ready and meet me outside."

The bike wasn't smashed flat. Except for a little tar, it looked as good as new—or at least appeared that it would look brand new once Daddy put the chain back on and reattached the chain guard.

An early fall wind blew through the breezeway. Shirley buttoned her sweater.

The training wheels lay off to the side. "Those will just slow you down—you don't need them anymore. You'll be riding in no time." Daddy dug in his toolbox. He whistled while he worked. "Look at that—" he pointed at the repaired bike— "done in no time flat."

Daddy closed the toolbox and set it to the side. "Come on, let's give it a test drive." He looked back over his shoulder, talking to Shirley as he rolled the bicycle out to the street. "You watch and see. You can do it. Easy. No sweat. In a little while, you'll be riding your bike so fast you'll be breaking the sound barrier—making sonic booms like those planes we heard when we moved in. Remember them?"

Shirley laughed. "Daddy."

He shrugged his shoulders. "I don't know why you don't believe me."

Daddy helped her onto the bike and stationed her near the curb. "Okay, we're ready. Put your feet on the pedals."

"Daddy?"

He kissed her on the cheek. "Yes, baby?"

"Daddy, is Mama going to be all right?"

He closed his eyes for a second and cleared his throat. "Yes, baby. Don't worry. She was just a little upset; that's human. She loves me. She loves you. She loves us. But she's going to be strong, and your uncles will be here. I'll be back home in no time. Good as new, just like your bike. You don't have to worry. Everything's going to be all right."

He winked at Shirley. "Now get on this baby and let me see you ride." He held the back of the seat with one hand and the handlebars with his other. When she had some speed, he let go. "Look at you, girl! You're free now. The speed barrier is gone! Boom! Boom! Boom!" She rode back, and he held her in his arms. "Everything is going to be all right. I promise." He loosed her and stepped back.

"Now, Shirley, I want you to promise me that when you ride you'll be careful. Just to the end of the block and back, unless you have someone older with you. If someone older is with you, you can ride to the end of the street and turn left to ride down Sixty-First Street, like the way you walk home. But not right, and no farther than that."

"Why, Daddy?"

"Promise me, Shirley."

"Yes, sir."

"It's for your own good."

"I promise, Daddy."

She held her mother's hand while they stood next to the car.

"Be strong for me, okay, Geneva?" Mama nodded then looked away. "I'll be back soon—I promise."

Daddy gave Shirley a crisp salute. "You be careful breaking that sound barrier. Keep your eye out for cars—you don't want to destroy 'em." He smiled. "I love you all." He started the engine then began to ease the car down the driveway. He stopped the car and put it in park. Then he shook his head. "No, we've had enough hugs and kisses, right?" A frown crossed his face; then it was back to a smile. "We're all kissed out, and I've got a plane to meet. You know what, Shirley? You watch for planes that fly over the house. When we fly out of Scott Air Force Base, if I can see you outside, I'll get the pilot to do just like Penny and her uncle on *Sky King*. We will tip the wings at you."

"Okay, Daddy."

He waved one last time. "I love you, Geneva. I love you, Shirley. Don't worry, I'm coming home soon, I promise. You take care of each other." He drove the car quickly down the street and out of sight.

When Mama went into the house, Shirley rolled her bicycle off of the breezeway and out to the street. She placed one foot on a pedal and used the other to balance like Daddy had shown her. *"You can do it. Easy. No sweat."* She took a deep breath, lifted her other foot, and began to ride. She rode to the end of her block—alone. Her heart pounded. Then she circled back to her house.

Shirley looked in the direction her father had driven. *Look at you, girl! You're free now. The speed barrier is gone! Boom! Boom! Boom!*

She was going to be all right.

EIGHT

*H*e would not share his name, not even with others of like kind.

His name was key to his defeat, so he was known only by his function and his assignment. Child killer. His sole purpose was to keep watch over his charge, a child. Keep watch and kill, spiritually and physically. He incited havoc around her until she submitted to some manner of evil—depression, frustration, doubt, anger—or until he caused her death. He was a child killer; his assignment was Shirley.

Child Killer Shirley hunched in the darkness of the Second Heaven. In another world he might have been thought handsome—if one avoided his one dead eye and the other eye that pulsed a sick yellow light. His tongue flipped from his mouth, wrapped round his face, and licked the wound that gaped open where his left ear had once been. He frowned up toward the Third Heaven, toward the realm into which he could not see, toward the realm that could see him, the realm that was bound or loosed by prayers.

He would make the child pay. He had almost had her, almost had his hand around her throat last night.

Her father was busy and her mother was distracted, so there weren't many prayers going up on her account. She was soft and weak. But always when he was close, so close, she sang that song. He drew his tongue back into his mouth and clamped his clawed hands over his ears—at least over the one remaining ear—he could still hear the song. The song that called down Glory. The song that called down her guardian, moving him into action. The child killer could still hear the song, and the resulting blows struck by her guardian from the Third Heaven. Even now, it plagued him. He could hear the soft thing's voice…

Rock me, baby Jesus,
Hold me, baby Jesus,
Keep me, baby Jesus,
So I won't be afraid

He growled. Like his master, he hated music, songs that spoke to heaven, songs that reminded him of where he had once lived, songs that reminded him he had once been in the presence of God. Songs that reminded him of his eternal mistake.

She would pay.

The child killer took a deep, dark, jagged breath and forced himself to stand. A hot jolt of pain shot from his midsection up through his chest. He stretched his arms in front to look at the charred scales that covered his muscles. His beautiful scales. Once green and blue, they were now blackened—burned, maybe permanently damaged. Child Killer Shirley cursed her Third Heaven guardian. The soft one would be sorry for what he had suffered, and so would her Third Heaven guardian who had inflicted the pain. Children's prayers! He spat into the swirling firmament under his feet. Insipid little prayers that activated the Host.

She would pay, and it would not be difficult. Shirley's mother was helping. Her mother loved the soft one, but all the child's life she had been speaking and teaching the child despair—one of the languages of death. The soft thing would be his.

Behind him the minions lurked and gurgled.

"May we serve you?" One of the shapeless things made sucking noises as it spoke. Not even worthy of form, the things existed—never to be promoted, never satisfied, and filled with ambition—only minions.

The child killer ignored it and continued surveying the damage to his form. He ran his hands along his heavily muscled thighs, up his slender hips, to his broad chest.

One of the minions slithered closer and reached a mis-shapen hand to tug at one of the child killer's loose and damaged scales. Something like spittle dripped from what must have been the minion's mouths. The child killer swatted the thing away so that it thudded then skidded into the rest of the waiting, slobbering pack.

"Not yet," the child killer growled. He turned and glowered at the minions. "Don't fix your mouths for me. I'm still alive." Then Child Killer Shirley turned his head so that he could fix his one good eye on the child far beneath him on the earth.

The soft, weak thing would pay.

NINE

"What can you teach me?" Ken snarled from the cloakroom corner where he sat. "You ain't nothing but a—a—little old girl!"

It was pretty clear that he didn't use Vitalis—his hair was dusty, blond, and dry, not slicked back and parted like the men on TV. His hair was uncombed and looked more like animal fur.

He looked away from Shirley and clamped his arms tightly across his chest.

Just a few more minutes, she told herself. *Just a few more and we'll be out of this cloakroom and going home.* She glared at Ken. It was hard, too hard. They couldn't remember the sounds or the smallest words, and Ken didn't even try. At least Barbara and Misty pretended to be interested or looked amused at her efforts to teach them to read—unlike Ken. Shirley wanted to punch him.

But if she could just hold out...just a few more minutes. School would be out early today. Just a few more minutes. Misty's hair was tied in the usual ribbons, but Barbara's hair was teased into a snarling, dishwater blond beehive. She wore harsh pink lipstick and bright blue eye shadow, and she felt for the packet of cigarettes in her sweater pocket.

Brrring! Brrring! The bell!

Ken stood up and left his chair where it fell backward on the floor. "You pick it up." He glared at Shirley and then slammed out of the cloakroom.

Barbara set the chair back on its feet. "Don't pay no attention to Ken. He's simple." She shrugged her shoulders and smiled. "Come on, Misty, so the bus won't leave us. I got somewhere to go tonight." Barbara nodded at Shirley. "Good teachin' today. See you Monday."

Misty waved good-bye while Barbara pulled her out the door by her other hand.

Mrs. Canada appeared in the doorway that led from the classroom as Barbara and Misty exited through the door that led out to the hallway. "Looks like they charged out of here on you. Well, I guess you're about ready to go anyway." She laid her hand on Shirley's shoulder and smiled. "Is this too much for you, Shirley? I don't want this to be a burden on you. If it's too much—"

"Oh no, ma'am. I like it," Shirley lied. She could not fail. She did not have the luxury of quitting.

"You'll tell me if it gets to be too much? Promise me, Shirley."

"Oh yes, ma'am. But don't worry, I'm doing fine."

Trina held her portable radio to her ear. "'Land of a Thousand Dances'! That's my favorite song." She started to shake it to the east and shake it to the west. She did the Jerk and the Monkey. Shirley joined in and did the Mashed Potatoes.

"Look at you. Look how stiff you are." Trina pointed at Shirley and laughed. "You dance like a white girl."

"No, I don't."

"Yes, you do. You think you so smart. You can't even dance. You can't stay on the beat." Trina pushed Shirley's shoulder. "Stop it. Stop trying to dance to my radio. This is *my* music."

"Forget you, Trina!" Shirley was scared, but she pushed back.

"No, forget *you*, Shirley!" Trina pushed again, harder. "You can't dance or nothing. I don't even think you are a Negro."

"Yes, I am."

"Could have fooled me."

"My daddy said I can dance *good.*"

"Well, guess what, Miss Smarty Pants? Your daddy ain't here, and I say you can't dance."

Trina was older, taller, and she had a reputation for fighting. But Shirley's forehead was pounding. "Don't you talk about my daddy! And forget you anyway, Trina!"

"No, forget *you*, Shirley!"

Her ankle was throbbing, and she felt like she wanted to go to the bathroom. "Forget you, forgot you, never thought about you!" Shirley stepped closer—it would be worth getting beat up.

"Oo-oo-oo-oo!" The other kids looked and crowded in. "It's going to be a fight!"

"You know what, Shirley? You're not even *worth* fighting. You too little—a little third-grade Negro. I don't even know why I bother hanging around you, you little kid. But since you forget me, forgot me, never thought about me, why don't you walk home by your *own* little self. *That'll* fix your little red wagon."

"I don't need you, Trina! I don't even *want* to walk with you!"

"Bye, then!"

"Bye!"

The other kids looked back over their shoulders as they followed Trina home. Shirley wanted to run and catch them, to tell Trina she was sorry. She didn't want to be alone. Didn't want to walk home alone. Didn't want to be snatched and killed like Emmit Till. She could feel tears welling in her eyes.

Up ahead, Trina laughed out loud—extra loud. "You all just wait, she's gone be bawlin' any second now. Crying her little eyes out…crying for her mama…wishing her daddy was home."

Shirley blinked. She licked her lips, threw her book bag over her shoulder, and sucked it up. She would walk alone. She had to. Shirley watched her image reflected in the shop windows she walked by. *Be brave. Don't look scared.*

She stopped in front of the IGA. Shirley looked ahead at Trina and the other children. She would make sure they didn't think she wanted to walk with them. She stepped on the automatic door pad and went inside.

The grocery store clerks—the checkers—looked at her like she didn't belong there. As though they wondered why she was there, if she intended to steal something.

On the candy aisle, she saw two children she knew from school. Shirley raised her hand to wave at them, then dropped it when she saw their mother.

The same faceless mom…like the ones who lived on her street, who lived in her neighborhood, who had children—her schoolmates, who played with her at school. But in the neighborhood where she lived, those children ignored her or became invisible themselves in the presence of their moms. In the grocery store, walking with their mothers, the same children who shoved and elbowed to play with Shirley on the playground did not know her. She had already learned the lesson. It had already happened over and over again. She had called their names, but they did not recognize her, or they pretended not to hear her when they walked near their moms.

Shirley's mother had taught her it was impolite not to speak when spoken to—it was an offense worthy of a spanking. But the moms did not upbraid their children for not returning her greeting; the moms did not speak themselves. Sometimes children called her *nigger* when they rolled by on carts pushed by their moms, and the women kept moving—nameless, faceless, voiceless.

Shirley knew the moms did not like her because they would not let her pile into their cars with the other children on rainy days. They would not let her join the Brownie troop at school—there was no room, they said. They tried to keep their children from her, told them not to play with her, and sometimes the moms let their dogs out to bite her and other Negro children when they walked past their doors.

Shirley had already learned the lesson.

But the moms did not know that at school, out of their presence, their children adored Shirley because she was smart and nice and fun. And she did not hate the moms, even though they hurt her because she knew that they were sickly and confused by the silence in which they lived.

It did not matter so much that the moms did not love her. She was the smartest child in her class that first year in

Centerville, and all the other children knew it. Shirley walked down the candy aisle, then walked quietly out of the store. Every adult eye followed her.

Shirley stopped outside and took a deep breath. By now, Trina and the others had to be home already. *I can make it alone. I can make it.* She started walking until she reached the corner. Then Shirley ran all the way home.

Standing in the breezeway, she dropped her book bag and then dragged her bike from the garage. Shirley wrestled the bike down the driveway and out to the edge of the street. Swinging her leg over, she rode down to the corner and circled back three times. She took a deep breath, looked both ways, set her mouth, then rode to the corner.

And a few feet beyond.

TEN

*I*t had rained that morning. The smell was still in the air. Early spring flowers were showing their faces—tulips, irises, crocuses. Shirley sat on the breezeway watching them. The house seemed empty without Daddy. With Daddy away in Vietnam, Mama hardly ever smiled, and she never laughed anymore. Not even when Big Uncle and Little Uncle went out of their way to entertain her. Most times she just stared into space; sometimes she mumbled softly to herself as though there was some problem she was trying to figure out.

Fall spilled into winter into new spring, and Little Uncle talked about heart transplants and exploding spaceships, riots, and UFOs—but he never mentioned Vietnam. Not unless he wanted to hold Mama when she began to shake and howl.

And school was no better. The Greenbirds were still as they were on the first day. Shirley's only consolation was the poem that Mrs. Canada had her studying. A poem by William Wordsworth—"Not Longfellow," Mrs. Canada said, "Wordsworth."—that Mrs. Canada sent her to recite to rooms full of third and fourth graders.

I wander'd lonely as a cloud
That floats on high o'er vales and hills,
When all at once I saw a crowd,
A host, of golden daffodils,
Beside the lake, beneath the trees,
Fluttering and dancing in the breeze.

The poem was nice, reciting it was nice, but it didn't make up for or explain why the Cooties could not read.

"Is it too much for you, Shirley?"

"No, ma'am."

"You just let me know if it is."

What made it a little better was baseball—there was nothing like the slap of the ball into the glove or the crack of the bat—and riding. Riding to the corner, riding farther. Maybe today, she would ride all the way to the end.

Her uncles sat in the living room with her mother, watching the newsbreaks, listening to the count. So many murdered, so many wounded, so many missing in action.

Big Uncle nodded. "Hey, Shirley girl. How's it going?"

"Fine, Big Uncle."

"You sure?"

"Yes, sir."

"That's my girl."

Mama looked lost. "Make sure you change your clothes, baby."

"Yes, ma'am."

She ran to her room, changed, ran back through the house, got her bike, and rode. She did circles and figure eights down to the corner and back. Then Shirley rode farther. Down to the end of the street and around the bend. To the right. She saw houses she had never seen and a field.

Daddy's voice whispered to her, *"Promise me that when you ride you'll be careful. Just to the end of the block and back... But not right, and no farther than that."* Daddy was just worrying, and there was no reason to worry. She only had to ride back the way she came—she could find her way back home.

In front of her were wonders that she would have never seen on her own street, like one house with a plastic, pink flamingo in front and another with a jockey. But most wondrous of all was a large rock, a boulder in the middle of the field—a boulder like the one she remembered at the picnic grounds at Monks Mound in Cahokia, Illinois. The land was flat where she lived, but Monks Mound was full of hills and trails and Indian arrowheads. And there was the face of the horrible Piasa bird on a bluff—or maybe the rock was in Forest Park, near the St. Louis Zoo or near the Jewel Box. She wasn't sure where.

Shirley had gotten lost near that boulder. It was a strange place, and she kept thinking of the Piasa bird—the huge, strange bird that ate men—and she cried. It was a bird with a strange face, long sharp talons, red and yellow feathers—oddly human-looking shoulders and head.

But she was a little kid then. She was older now, and she would not cry. *"Mama, Daddy, help me!"* She was older now, and there was no need to be afraid. She wasn't worried. Excited maybe, but not worried.

It was much easier riding the bike now, but she still struggled. She rode over the bumps on the field to circle the rock. The ground was still wet, and mud sucked at her bike tires and made the going slow. She laid her bike on a footpath that cut across the field and walked toward the boulder. Shirley touched the cold, white rock and began to circle it, staring at the houses. Just like on her street, no one seemed to be at home.

Still touching the rock, she looked down at the brown mud beneath her feet—if she wasn't careful, it would suck the shoes off of her. Shirley laughed at what it looked like on her Buster Browns. The green grass stuck out of the muck on her shoes, like green whiskers.

The rock was much bigger than it appeared from the street. She could not see over or around it. It was like the chat, the small white rocks on her street, only a million, zillion times bigger. Shirley kept walking, it seemed like forever, and still never came back to the place where she started. She did not see her bike, or the path, or anything that she knew or remembered. She had come too far.

Shirley did not cry out loud, because she was too far from home. If someone mean came to get her, to hurt her, no one would know where to look. Just like Emmit Till. No one would find her. She stood panicked, staring at the rock because she did not want to look at the street and the field she did not know. *How can I be lost?*

You went too far, her mind replied. *And they don't know where you are.*

She could hear her heart beating; she felt it. Everything slowed. Shirley could still smell the grass and feel the sun, but the day broke apart.

I have to find my way home.

You better stay still so someone can find you, her mind said.

I better move. And Shirley turned to rescue herself.

Then there she was.

Another little girl, just looking at Shirley. Her expression said that *she* wasn't lost, but she knew Shirley *was*.

"Hey, you girl," she said.

Shirley didn't answer right away. The little girl looked bad. Shirley wasn't afraid of bad kids; she was strong enough to take care of herself—she had beat up one or two bad kids before, when she had to—but not when she was lost.

"I said, hey, you girl. Cat got your tongue?" The little girl's clothes were dirty, and her hair was nappy and uncombed.

Shirley fixed her mouth so that she would not look afraid. "Hi."

"You crying? You lost?"

"No, I'm not crying. I was looking at the rock."

"Crying ain't no big fat deal," the little girl said. "You run away? I run away before. I been to new places before." She didn't seem so bad after all. At least not mean.

"I don't know where I am," Shirley said. Then her face broke.

"Don't cry, little girl. I know where you are." She walked to the rock and took Shirley's hand and patted her on the shoulder. "I been way farther than this before. And I was watching you. I know where your bike is and your street is really close."

"It's almost dusk-dark!" All kids had to be home by dusk-dark, even bad ones. The little girl nodded—she understood.

"I'll walk you to your street, little girl," she said, still patting Shirley on her shoulder. They held hands, and the little girl walked Shirley around the rock until she saw her bicycle on the path where she left it.

"There's your bike. See? I told you. You don't have to cry no more."

Shirley wiped her face. "I'm not crying. And I'm not a little girl. I'm as old as you."

"Come on, little girl. We better start walking."

Shirley kept in step. "I'm not a little girl. I'm as grown as you are."

"No, you not. You not old as me. You ain't never been nowhere, and I been everywhere. I can take care of myself. I'm small, but I ain't no little girl. You are a little girl. Look at you—" she pointed at the ribbons in Shirley's hair—"your mama comb your hair, wash your clothes, and cook for you. You ain't got no knife to protect yourself. I bet your mama even fight for you. You *are* a little girl." She smiled. "But I like you anyway. It's okay to be a little girl."

They stopped at the end of Shirley's street. "Thank you."

The little girl shrugged and smiled. Shirley liked her and smiled back, even if she was bad.

"You can come play with me if you want to," the bad girl said. "I be out by that rock all the time. You know the way there now. You won't get lost."

Shirley watched the little bad girl walk away. The girl turned back to wave, her hands gray and grimy. She blew Shirley a kiss, then shook her hips side to side and hooted. "Bring me some cookies next time!" Then she turned and ran into the coming darkness.

Shirley hopped on her bike and pedaled home, riding fast to beat the street lamps—to be home before they lit. She was up the driveway and had her bicycle in the garage before the lamp near her house turned on. When she opened the door and stepped into the kitchen, Mama was at the sink wiping the counter. "You made it home just in time. Just by the skin of your teeth." Mama's eyes were red. "Go on and wash your hands. Then go in there and sit down with your uncles. We're fixing to eat."

Mama's face looked like she was trying to force a weak smile. "Did you have a good time?"

"Yes, ma'am."

"All right then. Go on and get ready." The smile faded, and Mama turned back to the sink, mumbling to herself.

At dinner she kept saying, "I'll sure be glad when your daddy gets home. God knows I can't take anymore."

Little Uncle pointed at the television screen. "Look at all those people. Who would have thought all those people would be crowded around the Pentagon. Hippies, regular folks, protesting the war. All they need to round out the group is George Wallace or H. Rap Brown—" he laughed—"wouldn't that be something to see?"

Big Uncle shook his head. "I told you, people feel like they need to do something…something about a lot of things." Some of the protestors carried signs that said "Make love—not war." Some had signs that said "Bring our boys home." "Power to the people" other signs read. The footage showed them singing and chanting while they stood toe-to-toe with military police officers. Mama kept her eyes fastened on her plate; she pushed her food around with her fork.

Big Uncle stared at his brother. "Everybody needs to do something. We owe more to this world than to just sit here and breathe."

Shirley stared at the screen and thought she saw a girl her age marching among the protestors. The girl's back was turned and her sign could not be read. Shirley imagined herself there. Marching. Marching for Daddy, for the one who loved her, the one who danced with her. If she were there, she would protest, because Vietnam had stolen her love away and upset her home. The girl on the TV turned and faced the camera. *"Bring my daddy back alive,"* her sign read.

Shirley closed her eyes and began to daydream of her bicycle and the girl beyond the end of her block.

ELEVEN

*E*very day she thought about the little bad girl—between each consonant song, behind every vowel repetition, and under every word the Cooties could not read, the girl was there. At every recess, while Shirley watched the other children play, the memory of the little girl stood near her.

Shirley was alone because Trina, Tina Turner's niece, had waved her away. "You might as well go on, Shirley. You not playing with us. You better go on and see if you can find you some white friends, since we won't play with you. Maybe those Cootie kids you teach."

Shirley walked away and stood huddled on a mound on the playground where she could see the other children—the white children—flying in and out of each other's arms like bright, wool-coated butterflies. She could see the Negro children playing baseball. But the Cooties gathered near the green-painted school yard fence.

Hi-ho-the-derry-o, the Cooties stood alone.

The white children fluttered by her, while chilly midwestern air turned their breath to clouds. "Does it rub off, Shirley?"

"No, it's just in my skin."

"Are you sure? How did you get that way?"

"A witch did it to me. See?" She showed the undersides of her hands to the pink butterflies. "My palms are white, like yours. I'm not different."

"My mom says niggers are dirty and they steal."

"But not me." Something sank inside her. "Not me." *Hi-ho-the-derry-o, the Cooties stood alone.*

"But you play with them all the time."

"Negroes don't steal."

"Yes, they do. My mom said so."

"But not me. Not me." The butterflies flew away. The memory of the little bad girl stood beside Shirley and kept her warm. Vietnam had her father and the shadows were taking her mother—*hi-ho-the-derry-o, the cheese stands alone*—but she had the little bad girl for company.

Saturday morning—after Shirley quietly put away her Easy Bake oven, after she dyed Barbie's hair for the sixth time, after she whispered and acted out the voices for Barbie and Francie on their trip to the beach, after a bowl of Apple Jacks, after making it to the ninesies three times while she played jacks alone, after playing with the Do Bee ring she earned during her stint on Romper Room, after watching cartoons and then deciding against watching more cartoons—Shirley tiptoed past her mother's bedroom door. The curtains were drawn to keep out the sun, and there was no sound except her mother's breathing. She ran for her bicycle and rode down her street and to the right, to the place where she met the little girl. She waited, did not see her, and then rode back home.

"Oh, Lord! Oh, God, no!"

Her mother's shriek reached Shirley outside. She sat still waiting to hear what she had waited to hear since her daddy left. Months had passed, and her mother had drawn deeper and deeper into the shadows.

"How could they kill him?"

She could hear Big Uncle and Little Uncle trying to quiet her mother. "Hush, now, Geneva! The child's going to hear you."

"But why did they have to kill him like that? Why did they have to shoot him?" Her mother's moans didn't sound human. "What are we going to do now? What are we going to do now?"

It got quiet for a while. Shirley could only hear them murmuring. Then she heard Little Uncle's voice. "How could somebody kill him? How could they kill Dr. King?"

Shirley covered her face with her hands. First she thanked God it was not her father. Then she cried. Whose spirit would walk the children home from school now? Whose hope would be their beacon? Who would continue the dream?

That Sunday in church, the men's heads hung low, and the women covered their faces with veils. While the people cried and the preacher talked about Dr. King, Shirley sat quiet in her seat, snuggled next to Mama.

"We have to say good-bye to Martin, like we said good-bye to John. Like we had to say good-bye to Emmit Till, to Malcolm, to Medgar Evers—to all the other sons and daughters lynched and killed in this fight for freedom.

"Reverend King was a family man. He was a good man," the preacher said. "Only Christ in a man could make him stand for peace so long, could make him love those that sought to take his life."

"Amen," everyone said.

A teenage girl sang.

Why should I be discouraged?
Why should the shadows come?
Why should my heart feel lonely
And long for heaven and home?
When Jesus is my portion.
A constant friend is He.
His eye is on the sparrow,
And I know He watches me.

A woman shouted, then fainted, as men and women openly moaned. But even in the midst of their sorrow, people stood to give their testimonies—to thank God for all that He had done. Mama sniffed and wiped away tears with a soaked handkerchief. And though Shirley sat quiet, in her heart she was thanking God for the little bad girl who had found her and saved her. She could have been like Dr. King, like Emmit, murdered and thrown away.

But His eye is on the sparrow,
And I know He watches me.

Shirley held Mama's hand as they walked down the sidewalk from the church service. Big Uncle held Shirley's other hand, while Little Uncle walked behind them, stopping here and there to shake his head while he spoke briefly with groups of men.

Mama shook her head, and the black feathers on her hat danced around her forehead. "I'm telling you, Big, this is it. I swear I can't take much more. How much more do I have to take?"

"Now, Geneva, you know the Lord won't put no more on you than you can—"

"Just shut up, Big." Mama stopped short, and Shirley was pulled between the two adults. "How is that supposed to help me? I don't need nice little sayings right now."

"All right, Geneva. I just meant—"

"No, Big. I don't care what you meant. What I'm telling *you* is that I can't take no more. What did I do to deserve all this happening to me? I'm a good person. I go to church. I don't run around on my husband." Mama's voice was rising, and people walking by were looking at her sideways. "I love the Lord. You know I do. But I tell you that I have about had it." She started walking again. "I'm telling you, Big, one more thing and I swear that I'm going to snap."

"Geneva, you shouldn't talk that way in front of the child."

Mama stopped again. "Don't you tell me! What child do *you* have?"

Big Uncle's face looked pained. "Geneva."

"No, you tell me. What child do you have? I'm the one that has to raise this child with no father. I'm here all by myself, bearing this burden alone, and you want to tell me how to be her mother. I think you just made a mistake."

Big Uncle looked away. "You're right, Geneva. You're right. I don't have a child. I was just trying to comfort you."

Shirley felt sick to her stomach as she looked back and forth between the two adults.

Mama picked up her step. "Well, don't. I need more than words to comfort me. I need more than preaching and singing right now to comfort me."

"Hey, hey. Ho, ho. What's going on up here?" Little Uncle ran up from behind and cut in front of Mama, high-stepping as though he were Fred Astaire. "I can hear you all over the church grounds, Geneva." He smiled brightly, as if a big smile would pacify Mama.

"I was just telling Big—"

Little Uncle smiled down at Shirley. "Yeah," he said to Mama, "I could hear what you were saying to Big. Everybody could. What you need is a little pick-me-up. How about that? A little pick-me-up. Something to take your mind off your troubles." When they reached the car, Little Uncle swung the door open on the passenger side and bowed as Mama slid into the seat and began pulling off her white gloves. He shut the door, then opened the back door for Shirley while Big Uncle climbed into the driver's seat.

Little Uncle sat in the back next to Shirley. "Sit back, now," he told her. "You know what? They say in a little while all cars will have these restraint belts—seat belts—that will hold you back in your seat. They're supposed to help prevent people getting hurt in accidents." He pinched Shirley's cheek. "What you think about that?"

Shirley smiled and hunched her shoulders.

"Well, until such time as we have them, you sit all the way back in your seat for Little Uncle, okay?" He smiled again, then leaned forward to talk to Mama.

"You just calm down now, Geneva. You know that you're

not alone. Me and Big are here to help you. You know that. Haven't we always been there?"

"I know, Little. I just…" Mama looked down and shook her head. "Big, I'm sorry. I'm sorry for back there."

Big Uncle just nodded. "It's all right. All of us are upset about Dr. King and all, and you got even more on you."

Mama laid her hand on his arm and looked out the window of the passenger-side door. "I just feel so sorry for all of us, for Dr. King's family—such a young family—and especially for the people in the South. Things are bad enough for us, but at least we don't have to deal with all that segregation foolishness." She sighed. Little Uncle leaned forward and kissed Mama on the cheek.

He snapped his finger. "I got it. I got it. I know where we can go." He tapped Big Uncle on the shoulder. "How about that new drive-up? That new place with the root beer floats. I think it's Dog 'n' Suds, or something like that. It's a little ways out, but we got plenty of gas. And if you think we need to, Big, we can stop at the gas station and fill it up—I got five dollars I can put in the tank." He smiled at Mama. "You know you like root beer floats." She smiled and nodded.

Big Uncle pushed down the lever for the turn signal. "Hot dogs and root beer it is."

The car pulled out into traffic and headed down State Street. There was a train, like always, at the railroad crossing, so they waited. Mama began to hum.

Little Uncle leaned back and kissed Shirley on the forehead. "You hear that, little bit? It's going to be a fine day after all." Shirley smiled, then leaned her head on her uncle's shoulder. Little Uncle put an arm around her and hugged her. "Yes, just like the good Doctor said, we are going to overcome."

❧

The drive-up restaurant was way out State Street, just before Belleville. The red-and-black Impala they drove slid quietly into one of the parking spaces. Big Uncle rolled down his window, and an April breeze blew into the car, tickling the feathers on Mama's hat again. He leaned his head out of the window and pressed the black speaker button on the metal order board. "We'd like to place an order, please."

Some minutes passed, and Big and Little Uncles began to clear their throats. Shirley watched the carhops, teenage boys and girls, moving to and from other cars while they took and delivered orders—trays piled high with burgers, fries, hot dogs, and root beer served in jumbo-sized, frosty glass mugs—just like on the billboard above the restaurant. Shirley's stomach was growling, and she could almost taste the cold sodie in her mouth.

Mama began to move around in her seat as though she were uncomfortable. "Maybe we should just go on home. I can fix us up something to eat right quick. I kind of had a taste for chicken anyway."

Little Uncle tapped Big Uncle on the shoulder. "Maybe they just forgot to write down your request for an order or something. That can happen. Maybe you should buzz them again. Just because we're the only Negroes here, it doesn't mean that they're trying not to serve us. This ain't Selma."

Big Uncle leaned out the window again. He pressed the button, and the voice box squawked.

"Excuse me, but we're still waiting for service."

There was no reply.

Finally a teenage girl approached the car. She had on black

tights, a black skirt, a short white apron, and she wore her blond hair in a bouncing ponytail. She held an order pad and pen in her hands, and she kept looking back over her shoulder toward the restaurant. She bent slightly to look in the car at Big Uncle. "Can I help you?" Her face flushed a pale pink.

Big Uncle smiled. "Sure. Thanks for taking our order." He ordered hot dogs for everyone, plus two extra Coney Island hot dogs for himself. "Make sure they chop the onions up fine and put the chili on top," he said. "And root beer floats. Root beer floats for everybody."

The girl nodded. "Got it." She flushed again, then turned and walked back in the direction from which she had come.

Little Uncle settled back into his seat. "See? I knew it was just a mistake."

Soon the carhop came back to the car, struggling with a large metal tray that she carried on her shoulder. Shirley could smell the hot dogs. Big Uncle began to hand them out as soon as she hooked the tray legs onto the window.

The waitress blushed beet red. "Sorry about the paper cups," she said as she pointed at the drinks. "We've run out of glass mugs in the kitchen."

Big Uncle smiled at the girl. "That's all right. We came for what's *in* the mug anyway. Things happen." He paid the girl. As he tipped her, another carhop passed by balancing a tray with glass mugs on it. Big Uncle nodded at the girl, and she blushed again. "Those were the last four glasses." She shrugged her shoulders. Just then, another carhop passed by with a tray with glasses, then another. The girl looked at the other carhops, then back at Big Uncle. She shrugged her shoulders again, and began to walk away.

"Just a minute, young lady."

The carhop turned back and was about to speak when Big Uncle cut her off. "I don't think we'll be dining here." He turned to Mama and held out his hand. She rewrapped her hot dog and handed it to him along with her root beer float in the paper cup. Big Uncle placed it back on the tray. Then Little Uncle followed by handing his food forward. Shirley held hers, her mouth open and ready to take a bite.

"Come on, baby," Mama turned in her seat. "Root beer and hot dogs is no fitting kind of Sunday afternoon meal." She looked into Shirley's eyes and held out her hand for the food. Shirley felt a big ache in her chest, and her stomach growled again. Her face felt warm. She looked at the hot dog and the float, then handed them forward.

Big Uncle nodded at the waitress. "You can take this tray away. Thank you for your service." He started the ignition and left the carhop staring after the car with her mouth open.

Mama turned her head back toward her window. "I told you, I had a taste for chicken anyway." She took a handkerchief embroidered with pink flowers from her purse and began to cry.

Child Killer Shirley looked down at the family traveling in the car and began to laugh—actually, it was more of a shriek. As he laughed, some of the charred scales began to twist and meta-morphose, returning to their original shape and color. People were such fools. They made his job so much easier. Only he knew just how deep a scar could be left by a small incident like the root beer float debacle.

Pride, racism, cold and hard hearts… They made his work a joy.

He gurgled with delight while he watched Shirley, the soft one, stare out the window. Poor little dear—frowning and crying on the inside. He pounded his chest with one clawed hand. The minions crowded closer for a better look. As he moved about, a foul liquid began to ooze from beneath the new scales. When the stench dropped from his body and hit the earth's atmosphere, it steamed, then vaporized. Depression filled the air in the car in which the two men, the mother, and the child rode. The child killer licked his tongue out of his mouth toward the Third Heaven, and then looked back down at the car.

The soft one had just begun to pay. He would kill her before she knew who she was.

TWELVE

hirley squeezed the rock in her hand.

It was almost as large as her palm. She wanted to hurl it as hard as she could, to see it go smashing through the window. It wouldn't bring him back; it wouldn't make her feel any safer walking home. But maybe it would make someone else hurt the way she hurt. Maybe it would ruin their lives—even just for a moment. Maybe it would shatter their perfect lives, their perfect lawns, their selfish worlds that took no notice and felt no responsibility for her or for her dreams. Maybe it would crack the picture window so that they would have to see her and feel what she felt.

Shirley stood in front of the house two doors down from her own, a perfect house just like all the other perfect houses. And that day, like every day since his death, Shirley wept for Dr. King.

All week she kept thinking about the little bad girl. If she could just get to her, she would be able to forget. The little girl didn't really seem so bad. In fact, Shirley liked her. She wasn't sure why she thought of the other girl as bad—maybe there was a light in the little girl's eyes, or a smile that said no one covered the little girl. Shirley wasn't sure. Maybe it was her clothes—little, dirty, boys' pants; little, dirty, boys' shoes; nappy hair; and a dirty T-shirt with jelly stains.

Shirley went to school each day, walked home, then played with Trina and her other friends. Still she thought of the other little girl. Friday after school, Shirley got on her bike and rode from her house toward the bend in the road. As she pedaled, the wind lifted her shirt. Finally Shirley relaxed into the wind, into the rhythm of her riding, into the sound of the tires on the asphalt, even into the shiny blue color of her bike. She lifted her hands toward the sky and, for a moment, closed her eyes. Shirley was free.

She opened her eyes, put her hands on the grips, and continued on to the big rock. She didn't see anybody. Shirley circled the rock on the path and laid down her bike like she had before.

She wasn't there—the little bad girl wasn't there. On foot, Shirley circled the rock searching for her. She didn't know the little girl's name or her address; there was no way to search for her. Shirley sighed. Might as well start home and play with her old friends. The little bad girl was probably gone somewhere anyway—probably somewhere in trouble.

She walked around the rock until she saw her bicycle—this time she had no doubt that she would find it in its place. She walked toward it until she heard a voice.

"Hey, little girl. What you doin'? What you got on? Are those ruffles on your bloomers? Look at those! See! You are a little girl. You sure you not a little white girl?"

"No, I'm not a little white girl. See?" Shirley held out her arm so that the little bad girl could see. "What time does it look like to you?"

The little girl cracked up. "Dark time!" And the two of them laughed and laughed until she spoke again. "Why you come over here? You lost, little girl?"

Shirley turned her nose up in the air. "No, I am not lost. I was taking a ride around."

"You came to see me? Then where my cookies?" The little girl frowned. "I told you to bring me cookies."

The little bad girl smiled, but Shirley felt mildly distressed. "I don't have any cookies. But I got some Mary Janes."

"Mary Janes. Mary Janes! How many?"

Shirley held up all of her fingers and wiggled them.

The little bad girl smirked. "Okay, I'll take some of them." She sounded as though she were doing Shirley a favor.

Shirley lifted her head and took a deep breath. "I'll go home if you want me to. I got other friends."

"No, you can stay—if you want to, little girl." The little bad girl held out her hand. "Give me some candy, unless you stingy." The girl's eyes shifted between the candy bag Shirley pulled from the pouch on her bike and her outstretched hand. "You like school?" she asked Shirley while they divided the candy.

"Yes, I love school."

"Oo! Oo! Oo! Little girl, what is *wrong* with you? I bet you are the teacher's pet too." The little bad girl frowned and hunched her shoulders. "I hate school. They think they my mama. They not my mama. They don't like me; I don't like them. Most of the time, I don't go. They not beatin' me, and snatchin' me, and talkin' to me like I'm stupid." The little bad girl paused, looked Shirley in the eye, then continued. "But that's okay, little girl. You go ahead and like school. They like little girls like you." Using the hand that held no candy, the little

117

bad girl touched Shirley's pressed hair. "Clean with barrettes *and* ribbons." She fingered Shirley's hair again. "I ain't got no ribbons…" She shook her head. "Forget them, though. They don't like me cause I don't look right." The little bad girl cussed.

"Oo-oo-oo! You know you not supposed to cuss."

"Who's gonna stop me? I told you I take care of myself. Can't nobody tell me what to do."

Shirley's eyes were round. "What if somebody hears you?"

The little bad girl smirked and shook her head. "Ain't nobody around, little girl."

"Why do you call me *little girl?* My name is—"

"Your name is Little Girl," the little bad girl laughed. "That's all the name you need."

Shirley unwrapped a Mary Jane and popped it in her mouth. "Well, what's your name?"

The little bad girl put one hand on one of her hips. "You can call me…Miss Lady."

"Miss Lady? I'm not going to call you Miss Lady. You ain't no lady. You're not grown. You're just like me."

"No, I'm *not* just like you. I told you that before. You can't even cuss. See?" The little bad girl let go a string of expletives and smiled real big when she finished. "See?"

Shirley winced.

The little bad girl shook her head and wagged her finger. "You can call me Miss Lady, or just don't call me. It don't make me no difference."

Shirley mimicked the little bad girl's movements. "I won't call you nothin' then!" She stood with her feet firmly planted. The other girl might cuss, she might be bad, but there was no way Shirley was going to call her *Miss Lady.*

The two of them walked closer to the rock, sat on the ground, and looked at their Mary Janes. They watched the grasshoppers hop, the ants work, and the grass being blown. They forgot about everything except the moment. Under the cover of the rock's shadow, they were separate and safe, sure that they would not be found. It was just baby blue skies, cotton-ball clouds, and oven-warm sunshine.

"What about Dr. King?" Shirley said.

The little bad girl stopped smiling. "What about him?"

"Today I almost threw a rock through somebody's window because of what they did to Dr. King."

"I don't care. I don't care about him."

Shirley stopped chewing. "What do you mean, you don't care?"

"I mean I don't care. What does he have to do with me?"

"How can you *say* that? You're a Negro, and he was working…trying to make us free. You know—"

"I don't see Dr. King coming to my house to free me." The little bad girl looked away and dug her toe in the dirt. "Anyway, my mother says that Dr. King was just asking for it. He was out running around trying to be seen, and he got what he deserved. Good riddance, that's what my mother says."

"I can't believe—"

"I don't want to talk about it!" The little bad girl hit her hand down on the ground. She took a deep breath and then stopped and smiled. "Okay? Let's talk about something else, okay?"

Shirley opened her mouth, closed it, then they went back to their Mary Janes, nursing them in silence.

"Come on! Get up!" The little bad girl hopped to her feet and held out her hand for Shirley. "Come on, let's shimmy."

"Shimmy?"

"Yeah, like shimmy, shimmy cocoa puffs!"

Shirley laughed and the two girls giggled and wiggled until they collapsed on the ground out of breath.

Just before dusk-dark, Shirley collected her wrappers and then stood to her feet. "I'm fixin' to go."

The little bad girl rose. "Okay, me too." She hesitated and then smiled. "Next time you come, we'ya go somewhere." She stuck out her pinky, and Shirley linked pinkies with her and they shook on it.

"See you." As Shirley walked she thought she heard the girl calling her name. "Huh?" The little bad girl waved wildly, dancing about like Rumplestiltskin, then cupped her hands to her mouth.

"My name!" she yelled as she hopped around. "You don't know my name!"

When Shirley walked through the door, her mother was sitting at the kitchen table, head in hands, crying.

THIRTEEN

❧

Shirley looked from one adult to the other. Big Uncle sat at the table with Mama, his arms around her in a hug so big she was almost hidden. Tears hung on the rims of his eyes, while Mama's tears streamed down her face.

Little Uncle paced back and forth. "Look, you all, it's not like we didn't know that this was a possibility. We knew it was coming, right?"

Mama sputtered for a minute, like she was trying to catch her breath. "That doesn't make it any easier, Little! That doesn't make death any easier to take." Mama began to breathe, as if she were choking.

Big Uncle rocked her. "It's going to be okay, Geneva. It's going to be okay."

"No, it's not!" She pulled away from him. "Don't tell me that. It's not going to be okay, and you can't make it okay no matter what you say."

Little Uncle stepped closer and laid a hand on Mama's shoulder. "Geneva, now, we've got to stay calm about this." He nodded toward Shirley. "Getting hysterical is not going to help.

We've got to be logical about this."

"No, you be logical, Little. I don't have to be anything I don't want to be." Mama started yelling. "I'll scream if I want to, Little! You can't tell me what to do. Always acting like you got everything figured out. Like you so smart—"

Big Uncle shook his head. "Come on, now, Geneva. Don't do that. Little is just trying to help."

"Help? Help? You know what?" Mama hopped up from the table and knocked her chair to the floor. "I'm *sick* of the two of you trying to help. You're smothering me, that's what the two of you are doing. Trying to make me act like Donna Reed or somebody. You know what? Maybe I don't need your help. Help from the two of you is no help at all. Maybe I don't need help from any man.

"The two of you can just get out of my house! What good are you? Your being here is not bringing my husband home. It didn't keep Grandmama Lucy from dying, did it? Did it?"

Big Uncle reached for Mama again, and she jerked away. "Come on now, Geneva."

Mama screamed. "She's *dead!* And what did you all do about it? What could you do about it? Nothing!" She pointed at the door that led from the kitchen outside to the breezeway. "Get out of my house! Get out now!"

Little Uncle stepped toward her. "Calm down now, Geneva. You're just—"

"I just? What I *just* is that I want you two to leave…now!"

"Okay. Okay, Geneva. Come on, Big. We'll come back later."

Shirley felt as though all the air had been squeezed from her body. Her hands were cold, and she shivered as she watched her uncles dragging themselves to the door. She wanted to run to them, to beg them not to go. She looked at her mother. She wanted to grab the three adults and tell them to stop, but she stood still.

Mama frowned and shook her head. "No, you don't need to come back later. The two of you can just keep on going."

Little Uncle opened the door and walked out without looking back. Big Uncle turned just before he stepped out the door. "Geneva, you're going to say that one time too many—'don't come back.' Everybody's upset about Grandmama Lucy. I know you're upset. But you can't keep giving yourself permission to take it out on everybody else like we don't have feelings too. One day…one day you're going to tell us to leave just one time too many."

Mama stood quietly. She looked deflated. Big Uncle went on talking. "Now we've got to make arrangements to get to Texas and all. So we'll be back tomorrow." He looked in Shirley's direction, then back at Mama. "In the meantime, you get yourself together. You've got to think about more than yourself." Big Uncle nodded and gave Shirley a closed-lip smile, then turned and lumbered out the door.

Child Killer Shirley looked toward the Third Heaven and laughed. He couldn't see into it, though the Heavenly Host could see him. But he knew from what was going on beneath him that the soft one's angels were paralyzed. They wouldn't be making any raids into the Second Heaven on her behalf—at least not any time soon. On earth, there was confusion all around Shirley, and the child killer loved confusion. And fear. He could smell fear—in fact he could see a spot of it growing on the child's heart. The child killer threw back his head, laughed, and did a little dance. If he could not kill her today, at least he had stolen her joy—and in time he was sure that fear would do its work and destroy her.

He taunted the Third Heaven angels above him. "Why don't you come down now? Why don't you finish me off? Why don't you come and save the soft thing—Shirley—*right now?*"

He brayed and then squealed—what he considered laughter. As he did, some of his scales lifted and slime began to ooze from beneath them. When the rotten liquid hit the earth's atmosphere it sizzled.

Fear and dread filled the air in the kitchen.

FOURTEEN

⟨ornament⟩

The black-and-red Impala zoomed over the asphalt on U.S. Route 20 through Texarkana, just east of Tyler, just east of Cuney. Shirley sat in the backseat of the car, sometimes dozing, sometimes listening to Little Uncle talk, sometimes staring out the window.

There were farms with wooden fences and horses and cows, and sometimes the smell of fertilizer was overwhelming, even with the windows rolled up. "Not much has changed down here," Little Uncle said and then settled back into his seat. Trees rushed by the window. In his lap was a copy of *Ebony* magazine. He became engrossed in the feature story, which covered the life and death of Dr. Martin Luther King Jr.

Mama sat in the front seat with a picnic basket on her lap. She leaned toward her older brother, her hand outstretched. "Come on now, Big. You know you want this cookie. I made them just for you." She batted her eyelashes. "Don't be mad at me now, Big. I told you I was sorry."

"I'm not mad, Geneva. I just told you that one day you're going to tell me and Little to go just one time too many."

Mama pouted and smiled at Big Uncle. "Don't treat your

baby sister mean, Big. You know that's just how I am. I just get upset over things. But then I calm down, and everything's all right again. See?" She pointed around the car, cookie still in her hand. "Everything's just fine. Everybody's doing okay. *Copacetic,* as the beatniks say."

"You get everybody all worked up, Geneva. And it's not fair—"

"Oh, Big. Stop fussing. You're just blowing it out of proportion. Nobody's worked up. Are you all worked up?" Mama turned and smiled at Shirley. "Are you worked up, baby? You understand Mama, don't you? Tell your Big Uncle that you're not worked up or upset."

Shirley could feel her heart thudding in her chest. Her hands were cold again. She wanted to tell her mother that she was confused and that she was frightened. "No, Mama. I'm not upset." Shirley turned her head so that she could continue watching the trees buzz by.

"See, Big, I told you." Mama quickly stuck the cookie in Big Uncle's mouth when he was about to speak. "After you chew that, I'll give you some water to wash it down."

They rode the rest of the way talking, eating from the picnic basket, and listening while Little Uncle read from the article in *Ebony*—and Shirley tried to keep fear off her face and out of her eyes.

"It's a dirty shame," Little Uncle would say and then shake his head. When they reached Cuney, they pulled into Great-Granddaddy Demo's driveway. Big Uncle parked the car; then he and Little Uncle grabbed the luggage. The four of them went inside the country house to wash, do a little talking, then take a little rest.

Tony Taylor sat in a metal, fan-backed chair, his eyes half-closed, his bare toes drawing circles in the dirt while he watched his grandfather. Grandpa sat in a larger chair to the side of Tony, smoking a pipe. His chair faced the road and was positioned under a large sycamore tree. Tony's grandfather's friends, when they stopped by, always joshed about the old man holding court. Grandpa just sat in his seat, waiting for them to make their way to him. He ran things from under that tree, they said. Sometimes they called him the Mayor.

Someday, Tony knew he would grow up to be just like his grandpa. He would hold court. And when he was grown, he wouldn't have to call other grown people Mister or Miz or Aunt or Uncle or Cousin. He would be grown too, and he would be able to leave off the titles. He would still have to use titles with people older than him—but he wouldn't have to do it for *everybody*.

It didn't seem there was anybody younger than him. It seemed like half his life was taken up having to remember "yes, ma'am," "no, ma'am," and the like. When he was grown, he wouldn't have to worry that his grandmother or mother would spank him for calling his Auntie Rue, just plain old Rue. One day he would be just like Grandpa, smoking a pipe—or chewing tobacco and hitting the spittoon more than six feet away. But for right now, he had to remember the Auntie this and Uncle thats. To forget, his mama said, was uncivilized and nasty, like spitting on the ground. But someday...

An occasional car whizzed by on the highway, which cut through his grandfather's land, separating the barn and acres where his livestock grazed from his house and the land on which the two of them sat. Tony's grandfather was a farmer. He raised some cattle, some pigs, some corn. But he was well known for raising sweet watermelons.

Just to the side of Tony and his grandpa was a wooden wagon. *"Don't hang on the wagon, Tony!"* people were always telling him. The wagon was loaded, almost busting, with watermelons. Watermelons that his grandfather sold for profit. Watermelons that Tony wanted, whose hearts he craved. But not enough to take a whupping. That was something else Tony was going to do when he got grown: eat the heart right out of a watermelon. He didn't care what anybody said. He wouldn't have to care. He would be grown. Just plug the big old thing and dig right in. That's what he would do, and then leave the rest of the melon for ants or for any poor soul that couldn't grow his own.

But he wasn't going to be digging out any watermelon hearts anytime soon. Tony knew from his parents and grand-parents that it was rude and wrong to just eat the heart of a watermelon. The heart is sweetest, the prize, and it is to be shared. If you eat just the heart, you have ruined the rest of the watermelon for everyone else, they had taught him. Heart-eating is a greedy act. The heart tasted good, but it wasn't worth a whupping. But someday he would be old enough to spit, to eat the heart, to stop saying *yes, ma'am*. . . .

And someday, *he'd* be the Mayor.

Farther to the side of the wagon was a tree, and beyond that, the unpaved driveway—red Texas clay. The driveway led to Tony's grandparent's home. Tony looked from the road back down at his brown toes. Then he looked at Grandpa.

Color was always a funny thing to him. Especially skin color—funny just how it came to be. His grandma Taylor's skin was dark, with a reddish cast, probably due to the fact that her mother was Cherokee—or mostly Cherokee. Grandma Taylor, who was a teacher and a principal, was red, but she was black—a Negro. Grandpa Taylor was light skinned, almost white—whiter than some white men. But nobody seemed to think a thing about it. Grandpa was black—he was a Negro too. Tony shook his head. He just couldn't quite figure it out. But someday…

A pickup truck turned off the highway and onto the driveway. Not slowly, like most of his grandfather's visitors drove when they came to visit him or to rest a spell while Grandpa Taylor reigned in his outdoor chair. This truck spit rocks and clay dust. It was almost parked in the yard as soon as it turned off the highway. A white man got out of the truck, a man much younger than Tony's grandfather.

"Hey, Ant'ny," the white man said. *Anthony* was Tony's grandfather's first name. The man spit on the ground and put his dirty, booted foot on Grandpa Taylor's watermelon wagon.

"Hey there, Mr. Jim." Tony's grandfather took his pipe from his mouth and rose from his seat.

"I see you all got comp'ny." The man nodded toward the car that had recently pulled up and parked at a neighboring house—at Mr. Demosthenes's house—which was an easy yell away. Tony felt something in the air, something threatening, something uncomfortable.

"Yes, they're just here visiting for a little while." Tony's grandfather grinned. "You know, the funeral and all. If something was up, Mr. Jim, you know I would tell you. Just Old Demo's family. You remember his grandsons and granddaughter." The white man looked to be about Tony's father's age.

The white man spit again, then reached into his shirt

pocket and pulled out a folding knife. He unfolded it and stabbed it into the heart of one of Tony's grandfather's watermelons. The white man made a careful incision, then pulled out a large plug, which he devoured. He threw the rind on the ground, wiped his knife, and returned it to his pocket.

Tony waited for his grandfather to call the man a scalawag, to bop him across his pie-chopper. But his grandfather said nothing. He just grinned and kind of shuffled when he moved. Tony put a hand over his eyes.

"They won't be here long, you can count on that. If anything changes, you know I would tell you, Mr. Jim," Grandpa said to the younger man.

"All right, then, Ant'ny. See you do." The white man hopped back into his truck and sped away. Grandpa Taylor sat back down. He slumped in his chair, his head held down, his shoulders hunched forward. He drew in a deep breath, then recrossed his legs and stuck his pipe back in his mouth, sitting the way he had been before the white man came.

Tony hopped from his chair and dragged his toes through the dirt, making circles on the ground. Then he ran around the side of the house.

Child Killer Tony hunched his back and kneeled so he could watch more closely, so he could enjoy the show taking place beneath him. He was so delighted that he began to twist his massive head. He looked at the soft one pressed against the side of the house. See how it whimpered and covered its face with its hands. The child killer's tail coiled behind it like a snake.

The child killer was thrilled by his work, by his function. It was his honor to destroy children. Some of them had been killed in the womb—the child killer was known for his ability to deceive women when they were most vulnerable. Others— children of promise—he killed or destroyed by instigating havoc in their young lives, by creating strife in their families, by causing bullies to pick on them in school.

Promise children...the skin around what must have been his mouth curled. He sucked in air several times. He loathed promise children. They were children of destiny, children who were on assignment, who held within themselves part of the answer—children who would make it easier for others to return to God. They had to be killed. And each promise child was assigned a Second Heaven guardian, a child killer like him, to weaken or nullify that child's effect on the earth. Assignment was made before the child was even conceived in the physical world. The child had to be killed before the soft thing became aware of its purpose or its connection to God.

The child killer looked toward the Third Heaven—he could not see up, though they could see down. He shuddered and flinched just to think of the Most High. The end had already been written, but still he and the master's army had to fight.

They had to kill the children.

He gurgled when he thought of how much time the soft ones spent trying to figure out why bad things were happening to them, why they were under attack. It was simple: Promise children had to be destroyed.

Each promise child also had a Third Heaven guardian, and when prayers from the soft ones were flowing, the Third Heaven guardians were invincible. Child Killer Tony looked at the stump where one of his arms used to be—he knew first-hand. When there were prayers, the Third Heaven guardians raided and fought battles in the Second Heaven—raiding and taking back lost souls. But lately…

Lately there hadn't been many prayers, especially united prayers. And the child killer and others like him had been free to rule the Second Heaven.

Sometimes the humans made it too easy. They took the challenge out of it; they were so cruel to each other that he found himself taking note of their methods. Their hard-heartedness caused so much damage; the child killer often found himself reaping the fruit of seeds he had not sewn. Those kills were too easy, no fun. However, a kill was a kill. His tail flicked and writhed behind him.

He would have this boy. He would win this boy. A gill-like thing on Child Killer Tony's body lifted, and something slick and moist slid from underneath. When it reached earth, it vaporized.

Shame engulfed the little boy.

"I guess you all have already seen the *Ebony*." Shirley watched while Little Uncle held it up to show to Grandpa Demo. They all sat at the table—Grandpa Demo, Big Uncle, Little Uncle, Mama, and Shirley—eating oxtail soup from big white bowls, some of which were chipped and cracked. Big hunks of hot cornbread, resting on paper towels, sat next to each person's bowl.

Grandpa Demo shook his head. "No, I don't 'spect we have."

Little Uncle tapped the magazine in his hand. "You had to. It's been out more than a week now."

"The folks down here in the post office held it up. Said they didn't want no trouble to get started down here. You know, I guess they thought colored folks might see the pictures and get worked up." Grandpa Demo adjusted his glasses.

"It's *Negro,* Grandpa Demo, not *colored—*"

"Well, you know it's hard for an old man to remember all these name changes. But go on."

Little Uncle looked frustrated. "What do you mean they held it up? You mean, they're going to give it to you later?"

"No, son, I mean they not going to give it out."

"How can they do that, Grandpa Demo? That's against the law. They can't confiscate someone's mail, a citizen's mail."

Grandpa Demo took off his glasses and wiped them on his shirtsleeve. "Now, don't come down here getting all riled up, Little. You know where you are. You ain't been away that long. They do what they want to do. They're the law. Who's going to stop them? I know you don't have to put up with it up North, but that's the way it is down here."

Little Uncle slapped the magazine on the table. "See? That's what I'm talking about!"

Mama's face looked pinched. "Little, we came down here for a funeral. Grandpa Demo has enough on his mind. Now, don't get him all worked up."

Little Uncle looked at her and lowered his voice. "Who are you to talk?"

Grandpa Demo patted Little Uncle on the arm. "All right now, children. That's enough of that. Everybody's just feeling a little raw now."

Little Uncle shook his head. "I'm sorry, Grandpa Demo, but that is just way out of line. It's a federal offense—tampering with the mail."

Mama mashed her lips together and poked them out. "It's a

federal offense to murder certain folks too, but you see they get away with it all the time. Just leave it alone, Little, until we get back home."

Little Uncle lifted the magazine in the air, then let it drop from his hand to the table. "That's why it keeps going on, because we settle for it. There ain't no way I could *ever* live down here."

Big Uncle looked up from his soup. "You trying to say we don't have any problems in the North? It might be different, but you know it's just as bad."

"I'm just saying that I'm sick of it." Little Uncle laid one of his hands on his forehead.

Big Uncle leaned forward in his chair. "That's why I keep saying we need to do something about it."

Mama slammed her spoon down on the table. "That's it! I am sick of you all. I don't want to hear any more about any of this." She started to cry. "It's been enough, and I can't take no more. I knew I shouldn't have come down here with the two of you. I knew it would be a lot of mouthing off, a lot of big talk."

Grandpa Demo reached to pat Mama's hand. "Now, Geneva, the boys are just talking. It's all right for men to talk. They're supposed to talk about it, get it worked out. Calm down now."

She jerked her hand away and her voice raised. "No, don't you tell me to calm down. I have been through enough. My husband's gone, and who knows when, or if, he's coming back. Then Dr. King!" She got louder. "Now Grandmama! I can't take no more. I'm tired of my life. How much more do I have to take?" She thumped her chest, then pointed at Big Uncle and Little Uncle. "And the two of you are just good for nothing. Just worthless."

Big Uncle's eyes filled with tears. "Stop it, Geneva. You don't have to do this. Don't go too far."

Mama gave him a look that gave Shirley chills. "I'll tell you one thing I know for sure." She looked at Shirley. "You can't trust no man. Don't ever count on one, because you will be disappointed every time!" Mama put her hands on her hips. "You remember what I say now: Don't *ever* trust a *nigger!*" She looked back at Big and Little Uncles. "And you two are just the same." Mama wiped her mouth and stamped off from the table.

Shirley pressed her back as far into the hard, wooden chair she sat in as she could. She closed her eyes. Maybe if she closed them, it would go away. She would be invisible. Maybe if she closed her eyes, she wouldn't see. Maybe she wouldn't hear. And maybe if she was really, really still…she would just disappear.

Child Killer Shirley hacked and wheezed. He could feel something like tiny bat wings beginning to sprout on, to push from his back. The minions crowded around him as they looked through the firmament to the earth below.

The soft one would be his—she was growing weaker each day. The angry mouths, the hateful words around her were murdering her. Fools. People sealed their own fates. They went to church, but never searched the Word—the Word would have told them, "Everyone who hates his brother is like a man who kills a person. And you know that no one who kills a person has life that will live forever."

The child killer looked toward the Third Heaven. There wasn't even any reason to post a guard. No prayers were going up, so the Third Heaven angels would not be coming down.

There would be no war waged in heaven. He looked back down. Drool leaked from his mouth and turned to steam when it hit the earth's air.

The master would be pleased.

FIFTEEN

ig Uncle and Little Uncle had been quiet since the argument at Grandpa Demo's table. Shirley stood near her mother and watched her uncles helping their grandfather. The funeral seemed to have taken something out of Grandpa Demo.

"Do you want to come home with us?" Little Uncle had asked him. Grandpa Demo had said no, this was his home, and he would stay there until it was time to meet his wife on the other side.

It wasn't too long afterward that they dropped the bomb.

Little Uncle looked Mama in the eye. "We got you and Shirley bus tickets back home."

Mama snapped back. "Well, I think that's pretty childish. Like you can't ride back in the car with me and my daughter. You shouldn't be so mad. You shouldn't be so petty. I might have expected it of you, Little. But I'm really surprised at you, Big."

Big Uncle had been sitting with his head in his hands. He raised it and stared at Mama. "We're not going back, Geneva."

Mama's lips started moving, but no sound came out.

Sharon Ewell Foster

"People need us here. People can't keep living the way it's been down here. Afraid to live the way they want to in their own houses, on their own land. Bound up. Can't vote, or paying poll taxes—you know, making black folks pay money before they can vote in order to keep them from voting...taking their mail...terrorizing them. Somebody's got to do something. So me and Little made up our minds. We've got to do what we can. No matter what." He nodded at Mama. "Besides, you don't need us."

Shirley wanted to run to her uncles, to plead with them, to wrap her arms around them, to tell them *she* needed them. To beg them to stay with her. She looked at her mother and stood still. The muscles twitched in her mother's jaw.

Big Uncle stood up. "If you tell us you need us, Geneva—that Shirley needs us—we'll go back home with you. At least until your husband gets back. I know you've had a lot on you, and..."

Tell them we need them, Mama! Please! Shirley exploded inside but kept her face like stone.

Panic and fear flashed in Mama's eyes for a moment—but what lingered in them was a cold, hard anger. "Well, you know, like I said. You can't ever trust a *nigger.*" She squeezed Shirley's hand until it hurt, then led her away.

Grandpa Demosthenes sat in a chair shaking his head.

On the bus ride home, Mama was short tempered. "I said *move,* girl! Didn't you hear me? I'm not playing with you."

Shirley sat still. She barely breathed. Maybe if she was quiet, Mama would forget she was there. If she was quiet and still, it would be impossible for her to do anything wrong, to do any-

138

thing to make Mama angry. She would not ask for anything. She would not disturb Mama. Maybe if Mama rested…

Shirley wiggled, for just a second, in her seat. No, she wouldn't even use the bathroom.

Mama mumbled and talked to herself the whole trip. She jerked from side to side in her seat. Mama's eyes narrowed when she looked across the aisle at strangers, or even when someone accidentally brushed by her. Sometimes Mama's eyes narrowed when she looked at Shirley. That was when Shirley felt sick, felt like she might vomit.

Shirley closed her eyes and thought about her friend and about their meeting place by the rock. If only she could see her—if only she could see the little bad girl.

When Shirley walked in the kitchen, her mother kept cooking and never turned her face to acknowledge Shirley's presence. "Mama, can I go ride my bike?"

"Did you get everything unpacked?" She kept cutting chicken and never turned around.

"Yes, ma'am. I put everything away."

"Don't let me come back there and find anything still unpacked or out."

"No, ma'am."

"Be back before dark."

"Yes, ma'am." Shirley flew out the door, across the breeze-way, into the garage, and out to the street on her bike. Down the street and around the bend, she threw her bike on the ground and ran to the rock.

The little bad girl peeked out from the other side. "What's your hurry, little girl?"

"Nothing, Nothin'," Shirley said.

"Did you bring me something?"

"No, I did not. All I have is this candy necklace." Shirley pulled at the elastic string around her neck. It was ringed with brightly colored disks of sugar—red, orange, yellow, and pink. While she was still in her room at home, she had pulled it from the bag. The bag of candy she had hidden in her room. Candy that her uncles had given her when they put her and her mother on the bus—hidden sweets. She had stuffed the necklace in her pocket, then placed it around her neck once she was on the street and free. "This is all I have, Nothin'."

"Well give me some of that, then."

Shirley felt powerful. The little bad girl wanted her candy, and she still hadn't figured it out. Shirley had given the little bad girl a name. It was Shirley's turn to shake her hips. "Maybe I will. Maybe I won't, Nothin'."

The little bad girl put her hands on her hips. "Are you calling me Nothin'? I know you not calling me Nothin'."

Shirley smiled. "You said call you Miss Lady or a call you nothin' at all. So that's what I'm doing...Nothin'."

The little bad girl balled up her fists and took a step toward Shirley. Then she stopped and smiled. "Nothin'. Nothin'. I kinda like it."

Shirley slapped her leg. "Nothin' and Little Girl. It sounds like a story on the *Mickey Mouse Club*."

The two girls beamed at each other. Then Shirley held the necklace away from her neck. "Here," she said. The little bad girl leaned forward and began to suck on a small portion of the necklace. "Go ahead. You can bite it," Shirley said.

At that moment, Shirley didn't care what her mother would have said about germs and sanitation. She didn't care that the necklace was wet and slobbery when it fell back around her neck. The two girls sat on the ground and swished through the grass with sticks. The little bad girl hopped to her feet and poked the ground with her stick, as though it were a cane.

"Oh, I'm a hootchie-cootchie woman," she belted out at the top of her lungs. "Oh, I'm a hootchie-cootchie woman," she sang while shaking and wiggling her skinny hips. "Nothing on my mind. Oh, I can do the shimmy," she said while shaking all over. "Watch me bump and grind."

Shirley fell over laughing. "Where did you learn that song?"

"I made it up." The little bad girl started the song all over. After the third time, Shirley stood to join her.

"I'm a hootchie-cootchie woman," they sang over and over in the way that only children who feel free can do.

When they had run out of ways to scream and shake, the little bad girl said, "Hey, Little Girl, we supposed to go somewhere."

"I didn't tell my mama that I was going anywhere."

"That don't make no difference," the little bad girl said. "If you ask her, what she gone say? 'No!' She gone say, 'No!' If you want to go somewhere, Little Girl, you can't ask your mama." She winked at Shirley. "If you scared, just say so. I know you just a little girl."

"I'm not scared! I'm not scared of nothing, Nothin'! Let's go!" Shirley looked at her bike lying on the ground and stopped. "What about my bike?"

"Don't even worry about your bike. Won't nobody even see it here. Come on, we going!"

They walked places Shirley had only seen from her parents' car. Only in the car she couldn't see the path off the road by the railroad tracks. A path covered with weeds that led through the high grass to a ditch with a board that someone had placed across it. There was so much to take in. More green, more dirty, more wild than any place Shirley had ever been. She forgot to be scared that someone would see her—that someone would tell her mama. Shirley was far from her street. She was liberated.

There were no standards here. There was no race. There was no time—just the two of them in God's universe, on an adventure. That afternoon they discovered the fountain of youth, buried treasure, and the tips of several bad men's—now dead—bony fingers.

They ran through the jungle until they reached the sidewalk and the IGA. When they walked by the grocery store, Shirley did not look to see if she saw her friends and their moms inside. She and the little bad girl were in front of the IGA, but in another world…someplace Shirley had never been.

Shirley followed the little bad girl around to the back of the building. She nudged Shirley with her elbow. "Can you read?"

"I'm the best reader in my class."

The little girl pointed at some large letters someone had painted on the back of the IGA. "See those words? Can you read them?"

"No, I don't know those words. I can't read them. I don't read those kinds of words!"

"That don't make no sense to me. Seems like you should be able to read them," the little bad girl mocked Shirley. "They're not very long words. Four letters. Five letters."

Shirley could not breathe. She felt like something was pressing on her chest. "I don't know those words." Shirley felt like she couldn't see. She couldn't look at the words; she couldn't read them.

Suddenly she was too hot and too sweaty and too itchy. She had come too far. There were tears in Shirley's eyes.

The little bad girl put her arm around Shirley's shoulders. "It's okay, Little Girl. I was just messing with you. It's all right." She patted Shirley on the back. "You did real good. You came real far. We better start back home before it gets too late."

Shirley didn't say too much on the way back. Nothin', the little bad girl, tried to make conversation here and there, but Shirley didn't feel good. When they got back to where they could see the rock and Shirley's bicycle, she forgot about the IGA and the words.

"You feel better now?"

Shirley nodded. "Yes, I'm okay."

"Bet I can beat you to the rock!" They ran hard, like young horses. The little bad girl got to the rock a few inches ahead of Shirley. They slammed their child bodies into the rock in a way that would have injured adults; then they slumped to the ground.

Shirley held out her necklace to the other girl again. "Want another bite?" The little bad girl leaned in and opened her mouth. "You can take a big bite."

They sat and settled, discussing the treasures they had found. They sat back-to-back, their heads leaning on each other. Shirley pressed the daylight as far as she could. "I got to go," she said.

"Okay. Next time bring some better candy or food," the little bad girl said. "We might go somewhere more far."

They rose and parted company on their ways home. "Bye!" Shirley yelled. When she passed by the first unlit street lamp, she started to pick up speed on her bike—she had to beat the lights home. "God, don't let me get home too late," she whispered. And it seemed to her that He held back dusk-dark in the sky a little longer so that she could make it home. As she pumped the pedals, she heard the little bad girl yelling behind her.

"Hey! Hey, Little Girl! My name—my name is Sheri!"

SIXTEEN

⇛

*T*his week, Shirley, you're going to be reciting for the fifth and sixth graders!" Mrs. Canada beamed.

This week Shirley wouldn't be teaching Barbara and Misty. She would not see Ken's scowling face or look into his icy blue eyes. Instead, Shirley—cleaned, greased, braided, and barretted— stood in front of them, mostly white children, in the fifth and sixth grades. Mrs. Canada's smile told Shirley that she could do what they could not do. A child of integration would recite for them.

> *I wander'd lonely as a cloud*
> *That floats on high o'er vales and hills,*
> *When all at once I saw a crowd,*
> *A host of golden daffodils…*

Shirley was special, her teacher's behavior said. It did not matter that most of them looked at her with blank faces or as though they couldn't understand the language. She was speaking. And she knew Mrs. Canada was pleased with her. Pleased enough to let everyone else know that she was pleased. The spotlight was on Shirley. Someone loved her, found no fault in her. She loved it, or needed it—maybe both.

> *Continuous as the stars that shine*
> *And twinkle on the Milky Way,*
> *They stretch'd in never-ending line*
> *Along the margin of a bay:*
> *Ten thousand saw I at a glance*
> *Tossing their heads in sprightly dance.*

Shirley wanted to be liked, to fit in in a world where hair—long and blond, or soft, straight, coal black curls—where eyes—big blue or large brown with long curly eyelashes—where size—tiny—and skin color—white or "light, bright, most nearly white"—carried the day.

She was none of those things. At church, the mothers, grandmothers, and aunts loved her, and her deficiencies did not matter. But at school, where white was the standard—and at home, where the standard was unspoken—she could not win, place, or show.

She was none of those things. Her hair was black and nappy. It had to be pressed with a hot, iron straightening comb. Her eyes were brown, but small, with almost no lashes. She was tall, and though she sometimes felt pretty, it was never long enough to make the grade.

> *The waves beside them danced, but they*
> *Outdid the sparkling waves in glee:*
> *A poet could not but be gay,*
> *In such a jocund company:*

I gazed—and gazed—but little thought
What wealth the show to me had brought:

She could not compete against the standard, but in the classroom she left them all behind. She ran like Wilma Rudolph. No one could touch her. Mrs. Canada had helped to find the way. Now she was lapping the field.

All the wordless behavior told Shirley that she had left the blond-haired, blue-eyed, curly-haired, light-skinned pack in the dust. The other children's eyes told Shirley that they knew it—she had outrun them. It was only fair, after all, because on other days, in other arenas, her eyes—and all the eyes of the other kids who did not meet the standard—flickered and then failed. Sad eyes said that they knew they had disappointed their parents, had not won the prize.

But today was not that day. Today Shirley was in the light, and she was winning—running faster and faster. So fast she could break down walls. And Mrs. Canada had made Shirley's race, her event, the main focus.

For oft, when on my couch I lie
In vacant or in pensive mood,
They flash upon that inward eye
Which is the bliss of solitude;
And then my heart with pleasure fills,
And dances with the daffodils.

Mrs. Canada directed all attention to Shirley's track, and she did run well. From some place high in the room, almost above the ceiling, she watched herself reciting. Shirley did run well, and they could not touch her—not even the moms. They couldn't grab her, they couldn't stop her.

When she got home, her mother was sitting at the table laughing and shaking her head. It was not good laughter. She held a letter in her hand. "Well," she said. "I might as well tell you. I knew it was going to happen. I knew things wouldn't get any better." She stopped smiling and sighed. "I told my fool brothers…" She shook her head. "Your uncles, the heroes, the freedom fighters, got in the middle of some protest and now they're in jail." She frowned and shook her head. "I told you. You listen to me, never trust…"

Inside, Shirley began to sing her song.

Rock me, baby Jesus,
Hold me, baby Jesus,
Love me, baby Jesus,
So I won't be afraid.

On Saturday, Shirley could hardly sit through the cartoons— Beanie and Cecil seemed to drag on and on. If only she could see Sheri. If only they could go somewhere again. She wasn't sure if Nothin', if *Sheri*, would be at the rock. But just to be where she had been or just to be on her own at the rock would be good, would be enough.

She suffered through another half hour just so her mother would not be suspicious. Not that Mama would notice—she seemed more like a shadow each day. During the first commercial break Shirley got two apples—there were lots of them in the bowl; the two wouldn't be missed. At the next break, she got some crunchy, salted Bugles and filled two baggies so full she could hardly close them. During the last break, she got

Oreos. She sneaked her booty out the side door and into the saddlebag on the back of her bike.

Shirley waited by the rock for what seemed like forever. The sun moved. She looked around, kicked dirt, and rubbed her hands through the grass. She counted clouds, piled rocks, laid on her back, flipped to her stomach, repiled rocks, and picked her oldest scabs—still Sheri did not come. Shirley sighed.

"Hi." Sheri flopped down beside her. She looked away and wiped her face.

"What's the matter?"

"Don't worry about it. Nothing, that's what's the matter. Nothing."

Shirley tried to put her arm around Sheri's shoulder, but the little bad girl shrugged her off. "Don't pet me up."

Shirley looked around for something to say. She remembered the food. "I got some stuff. Some apples, some Bugles, some Oreos—we can go somewhere."

"No." Sheri shook her head. "I've got to get back home. My mom..." A tear squeezed from her eye. "I've got stuff to do."

"I thought you lived by yourself."

Sheri shook her head. "No. With my mom and dad and my brothers. But sometimes..." Then Sheri cried. "I'm not supposed to talk about it."

Shirley told the little bad girl that it was all right. She would never tell. "It would be like telling on myself," Shirley said. Sheri hid her face and then she told Shirley the story. And when she was finished, she went home.

Sheri held her breath and walked like cotton to the side door of the house that she lived in. If she was quiet, she might not wake her. If her mom was already awake, then if she was very quiet she might not make Mom angry. If Sheri was quiet and she could feel in the air that her mom was already angry, she might be able to sneak back outside before her mother sensed she was home.

She turned the door handle slowly and peeked her head in first. Then Sheri stepped inside and eased the door closed without a sound. She tiptoed to the living room, then to the laundry room, but everything was still. When she was satisfied that she was safe, she stood on her tiptoes and reached for a red metal cup in the cabinet. She filled it with tap water from the faucet.

Sheri heard a noise behind her, startled, and dropped the cup, spilling water on the floor.

"I thought I told you I didn't want you making a mess!" It was her mom. "You know I need my rest—I got a lot on me and I don't need any noise. It's enough that your daddy's gone away…I have to do everything by myself—left you here on me. I'm doing the best I can. But I'm not having any mess." Sheri could not have told anyone how her mom got hold of her. She could not have told anyone when she started holding her breath or when she started expecting the blows. First it was her mom, but then it was the beast, and the dark angels. Sheri knew the beast, so she surrendered.

The beast dragged her around the room and shook her, and Sheri did not say a word. The beast slapped her and called her names, and Sheri did not say a word. She saw its teeth and smelled its breath. Once she accidentally looked into its eyes. Sometimes it pretended to be her mom, but then she would know it was the beast. And when it was finished, Sheri did what she always did. She picked herself up, went to her room, and went to bed. She wasn't sure how much more she could live through, how much more she could take.

Shirley stayed at the rock long after Sheri left. She bit an apple, toyed with the Bugles, and ate an Oreo. She rolled in the grass until the sun said it was time to go home.

When she pulled into the driveway, there was a strange car parked there, and she could hear her mother screaming. Shirley walked into the house and heard one of two men in the living room talking to her mother.

"He was evacuating the wounded. There was heavy fire," the man said. "He knew it was going to be dangerous, but the troops were caught in crossfire. You should be proud. Your husband was brave," the man said.

Shirley watched her mother faint, and saw her body slip from the couch onto the floor. There was a sickening thud. Shirley did not speak; she did not breathe. She just turned and walked back out of the house, got on her bike, and rode back to the rock.

Sometime during the night, she thought she awoke. First she thought she heard Sheri. That Sheri was crying and that she held her hand. Shirley fell back into blackness, and then she thought that she saw her mother walking down the street—her mouth like an *O* and her pink chenille robe half on half off. Shirley thought she saw her mother walking past the rock—the rock like the rock at Monks Mound, the rock like the rock with the Piasa Bird—and her mother was wearing only one house shoe. She thought she saw her mother's arms in the air and that she saw her mother tearing at her hair. Shirley thought she saw her mother walking right past her.

She shook her head, huddled closer to the rock, and went back to sleep.

"Wake up."

Someone shook her. It was a man, and he scooped Shirley up and carried her away from the rock.

She just wanted to see Sheri. She tried to turn her body back toward the rock. If she could just see Sheri again.

The man put her in the backseat of a car. There was a nurse wearing starched, crisp white and a white cap in the backseat beside her. She could hear the man talking to another woman outside.

"I'm not sure what we're going to do with her," he said.

"Do you think she's dangerous?" the woman said.

"I don't think so, but she has to have done it. There were matches beside her and her hands are covered with soot. Who else could have done it?"

"Well, my goodness, then, I don't see how you can say she's not dangerous. It makes me sick to think about that house burned down and that poor old woman inside," the woman said. "What would make her do something like that—burning down a house?"

"Well, don't be too hard on her. Remember, she just lost her father, and her mother's been hospitalized." He said *hospitalized* in a strange way. "I don't think she's going to be out anytime soon." He sighed. "I don't know what we're going to do with the girl."

Shirley sat on her cot, her legs drawn up under her, her back pressed to the wall. The room was dark, like the cloakroom at school, with only one window. She hated the McGinty home and wondered what she had done to be sent there, to have lost everyone.

For weeks, they—doctors and people in suits—had been grilling her. Asking her about the matches, about the house, about her mother, about her father. And when she told them about Sheri, they looked at each other and shook their heads. "You have to tell the truth," they told her.

"I am telling the truth," she said.

"This is not a good time to pretend," they told her.

"I'm not pretending," she told them.

"What was her name?" they asked.

"Sheri."

"What was her last name?" they asked.

"I don't know."

"Where did she live?" they asked.

"I don't know."

They shook their heads, and then she told them the story again. And she told them about the dream, about the last time she saw Sheri and about how she saw her mother walking down the street and tearing her hair.

They looked at each other and shook their heads, and then they started giving her shots. And when they gave her the shots, at first it burned, and then she fell asleep.

That was when she decided she would stop talking—not any more than she had to. And that she would disappear. Maybe if she was quiet, more trouble would not find her. Maybe whatever or whoever—maybe it was God—was angry with her would think she was dead and then go away. She lay down on the cot and covered her head.

Maybe it would all go away.

‹❧›

Child Killer Shirley watched the soft one sleeping. He squinted his one good eye and jerked his head toward the Third Heaven. He licked out his tongue.

It was almost over. She was almost gone. He could feel her spirit weakening. He turned his one good eye back to the firmament portal where he could see her. It had been a while since she had sung that blasted song, since she had activated the movement of Third Heaven angels. She was almost gone, and there would be a handsome reward for him for destroying the promise child.

It would be over. Soon! Soon! He stood up and did a teeter-tottering dance around the mouth of his window into the firmament below. She was losing her strength; she was being neutralized.

There was nothing he loved more than the death of a child.

SEVENTEEN

*other Johnson sat across the big mahogany desk. She was almost swallowed up by the big maroon-colored chair she sat in. Her cotton dress was starched and pressed. Her support stockings were beige—the only color she could find in Tyler—they were rolled and knotted just beneath her knees. "So, are you trying to tell me I can't take the child?" One of her eyebrows raised.

"No, you're her closest blood relative." The doctor made his fingers into a tent. "It's just that we're concerned about her being off the medication."

The old woman smiled. "Well, I'm concerned about her being on it."

"That's understandable. You're not a physician and have little knowledge of such things."

"You know what, doctor? You might be right about me. But I do know the greatest Physician that ever lived, and I'm pretty sure that He will take the case."

The doctor smirked. "That's just what she doesn't need. She's already been through a severe trauma, and she's having difficulty determining exactly what reality is. The last thing she needs is to be exposed to superstition."

"How long has she been here, doctor?"

"Nine months."

"Has she gotten any better? Have you been able to lower the amount of medicine you're giving her?"

"It's not that simple, Mrs. Johnson. These medicines are very complex, and while we've had to adjust them several times, Shirley hasn't made sufficient progress to justify lowering the medication. We have to be patient."

Mother Johnson leaned forward. "Well, I tell you what, doctor. You just pack up my baby's things and bring her on. We've got a bus to catch. And if we leave right now, we'll get to the Trailways station just in time."

Shirley wasn't sure if she had ever seen or met Mother Johnson before. She had heard the coffee-colored woman's name and knew she was a relative, but that was all she could recall. It was hard to remember anything right now. When she boarded the bus, it reminded her of the last time she saw Big Uncle and Little Uncle. She wanted to cry, but the tears would not come. Besides that, she was sleepy...so sleepy.

Mother Johnson sat in the seat next to hers. She patted Shirley's leg. "Don't you worry about a thing. You go on to sleep. You'll be waking up soon enough." The funny-looking old woman put her arm around Shirley's shoulders.

"I don't know everything, baby. But I do know that you have been through a lot. It will probably be some time before you feel like talking—before you're ready to tell the tale. That's all right. Everything's probably looking dark to you, looking like night, like you can't make heads or tails of where you are."

The old woman looked out the window, as though she were looking back on someplace familiar. "What I can tell you is that God never sends us any place by mistake. He never puts us in somebody's life by accident. One time, I walked through a dark place. There were shadows everywhere, and in every shadow it looked like there was a boogeyman. But God was in the shadows too. I couldn't see Him, but every once and a while He would reach out and touch me...let me know He was there."

She squeezed Shirley and kissed her on the cheek. "I walked out of the bad place." Mother Johnson smiled. "And now I'm free indeed. I walked out of the shadows. Baby, count on it—you're coming out too. And you just remember I told you so."

Shirley was too sleepy to talk, and for some reason she couldn't feel a thing—just emptiness...grayness. Her head fell forward. Then Shirley closed her eyes and slept.

EIGHTEEN

Huntsville, Alabama, 1986

The key turned in the ignition, and the engine turned over. Shirley turned to check her children in the backseat. "Mika, make sure Lex's seat belt is tight. And Lex, don't keep picking at it."

Lex frowned, and Shirley turned to face him more directly. "Like I said, Lex, don't be picking at that seat belt. I'll get a ticket if you don't have it on. And if I were you, Mister Lexington—" Shirley lifted her hand and shook it like she was rolling dice—"I would stop rolling my eyes."

Lex stopped frowning and stared straight ahead.

As she turned toward the steering wheel, Shirley saw Mika pat her little brother on his arm as though to tell him it was okay. Shirley was pleased.

"So, Mommy—" Mika wiggled in her seat—"when will we be there? California is a long way, right?"

Shirley sighed, but not too deeply. "Well, it's a long way. But—" she smiled into the rearview mirror—"we're going to have fun all the way there. We're going to just take our good, old, sweet time." She laid a hand on the envelope on the seat next to her. They would take as long as eighteen hundred dollars would hold out—less one month's anticipated rent and a few groceries. "We're going to have a good time!" she smiled and insisted.

She eased the car from the curb onto the main street, then onto the highway heading west on 72. Shirley stole glances in the rearview mirror. Mika and Lex were playing a game. Mika counted the red cars that passed them, and Lex counted the blue ones. "Blue is for boys!" he crowed every time he saw one.

He was taking a lot of pride in dressing himself lately, and he had on a pair of blue, knee-length shorts underneath a pair of shorter green shorts with black-and-gold stripes—all matched with red, high-top tennis shoes and a purple T-shirt. So much for the line of clothing that boasted animal labels that would "Help your little ones match the perfect tops and bottoms."

Before they could reach Mississippi, Shirley was sure that Mika would have found a million reasons to swing her head, which sent her hair wings flying. Her daughter was fascinated with her thick, upswept bangs. Parted on the top of her head, they flowed from the crown of her head to just behind her ears. "Mommy, I love them!" she had cooed when the beautician cut and shaped them. The child's neck had not rested since.

Mika and Lex giggled and tickled each other, and Shirley took the opportunity to disappear. She cranked up the radio and put on her sunglasses.

He's gone. You might as well get over it.

Her husband was gone, but the feelings hadn't died…and Shirley wasn't sure what to do with them. She kept waiting for late-night telephone calls, for his voice on the other end. Sometimes she wakened, startled and sure that she had heard the phone ring. But when she picked it up, there was just dial tone.

Even if he was drunk or angry, she would have given almost anything to hear his voice one more time. And she wanted to warn them—all the women she passed in stores who were irritated because their husbands moved too fast, moved too slow, or picked up too many things not on the list… She wanted to tug at the sleeves of all the women frustrated because their *him* would not pick up his socks or take out the garbage. She wanted to whisper to the women who threatened to leave because he never bought cards, never remembered birthdays, or never brought home a gift or Valentine. She wanted to sound the alarm, to tell them that he might be gone in a second. To tell them that, if they were like her, they would be wishing him back. They would be looking under beds and behind dressers for a pair of old underwear to sleep with…searching for a pair of dirty socks so that they could smell him—bring him alive for just a minute, for a moment.

She would tell them to be grateful. To take time to inhale their *him,* to touch him, to remember the weight and sound of his steps, the feel and the press of his elbows and thighs. She would tell them to study hard the timbre of his laugh and to appreciate the feel of his arms around them. She would tell them to fall on their knees and thank God for the smell of his breath in the morning and the roughness of their man's feet on their legs at night—to be grateful for their *him* now, because in a second he might be gone.

But the love would not be gone. She could tell them that. And the love was hungry. It crawled up her back, underneath her shoulders, until it sat heavily on her chest. Then it walked down her chest to her stomach, and pressed lower—reminding her her womb was empty, crying to her that it would never be filled again.

And people would not understand, she would tell them.

"Don't grieve too long," people would say, as though they could not see the gaping wound that bled and ached. It was the hole in her side where she and he were once connected.

"You've got to live on," people said, as though they could not hear her heart crying that it could not believe it was still beating without him. Her heart could not believe it had been left behind to continue their rhythm as one.

"I knew he wasn't going to be your mate for life," people said.

"God has someone better for you," they said, as though they could not feel how she ached for him. Words flew from their mouths, as though they could not bridle their dislike for him even long enough to keep rusty forks from picking at the soreness she felt.

"You're a young woman," they would say, as though that knowledge was supposed to comfort her rather than remind her of the lonely years that stretched in front of her.

Widow. Shirley formed the word with her lips. Then she pursed them. It was too hollow, too lonely, too final.

She reached for a tape and popped it into the cassette player. Hall and Oates's voices danced and rocked from the speakers as they sang "Private Eyes." Lex and Mika picked up the tune and joined in singing. Shirley turned on her blinker, moved to the right lane, and exited onto Highway 55 north. She forced herself to sing and smile.

PART 2

NINETEEN

Tyler, Texas, 1969

The Trailways bus bumped over the red brick streets that surrounded the square and rumbled into the station in downtown Tyler. The bus door squealed when the driver opened it. Shirley watched from her bus seat window until she and Mother Johnson grabbed Shirley's few things, walked down the aisle, down the three steps, and onto the sidewalk. Shirley looked briefly to see what was "downtown." There were no tall buildings, no buses, no racing engines, no stoplights. No traffic cops with gloves and whistles, and no thronging crowds.

It's like Mayberry.

Then she followed Mother Johnson through the double doors and into the station. "I know you're thirsty," Mother said. "We'll just stop and get you a little something."

The station was laid out in a square. To the right was the baggage area, followed by one or two ticket agents with folks standing in line, then on around to a little restaurant in the far corner. Shirley and Mother Johnson shared a little hamburger with a thick slice of onion—it was a shame, Mother said, for them to charge seventy cents for that little bit of meat on that little bit of bread—and Shirley drank a cherry cola while Mother drank water. "Come on," Mother said after they paid the check. "We might as well make the most of the day. We don't get downtown often, and school will be starting any day now." She stuck out her hand. Shirley held it, and they walked out to the street.

At opposite ends of the square, there were two banks—People's and Citizen's—and situated at intervals as Mother Johnson and Shirley walked were Kay Woolen's women's store, Kress five-and-dime, Leon's Shoe Store, and Perry Brother's five-and-dime. The pair walked past the Tyler Theater and the Arcadia until they came to the Myer and Smit department store. "Come on, baby," Mother Johnson said.

They walked through the glass doors, and Shirley started through the lobby toward the main shopping level. "Oh no, baby," Mother said. "We're going down here. It's better down here." Shirley followed Mother Johnson down the stairs into the basement shopping area. A variety of goods were compacted into the basement area.

All of the shoppers were Negroes.

"How you doin'?" They nodded to each other.

"Just here trying to get my children ready for school." Hands waving.

"I know *that's* right."

All of the clerks were white. "Can I help you gals?" they said, no matter the age of the customer. Shirley stared and wondered why no white people were shopping. Why they didn't have to get their children ready for school. And something about it reminded her of the root beer place, the place she had gone with Big Uncle and Little Uncle and Mama. Something did, but she could not remember what. But what she did remember was the lump—the lump that was coming back to her throat now.

Mother Johnson picked up underclothes, blouses, skirts, socks, and leotards. She picked up a red sweater and held it up against Shirley. "Yes, that will do." She smiled. "We'll get you a coat a little later." Then Mother selected some shoes, a book satchel, and a lunch box with Barbie on it.

A young clerk with a smile like honey and eyes like flint walked up behind Mother Johnson and touched her on the shoulder. "You sure you can afford all that, gal?"

Mother stood up straight and opened her mouth to speak. Something crossed behind her eyes, seemed to travel to her stomach, then back up to her mouth. "Yes, miss. Yes, I'm quite sure I can."

"Well…all right." The clerk looked a little uncertain, as though she was not sure if Mother really had the money, as though she thought Mother might have been offended but couldn't figure out for the life of herself why.

Mother Johnson nodded at Shirley to follow. They moved quickly to the counter, checked out, and climbed the steps to the lobby. As they walked out the door, Shirley looked at a family walking in.

"I'm going to get different colored book satchels for each one. And maybe I'll get sweaters to match the satchels," the woman said to her husband. Instead of walking downstairs, they walked straight ahead to the main showroom floor. When Shirley looked behind her and into the main room, she saw other families shopping, just like the ones downstairs in the basement. Just like them, except they were all white.

"I appreciate you coming to pick us up," Mother said when they turned left onto Lincoln. "That's the good thing about church folk—at least some church folk." She laughed. "We look out for one another."

"Yes, indeed," the man said as he turned right onto Grand, then left onto Twenty-Ninth Street. As they drove down the street, Shirley pressed her nose to the window then mouthed the words *Texas College* as they drove past. This was Tyler, but it was a different Tyler. There were Negroes in this Tyler, only Negroes—and they walked and laughed and talked out loud as they moved in and out of Moon's Cleaners, Moon's Grocery Store, Daniel's Record Shop, Wilson's Hamburger Stand, and Humphrey's Photography Studio.

When the car stopped, Mother Johnson thanked the man. The house on Carter Street sat far away from the street. There was a long driveway and a front porch with two metal fan-back chairs. The man stepped from the car, grabbed the bags, and set them on the porch for Mother Johnson and waved away her hand when she tried to pay. "Don't make a gentleman feel bad."

"Come on, baby," Mother said, and the two of them made their way into the house on Carter Street. "Now, it's not fancy," she said. "But it's all we need. Shades go up to let in the sun; curtains draw in to keep out the prying eyes. A few throw rugs so your feet don't get cold when they hit the floor, and enough gas heat to keep you warm when winter comes." She crooked her finger. "Here goes the bathroom. Nothing fancy. The water drains from the tub just fine, and there goes the plug over there in the corner. Don't flush nothing big down the toilet because the plumber charges an arm and leg, and I ain't got none to spare."

Mother Johnson grabbed Shirley and hugged her tight. Shirley did not know what to do—she could not remember—so her arms dangled at her side. "It's okay, baby. Don't worry. My home is your home. Nothing to fear here. And in time you're going to be coming out of that dark place. You remember I told you so."

Mother kept hugging, and Shirley held her breath. "All right now," Mother Johnson said. "Let's get you unpacked. Get your things in your room. Then I'm going to show you the way to school, let you meet some children you can follow, so you'll be ready when Monday comes."

Sunday night it rained. But Monday morning was bright, and Shirley was fed, dressed, and out the door waiting for the other children—the ones she was to follow. She would be okay today. She was going to school—a place where she was certain, a place where she was safe, a place where she was at home.

Shirley sat on one of the metal chairs. She ran one of her hands over her new white blouse, blue pleated skirt, and socks so white they almost glowed. Shirley had matching blue ribbons and barrettes in her hair.

"You look like you're going to school to really take care of some business," Mother Johnson had said when she finished brushing, combing, and braiding Shirley's hair.

"Hey!" the children said when they arrived and threw up their hands in salute. Shirley got up from the front porch swing. She nodded but did not smile as she followed them down the street. Shirley felt in her pocket for the quarter Mother Johnson had given her. *"Here, you take this because the kids always stop at the Blind Man's Store on the way to school. You might want to pick up a little something."*

She followed the group down Twenty-Ninth Street, in the opposite direction from Texas College and Wilson's Hamburger Stand. They came to a white frame house—white, tinged with years of East Texas clay. The group turned and walked around the back to steps that led to an open back door.

Shirley could hear her mother's voice, her warning…

"Shirley, don't you let me catch you running in and out of anybody's house. And don't even let me hear about you going to some stranger's house. How would I ever find you? You could be lying there dead and I would never find you." Just like Emmit Till.

She stopped and watched the other children piling in and out of the house.

One of the children she was following to school—a little skinny girl with long, skinny braids—came and stood in the doorway. "Ain't you coming in? Ain't you going to get nothing at the Blind Man's Store?" She waved at Shirley. "Come on in."

A store? This was the blind man's store—a house that children ran in and out of? Shirley felt the quarter in her pocket. Mother Johnson knew about the store and had given her money. She heard her mother's voice, but she climbed the stairs and went inside.

The only light in the room, in the kitchen, came from outside. But the countertops and the kitchen table were covered with all kinds of treats. Shirley got in back and followed the line of children who circled the room, then made their final selections from the table. At the end of the table, near the door, sat a man. He looked to be just a little older than her father. He wore black sunshades and held in his lap a green metal box in which he collected money—pennies, nickels, dimes, quarters—and from which he issued change. A woman who looked to be his wife stood closer to the door, quiet and almost invisible.

"What you got?" the blind man asked. He quickly figured the total in his head. Held out his hand for the money. Even more quickly felt it and determined what was due him or his young customer in change. Shirley could hardly decide what to buy because she was so busy watching the man. She had never seen a blind man before—not in real life.

She passed by the Sugar Babies, by the Turkish Taffy, and by the Banana Bites. She let her fingers trail over the wrappers and boxes for the Red Hots, the Baby Ruths, and past the Mr. Goodbars. Shirley was undecided until she saw them—cookies almost as big and as round as the moon that had looked in her bedroom window in East St. Louis…cookies bigger than her palm.

"You better get three," the little skinny girl leaned back and told Shirley. "They're three—three moon cookies for five cents." Shirley bought three.

When she held out her money to the blind man, she wondered what was behind his glasses, if he was only pretending to be blind. The blind man handed Shirley her change, and his wife handed her a bag for the cookies as she started out the door. She looked into her brown paper bag at the moon cookies one last time, then stepped back out the door.

Shirley followed the children back around to the front of the Blind Man's Store past the red brick house next door. They made their way over a footbridge that spanned a gully—crossing the branch, they called it—and then began to cross a field full of red Texas clay, clay mixed with last night's rain.

The children moved quickly, dodging this way and that, until they crested the top of the hill. Shirley followed as quickly as she could, and just as she was at the top, just as she was about to reassure herself, the red Texas clay sucked off one of her new shoes. Now one of her glowing socks was red, wet, and sagging around her foot.

One of the children she followed—a boy—turned and pointed at Shirley. "Look at that, you all. It got her shoe! She let the mud get her shoe." The children laughed at Shirley, even the little skinny girl with the skinny braids. Then they piled down the hill and crossed the street to enter the school.

Shirley stared after them. One foot in and one foot out. One foot dry and one foot wet. One foot white and one foot red. She pulled her shoe from the muck and limped—one shoe on, one shoe off—until she got to the street. Shirley stripped off her socks and used them to wipe the muddy shoe. And then she made her way into the building. If she could just get inside, she would be okay. She would see Mrs. Canada again. She would win again.

There was no one in Tyler like Mrs. Canada, at least not at Mamie G. Griffin Elementary School, at least not on Glass Street. On Glass Street, in Griffin Elementary, none of the teachers had pink cheeks. They all were Negroes. All of the children at Griffin were Negroes, so were the principal, and the janitor, and the cafeteria workers. Shirley wondered where the children were that she had seen at the department store—at Myer and Smit. And at first Shirley felt calm, felt like she was at church, felt like the brown hands would enfold her.

But that did not last long.

"What's your name? And where are you from?" the teacher

asked her. And by the time she had stood and said that she was Shirley, that she was from Illinois, and that she loved school more than anything in the world—all the children were staring.

"Why do you talk funny?" they asked her at recess. "Why do you talk proper?" they asked her. "Why do you try to talk like white folks, all proper? Maybe you need to go to the white folks' school." Even the little skinny girl with the skinny braids laughed. By the end of the day, Shirley was sure she would never speak again.

The little girl and the old woman walked along the edge of the road headed for the grocery store. Mother Johnson looked over her shoulder at Shirley. "Come on, sugar. Pick up your step. The more you walk, the sooner that junk is going to be all out of your system. You'll feel better. Get your wind back." She carried a folded cart in her hands.

Shirley didn't even have enough air to say "yes, ma'am." She just nodded her head and tried to keep up—with the walk and with where her life was headed. No daddy, no mama, no uncles, no home. And school…

Her lip started to tremble.

Mother Johnson looked back at her. "Don't worry, baby. It might not be easy to believe right now, but trouble don't last always. It might look like the rug's been pulled out from under you, but everything's in Divine Order. You remember I told you so." They walked past the Blind Man's Store and on for what seemed to be miles.

How could the old woman—Shirley wasn't sure if she was an aunt or a cousin—know what she was thinking, how she was feeling?

"You know, sugar, I make this trip at least twice a week. I always have fresh food, and walking is good for body, mind, and soul. People think I'm crazy for walking this far, but he who laughs last, laughs best." The old woman pointed. "There it is, up ahead. The Lassiter's market. We're just going to run in and get a few little things."

Shirley followed Mother Johnson into the store, and the first thing that hit her was the smell of apples—ripe red apples that smelled like cider. The old woman pushed a cart up and down the store aisles, checking items off her list. On every aisle there seemed to be someone who knew her, who stopped to chat.

"Hello, Mother, I've been meaning to come and see you."

Mother Johnson would smile. "Well, you come on then. You know where I am," she would tell them. When the cart was half full, Mother rolled into a checkout line and waited. "He looked beyond my faults and saw my need," she half sang, half hummed.

Shirley was quiet. How was she going to find her way home? The old woman seemed nice, in a funny sort of way— her hair was slicked down on her head like a helmet, with a tiny row of tight curls that framed her face. Shirley was not sure if she liked her, or if she should wait for her mother.

When they reached the counter, Mother Johnson began to put items on the rolling belt. "You can reach and put some on if you want to."

Shirley bent over the buggy and put items on the counter, one at a time.

The sales clerk smiled at Mother Johnson. "I declare, Mother, you are in here four or five times a week." He shook his head and ran his hand over his crew cut. "One day, you're going to get more organized and only come in once a week."

"Well, why do you say that, Mr. Jack?"

"I just think that would make your life more orderly. I'm just speaking something helpful to you. Why, the power of life and death is in the tongue, Mother."

"You suppose so?"

"Of course." He laughed. "Everyone knows that, Mother. That's why it's so important to study the Word of God, not just get involved in a bunch of emotional acting out, like…well, you know…like you see in some of you people's churches. The Word says it clearly; the power of life and death is in the tongue." He smiled more broadly. "No two ways about it."

"That so?"

He nodded.

"Well, bless the cities, then."

Shirley looked at Mother Johnson, then back at the clerk. She looped her fingers through the metal bars on the cart.

The clerk frowned. "What, Mother?"

"I said, 'bless the cities.' If the power of life and death is in the tongue, don't it make you wonder?"

Mr. Jack looked over Mother's shoulder to his next customer and started bagging more quickly. "Wonder what, Mother?"

"It just makes me wonder why, if people believe in the power and all, why they holler out, 'The children are going to hell,' instead of, 'Bless the children.'" She started placing grocery bags in the bottom of her cart. "It makes me wonder why people keep saying the cities are going to hell, instead of saying, 'Lord, rebuild the cities. Lord, bless the cities.'"

"I don't know what you mean, Mother."

"Well, if lots of people start saying that, that's lots of power to good—lots of good prayers and blessings. And that's something easy and free that everybody could do to help people that need their help. Good would have to come from that, wouldn't it? Just like evil come from mean things people say. You know, 'Those blankety-blank Indians, those lazy Mexicans, those shiftless n—'"

The cashier held out his hand for the money. "I don't mean to rush you, but I have other customers waiting in line, Mother."

Mother Johnson pulled a worn coin purse from her purse. She undid the snap and removed some bills and handed them to the man. "Sorry, Mr. Jack. What you said just got me to thinking. Maybe it's something you could ask the people about—the ones that you study with—for me. Maybe we need to think about what we say every day." Mother smiled sweetly.

Mr. Jack had stopped smiling. "Excuse me, Mother. Thank you for your business." The man turned his back completely on Mother Johnson, as if she didn't exist. "Good morning, Mrs. Calhoun." He began to total the next woman's groceries.

"Excuse me, Mr. Jack," Mother Johnson said. "Don't forget my green stamps." She held out her hand.

Outside, Mother Johnson unfolded the cart and piled the bags on it. "Come on, sugar, you help me pull." They gripped the cart and pulled it along behind them. "I wasn't about to leave my green stamps. Enough of them and I can paste them in a book and get me a set of dishes, or towels, or whatever." She stopped to adjust the cart and then started walking again. "He's right, you know? The power of life and death is in your tongue. And that's one thing that's going to help you, Shirley.

"I know you been through a lot. I can't tell just what, but I know you got a burden on you older than your years. You might not feel like talking about it right now, but you just give it time." She smiled at Shirley. "You're going to come shining through. You count on it. God's going to lead us, giving us the words to show you the way home."

The two of them walked past the old man, on and on until they reached home. They walked up the walkway. "I've been through a lot of things. And I know how it is to feel like you're in a place you can't figure your way out of. Like you're down in a pit or in a fog. Or like you're chained to a wall and can't get free." She stopped and put a knotted hand on Shirley's shoulders. Mother Johnson used the other hand to cup Shirley's chin so she could look deep into her eyes. "Always remember, Shirley, not to give up. If you just sit still and you don't hope, you're never going to get free. But if you keep pulling at those chains—minute after minute, day after day, year after year— eventually the chain's going to break or the wall's going to crumble, and you'll be free. That's the power of hope. Believe me, I know. And you remember I told you so."

When they finished unpacking the groceries, Mother Johnson grabbed two peaches in one hand and motioned for Shirley to come outside. Shirley followed and sat down on the steps next to Mother. "One of the first things you're going to have to do is to be happy on purpose." Shirley frowned and Mother continued. "I bet you used to just smile all the time. I'll bet you were a happy little girl. Bet you talked all the time, too, just like little girls do."

Shirley shrugged her shoulders.

"Well, you know what? In order to get your smile back, to get your joy back, you are going to have to be happy on purpose." Mother Johnson took a napkin out of her pocket. "Did you go to church with your people?"

Shirley nodded and then said, "Yes, ma'am."

"Good. Well then, you know about heaven, about God, and about Jesus?" Shirley nodded. "Well then you must also know about the Bible?" Shrug. "A little bit?"

"A little."

"Well, you don't have to frown up your face like that, for goodness' sakes." Mother Johnson laughed. "That's okay. Small beginnings are good beginnings." She looked at the peaches, then looked a little more sober. "So, you also know about the devil—about the enemy. Some people call the devil *the enemy* because he is the enemy of our souls."

Shirley didn't feel like talking.

"Don't worry, baby. You don't have to be concerned or scared. I just bring him up because I want it to be clear in your mind just who it is that's your enemy. Who it is that doesn't want you to be happy. You see, some folks tell themselves that the devil is not there, so he wreaks havoc in their lives, and they don't even try to fight back because they think there's no one to fight. Or they try to fight people, when our enemy is not people—it's the enemy and his dark forces."

Shirley ducked her head and hunched her shoulders.

"Oh no, baby. You don't have to be afraid, either. The devil wants you to be afraid. And I know we see all these horror movies where the monsters always win and never die. But God always tells me to let people know to not be afraid. God says that He is here with us, Jesus is with us—"

Shirley jerked her head up and turned to look at Mother Johnson.

"That's right, baby. Jesus is with us. He and His Father are in heaven, but the Spirit is always here with us praying for us and helping us. And God is always looking over the earth, just try-ing to find someone He can help, someone that He can fight a battle for, someone He can deliver. Someone who's hollering for help." She nodded. "So don't give up talking."

Shirley looked at the woman and wondered how she could have known about her silence.

"That's right. Don't give up, because He wants to help you. That's why it's important for us to pray, and sing, and praise, and know the Word of God—it helps to defeat the enemy." She held out a peach to Shirley. "So the first thing we're going to learn how to do is to be happy on purpose and to say it out loud."

Shirley took the peach and rolled it in her hand. It was warm, firm, and fuzzy.

"Don't roll it around too much, baby. Peach fuzz will make you itch." Mother Johnson held her peach up to her nose and smelled it. "Now, go ahead. Take a big bite."

Shirley smelled her peach and then held it to her mouth and bit. Her teeth cut into the flesh and the juice exploded inside her mouth. Some of it slipped from the corners of her mouth and down her chin. She used the back of her hand to wipe it away. Shirley couldn't remember anything tasting so good…not in a long time.

Mother Johnson laughed. "You should see your eyes, baby! They are big enough to swim in. Ain't that a good peach?"

Shirley nodded.

"I tell *you* it is. Now, Shirley, all you got to do is say it out loud. Just let your heart be happy about that peach. Just take a moment to enjoy it and appreciate it." Mother Johnson shook her head. "This is a good peach." She smiled. "Now watch what I do." She closed her eyes for a second and then shook her head and looked up in the sky. "Lord, this is *some* good peach. And I'm happy about it. And I appreciate You just putting this peach in my way."

Mother Johnson looked back at Shirley and smiled. "Some folks would tell you that's going too far, being grateful for a little old peach. But I think God loves it when we are grateful for little things. It makes Him take notice. And when you been sad or hurt, sometimes you got to be happy on purpose, and all you can do, starting out, is to be grateful for little things. There's something about thanking God and taking time to pay attention to the little things that will, if you do it time after time, make you start to feel glad. And if you're glad over little things, wait and see if God doesn't give you something else bigger to be glad about." Mother Johnson touched her hand to Shirley's cheek. "But to let Him know you appreciate it, you got to open your mouth. You're going to learn how to speak life. You remember I told you so.

"Every day people make choices. Some choose to be mad. Some choose to be sad. It's just as easy to choose to be grateful and glad. Sadness will make you grow weary and weak. Anger will make your life dark and hard. But joy will make you strong and healthy. Remember, I told you so."

The child killer grabbed one of the shapeless things near him and flung it as far as he could see. The spirit in the old woman was strong, and she was focusing on the child, attempting to rescue the soft one. He would reach down and strike her, but the hedge of protection around the old one was strong. Shirley, the soft one, was *his*—he would not give her up.

He jumped up and down. Then he cowered. The master would be angry. The master would accept no excuses. The child killer would do whatever he had to—he could not let her get away. Child Killer Shirley turned his one good eye toward the Third Heaven. And above all—even if he had to invade her dreams to do it—he must not let the soft one begin to praise and pray. Not a single prayer.

TWENTY

❦

*S*hirley bolted upright in her bed. Her chest heaved. She could not remember her dreams, the nightmares, but they had sucked the air from her chest. The curtains at the window stirred and looked ghostly white against the black night. A mewling whimpering climbed from the ground beneath, up through the window. She held her breath.

"Mr. Jack? What you doin' out here?" Mother Johnson's voice cut through the eerie sound. "You goin' to wake the dead. What you doin' out here?"

The mewling turned to sobbing. "I-I didn't know where else to go."

"Get in here, Mr. Jack. Goodness gracious. If this don't beat all." Footsteps dragged from the edge of the porch to the front door. Shirley could hear Mother Johnson lock the door while the two adults whispered. "What you come to me for?"

"I feel like I'm going to lose my mind."

Shirley could tell from the way Mother Johnson called him Mr. Jack, and from the sound of his voice, that he was not a Negro, but she wasn't sure if it was the man from the market. It was a strange place and time for a white man.

"Hush, now, Mr. Jack. You going to wake that child, and she needs her sleep."

Through the thin walls, Shirley could hear every word, could hear Mother Johnson dragging her sulting table nearer to her favorite chair, could hear Mother Johnson turn the lamp switch—just one click—so that the living room must have still been dim.

"I know you didn't come way out here just for ice tea, so I'm not gone waste your time and mine offering you none. So let's just get started."

Mr. Jack's voice broke. "I don't know where to start, Mother Johnson. I feel so foolish—"

"Well, you had enough sense to come out here. Just jump on in and tell your story. Ain't nobody to hear but me and you."

"I don't know who I am."

"What you mean? I been knowing you all my life. I know your people—"

"No, Mother, I mean, I don't know if I'm a…a man."

Shirley could hear Mother Johnson rocking. "Do tell."

"I don't know how to say this."

"Well, who do you say that you are?"

"Always a man. I mean, I know I'm different. Quiet." Mr. Jack's voice broke again, sounded as if he was struggling to maintain a whisper. "Softer. I know I'm sensitive, but…" He sobbed for a while.

"Go ahead, now, Mr. Jack. You came here to get something out." Mother Johnson's voice was low and even.

"I'm a man. Ain't I?"

"Who says you ain't?"

"It started in high school, men approaching me, asking

me…trying to touch me. Telling me that I was lying to myself, that they could see the signs." '

"Who were the men?"

"I-I don't want to say. I don't want to cause anyone any trouble. I just…I just have to know. And I came to you because I know you can see. You can tell me. What's wrong with me?"

"Why you think these men know you better than you know yourself?"

"Over and over. It happens over and over, no matter where I am. And I never fit in, never played football, just sort of stayed to myself. Just with my mother and grandmother, what with my father being dead." Mr. Jack sighed. "I know I'm not hard, Mother, but I…now I'm not sure."

"Why you not sure? No girls like you?"

For the first time since Shirley heard him outside her window, Mr. Jack laughed. "Yes, Mother Johnson, girls—women like me. I love women. I've had relationships. I've even met a girl I would like to marry…I've been dreaming since I was a little boy about being a father and a husband."

Mother Johnson's chair stopped creaking. "Then you got to explain it to me, Mr. Jack. You got to tell me why you stumble up on my porch in the middle of the night, because I still don't understand it."

"It's just all these men making jokes and calling me names, other men telling me they see signs." Mr. Jack paused and sighed. "And I haven't slept with a woman."

The chair started creaking again. "What your mama tell you about women and things, Mr. Jack?"

He cleared his throat. "She told me I should be respectful of the woman and of God…that I should wait. Wait until I'm married."

"Sounds right to me."

"But the men say I'm soft and weak, and they say I couldn't have waited if there wasn't something wrong with me." His voice sounded resigned. "I'm thirty years old, Mother Johnson. And I don't know, maybe I'm not right, maybe I shouldn't risk trying to marry…for her sake. I have to know."

"You trying to tell me you ain't got no feelings, ain't got no stirrings for women?"

Mr. Jack chuckled softly. "No, I'm not saying that, Mother. I just made myself wait. That's all."

"So, you trying to tell me you going to give up what you been waiting for because of what some other trifling folks say?" Mother Johnson kept rocking and sighed. "I don't guess I will ever understand how some folks let other folks tell them who they are." She grunted.

"But, Mother, it's not that easy. I tried to fit in with the regular guys—they called me names, didn't want to be around me…sometimes they wanted to fight."

"Yes."

It got quiet for a while. Then Mr. Jack spoke again. "When I was away in college…sometimes I was so lonely, Mother. No friends. It just felt like I didn't fit in anywhere. And I got to thinking maybe I was wrong. Maybe I should stop fighting it. Maybe I should be honest with myself, maybe own up to who they said I was.

"I went to this little club, Mother. To this place I had heard people talking about. I was so lonely. I met a man there. He was friendly, nice. We left, had coffee… I don't think I can say any more, Mother." Mr. Jack started to cry again.

Wind gusted through the window in Shirley's room. In the other room, Mother Johnson's rocking slowed. "So, what you telling me, Mr. Jack?"

"Ever since then, I've doubted even more. It never felt right with the man, I always felt a little sick, a little uncomfortable. Felt like I was losing control. And now I don't know who I am, and I don't think I can ask God about it. I don't even know how He feels about me. I don't know how I feel about me."

"Well, it's awful late at night, and you come a long way. 'Fore we do anything, we got to pray. God can't help us if we won't let Him draw near. Give me your hand."

Shirley strained but could not hear the words they murmured, only the timbre of their voices until they said in unison, "Amen."

"We just asked God to forgive us of our sins, didn't we, Mr. Jack?"

Shirley listened closely to hear the man's voice. "Yes, Mother Johnson."

"Well, we asked, and the Word says God is faithful and just and will forgive us and cleanse us. He does it right away. That's what the Word says. You believe it? That what your mama and grandmama taught you?"

"Yes, ma'am, I believe it. That's what they taught me."

"So, He forgive us because God is a mercy God, and then we ask Him to make us wise on this matter before us. And the Word says if we lack wisdom, ask and He will give it to us. That what your mama taught you?"

"Yes, ma'am."

"Believe it?"

"Yes, ma'am."

The room got quiet again, except for the sound of Mother's rocking chair. Then she cleared her throat and spoke. "Seem like to me can't nobody tell you who you are except for you. You already done something one time trying to conform to who somebody said you were—and that something just about broke your heart. You need to know you ain't the first person ever got confused about who they were, and you ain't the last."

It sounded as if Mother was leaning forward in her chair. "Satan is the father of lies, and you can bet that whenever he starts to tell you a lie, one of the first things that happens is confusion. Satan telling lies; Spirit telling the truth. If a body don't know the Word, he can get turned around for sure."

Mother Johnson made a clicking sound with her tongue. "You also need to know that whoever you was, whatever you done, that's in the past right now. You sitting over there in that chair a new creature, and God loves you. Loves you enough that He sent His Son to die for you. Didn't just die for me, didn't just die for big old husky men, died for little you too. Ain't no sin in this room. You been cleaned out.

"Don't be miserable trying to be something you not. But don't be miserable trying to fit up to who somebody say you ought to be. All men not hard and tough. God made David gentle, made him a man that would praise Him. I guess it's okay if you follow after David, don't you?"

"Yes, ma'am."

"David was a little bitty thing like you. Sang all the time and played the harp. How many men you know singing and playing the harp? What you think some men might say about a man singing and playing the harp? To top that off, David danced for the Lord, out in public, in front of everybody. How many men you seen dancing so hard they come out they clothes? You know it had to be some folks whispering about David being naked.

"It's sad, but sometimes folks don't like it when you not who they thought you would be. Old Saul liked David when he was just a soft little boy. But when it turned out the soft little thing was a mighty man of God, Saul went crazy and wanted to kill David.

"Don't let what somebody say keep you from being who you are, or from enjoying what you been waiting and preparing for all your life. God's counting on you being who *He* called you to be."

Mother Johnson hummed softly for a moment. "I don't see nothing wrong, Mr. Jack. You just keep your hand in the Master's hand. And don't you worry about that man you met at the club, Mr. Jack. Just like God got the perfect right somebody for us, the devil got the perfect wrong somebody for us, and the wily devil is always waving that wrong person under our nose. The mean old devil tricks everybody some time, even me."

Shirley could hear Mother Johnson rising from her chair. Then she heard the two adults moving toward the front door. "You just got tricked for a minute. And all those men coming to you, whispering to you, trying to touch you—" Shirley heard the front door open—"they just trying to touch the goodness inside you. They don't know what it is, but they hungry and starving. They see your good fruit, fruit God's Spirit give you—goodness, kindness, gentleness, meekness. They just hungry and want what you got. Don't worry; just keep your hand in the Lord's hand. And if they come to you again, you just tell them about the Savior, about the Bread of Life, about the Living Water."

"Thank you, Mother. Thank you."

Mother Johnson's voice sounded muffled. "Don't hug me so hard, Mr. Jack. I ain't done nothing special, and you gone squeeze the pure life out of me."

"Thank you, Mother."

"Now, don't be trying to give me no money, Mr. Jack. Put your money away. You know your people taught you better than that. I ain't no witch. I just lean on God's Word for His wisdom. We are helpers one of another. Now go on and let me get some sleep. An old woman got to get her beauty sleep too."

Shirley heard the man's footsteps leaving the house. A car started, and his voice sounded from far away. "Good night, Mother. God bless you." She heard the car pull onto the highway; then it was gone.

A strange woman. A strange place. A strange night. Shirley nestled her head into her pillow and fell asleep. It was the first time but it would not be the last time a stranger appeared outside her window late at night.

TWENTY-ONE

One last apple hung from the tree on a branch beyond her reach.

Shirley had been watching it for weeks now. It was not going to move. All the leaves were gone, and it still clung stubbornly to its limb. She stared at it, then looked around for a stick long enough to poke it down. Finally, Shirley gave up and moved on to more accessible diversions. She danced around the trees in the yard, kicking the fall rainbow of leaves—yellow, orange, brown, red—until some of them flew high enough to drift down on her head. Her dance was interrupted every few minutes as she stopped to tug at her thick, black tights, which threatened to creep down her hips to her legs while pulling her underclothes with them. As she returned to her dance, she was careful to avoid kicking the pail of pecans she had collected.

Shirley stopped and looked at the apple one more time. Sheri would have come up with a way to get the apple down. The two of them together could have…

She missed Sheri. She looked through the branches to the sky. It looked like snow, but it wasn't cold enough. Shirley reached for the bucket and carried the nuts to the side door of the house.

"I know, Mother, but I don't understand why my life is so hard. I keep praying and praying. Why doesn't God answer? I can't take it anymore."

Shirley stopped short and pressed her back to the wall. She was afraid to open the door and afraid to look inside to see the woman who was speaking. For some reason, Shirley could hardly breathe.

"I can't take it anymore, Mother. I've loved him so much; I did everything for him. I-I-I…and now that I've had the baby, he's going with another girl. And she stopped me on the street, Mother. She told me I better leave him alone. And you should have seen her mother. She was a—I don't know what to call her. Why would he want a woman like that? I've done everything for him. People are talking about me, and he's with somebody like that. I just can't take it anymore, Mother."

The young woman's voice sounded younger than Shirley's mother's voice—and it sounded panicked. The smell of baking cornbread and cooking collard greens wrapped around the voice and drifted through the window next to Shirley's head.

"I hate him! Look what he's doing to my life." For a while there were no more words, just choking sobs. Then she spoke again. "And what about the baby? It's his baby too. He's forgot all about the baby. Nobody says anything about him not taking care of his baby. They just talk about me ruining his life. And where is God? I can't take no more, Mother."

When the girl paused, Mother Johnson spoke. "I know you upset, honey. But you got to stop saying you can't make it. The power of life and death is in your tongue."

"But Mother, you don't know how I feel. I feel like I'm losing my mind. I just want it to be over."

"Mind what you say, Naomi."

"Mother, I think about it all the time. About it being over…and how to do it. I just want it to end, Mother."

The girl wailed. Then her sobs sounded muffled. Shirley shuddered while she listened outside the window.

"I know it's hard right now, but you going to make it. You can't give up over something like this. It seems like it's the only thing in the world that matters right now. But believe me, that ain't so."

"I just want him to come home, Mother. I need him—the baby needs him. And look at what he's done to my life. And everybody hates me—it's not my fault. They think I tried to trap him. He said he loved me, Mother. I need him to come home…don't you have something to make him come home?"

Mother Johnson's voice sounded angry. "Is that why you come here, girl? You think I'm some root worker? Here I am thinking you've come for prayer. But if that's why you come, you might as well leave now."

"No, Mother, no. Don't you turn your back on me now too. I'm sorry, Mother. I'm just so desperate. I'm about ready to do anything. One minute he tells me he loves me and he's going to marry me. Ernest says he wants to do what's right. That he knows I love the Lord and he's not going to let people be laughing at me. Then the next minute he's with that other girl. I can't live without him, Mother.

"I love him, Mother. Me and the baby love Ernest. I just…I just don't know what else to do, or who else to talk to. I feel like I'm going to lose my mind."

Shirley wanted to run and run and keep running. She felt sick at the stomach, and she remembered her mother—could see her stumbling down the street, tearing at her hair…

She wanted to be any place but where she stood. *Run!* her mind shouted. If only she had a friend to run with her, someone to be strong with. Sheri. But Sheri was not there, and Shirley was afraid—she had been standing by the window so long now that if she went inside they would know she had been listening. Shirley wasn't sure if she was more afraid of what she was hearing or of Mother finding out that she had been listening. She stood frozen and listened.

"Take this towel, Naomi, and wipe your face. It's been a while since you remembered who you are. And for your sake—for the baby's sake—you going to have to get yourself together."

"I can't, Mother."

"Yes, you can. You have to."

"I can't make it without God, Mother. And I know He's not hearing me; He's not answering my prayers."

"Do you know who you are?"

"Of course, I do, Mother." Naomi's voice sounded shocked.

"Well, you not acting like it now. You're not acting like you're the daughter of the Most High God. Look at you. Sniveling and looking desperate."

"Mother!"

"Naomi, I'm not trying to be mean. But you need some sense talked to you and you need it quick, and there's no time to mollycoddle you. I don't think you've known who you are for a long time now. When you took up with that man, did you ask God first, Naomi?"

"I prayed about it, Mother. I told the Lord I wanted him."

"Did you wait to hear what the Lord had to say?"

The girl's voice sounded miffed. "I told you I prayed, Mother."

"Maybe so, but I don't believe that you waited to listen. Now you got you, that boy, and your baby in trouble."

"Why is everybody blaming me, Mother! What did I do so wrong?"

"Is that boy saved, Naomi?"

Naomi cleared her throat. "That's what I told the Lord, Mother Johnson. That I would help him get saved, that I would tell Ernest about the Good News, about the Lord. And I did. I kept my promise. I told him about it, and I took him to church with me."

"So when did you tell Ernest about the Lord, Naomi. Did you tell him when you were in bed, breaking the Lord's rules?" The sound of broken sobs fell from the window. "How was he supposed to learn who God was? You were the example; he was looking to see God reflected in you."

"But Mother, I did it for him."

"No, Naomi, first you got to tell the truth to yourself. You did it for you, baby. Not for him. What would have been best for Ernest would have been to find Jesus first. Tell yourself the truth, Naomi. You wanted him for yourself more than you wanted him for God. You took your eyes off God's will and started looking at your own will first. You took Ernest to you before he was ready. You know he wasn't ready for a woman of God like you. He was out there, running around lost, dead in his sins. Naomi, use your head. What's a woman of God doing with a sinner? You know when something holy touches something unholy, something's going to die. Bless his soul. We got to pray."

Shirley could imagine Mother Johnson patting the woman's hand. "When God didn't speak to you when you prayed saying you wanted Ernest, maybe He was saying, 'Not now.' Maybe

He was telling you Ernest wasn't ready. Maybe what He was giving you was one of the most trusted jobs He can give a body—bringing a lost sheep to Christ.

"You wanted the cake before it was through baking. Now, what you got is a mess. And I tell you for sure, killing yourself ain't gonna make the mess get straightened out. That's just more wrong on top of the first wrong, and you don't want to leave that as your baby's inheritance. And you know for sure that man won't be able to get saved with that kind of millstone around his neck."

A lonely howling sound came from the window. A howling that became a shrill shriek. "Oh, Mother. You're right, Mother. God forgive me. God help me!"

"God is gone help you, baby. I promise you that. God is a mercy God. He loves a contrite spirit and a broken heart. The Word says so. He loves you, He loves your baby, and He loves Ernest. Now I can't say for sure that you're going to have Ernest's name. That may be something you just have to bear. But the Lord *will* receive you back in His arms. You know His Word promises that. What's important, He will fix."

"What can I do, Mother? Look what I've done. Look what I've done to the baby."

"Naomi, you know that God does not want you full of shame. He wants you to return to Him, to love Him first, to trust Him. Then you're going to have to just walk through each day and let the Lord work it out. I'm not telling you it's not going to hurt. But you're going to just have to keep pressing, keep looking to God. You're going to have to trust you and the baby to the Lord and surrender your will for Ernest to God's will for his life. You are going to have to trust that the Lord has a good plan for each one of you. You going to have to believe that no matter what happens—even if Ernest marries that other girl—that the Lord means it for your good, the best for you, not your harm. That's what you got to say to yourself. God's got a good plan for you, and you and the baby are going to be all right—life and death is in the power of the tongue.

"Now come on, Naomi. We got to pray. For you, for the baby, and for that man."

Shirley's back slid along the wall until she was squatting on the porch. She laid her head in her hands and cried, quietly so that Mother Johnson would not hear. She was tired, so tired.

The light outside had dimmed but not faded. "What you doing out here, baby?" Mother was shaking Shirley's shoulder. "Wake up, baby. Mercy! It's too cold for you to be laying down out here. How long you been here?"

Shirley was still too groggy to talk, and she stumbled along while Mother Johnson's arm around her shoulder directed her into the house. She pointed back at the bucket of pecans, but was too tired, too cold, to make sense, to tell her about the nuts.

Mother bustled Shirley into her bedroom and turned on the lamp. "My goodness, baby. Come on so we can get you in the bed. I'll bring you a hot plate and some hot tea. Let's skin you out of these clothes, and you put on this warm nightgown. Mercy, mercy. Look at you, just shivering."

Mother squeezed her tight, and Shirley surrendered to the hug. She felt as though she had been found, returned from some place far away. "I'm sorry, Mother Johnson. I—"

"No, indeed. No, don't you be sorry, sweetheart. Goodness, I thought you were out there playing in the yard, playing in the leaves. The last time I looked out the window at you, you were kicking up leaves." Mother Johnson pulled the nightgown down over Shirley's head. It was warm and soft; it smelled of baby powder. The old woman leaned over the bed and pulled back the covers, then tucked Shirley underneath.

Mother Johnson leaned over to lay her hand on Shirley's forehead. "Thank God, I don't feel a fever." She kissed Shirley's forehead, then dimmed the lamp next to her bed. "You lay quiet now. I'll be back with your plate of food and the tea."

Shirley did not want to wake up, but a hand kept shaking her shoulder and a voice kept calling. "Come on, Shirley."

The voice was deep, but not deep enough to be Big Uncle. "Wake up, Shirley, so you can drink your tea." She opened her eyes. Mother Johnson sat next to her on the bed. Deep, blue night had replaced the gray afternoon.

"You been asleep a while now. I was gone just let you sleep, but I think you need to have a little something in your stomach. Come on now, sit up." Shirley pushed herself up, then accepted the cup of tea Mother Johnson offered. It was sweet and hot—not hot enough to burn her tongue, but hot just the same. "Is it good?"

Shirley nodded. "Yes, ma'am."

"It's got rock candy in it. When I was a little girl, my daddy kept a little rock candy stashed away. Whenever I was sick, he would break off a little piece and drop it in my tea with a little lemon." Mother laughed. "Sometimes I would wish for a cold just so I could taste that rock candy. Thought you might like it too."

"Yes, ma'am. I do."

Mother reached her hand and brushed the hair back from Shirley's forehead. "I guess you were outside the door for a while."

She nodded.

"Well, I guess you heard everything then. Probably some things you understand and some things you don't." Mother Johnson sighed. "You know, Shirley, I have just give up trying to tell the Lord His business. It's some reason why you're always around to hear grown folks talk. I guess He figures you got grown-folks-size trouble. All that woman's misery probably made you weary, Shirley. But I promise you what I told her is true for you too. You been through a lot. More than a child should have to bear, it seems to me. But sure as I'm sitting here, and as sure as I love you, the Lord loves you more. And no matter what you been through, the Lord loves you and He's got a good plan for you. A good plan that's going to bring you out of your trouble."

She rubbed her hands over Shirley's fingers. "I can't promise you when it's all going to be over. But the Lord is going to raise you up to be a strong woman, a good woman. And one day, you going to look back and count it all joy."

Mother Johnson handed Shirley a small plate full of a large spoon of collard greens with small pieces of ham, cornbread, and a dollop of sweet potato pudding. "You don't have to eat it all. Just get a little something warm in your stomach."

She sat on the edge of the bed and told Shirley the Bible story of Moses crossing the Red Sea. "And after all the troubles they been through, the Lord heard the cries of the children of Israel. One day when they felt like giving up, when everything looked bad—Pharoah behind them and the Red Sea ahead of them—He made a way out of no way. He parted the waters. Opened the

Red Sea right down the middle, and all the people—men, women, children—their animals and their goods crossed over on dry ground, shouting, 'Glory! Hallelujah! Troubles over!'"

Mother Johnson sat on the bed telling the story until Shirley drank all the tea and fell back asleep with the plate in her hands.

The next day was Wednesday. And as was their habit, after she got home from school, Shirley followed Mother Johnson to the prayer house.

"Come on, Shirley. We got to make some noise today. We need the Lord to hear us."

As always there was no one around, and for some reason Shirley felt freer. She shook the tambourine and danced. She sat silently while Mother Johnson prayed; she did not move when Mother said words she did not understand.

Mother turned her head toward heaven and began to shout. "'Lift up your heads, O ye gates, and be ye lift up, ye everlasting doors; and the King of glory shall come in!" She wagged her gray head. "Who is this King of glory? The LORD strong and mighty, the LORD mighty in battle." She lifted her hands. "Lift up your heads, O ye gates; even lift them up, ye everlasting doors; and the King of glory shall come in. Who is this King of glory? The LORD of hosts, he is the King of glory.' Come, Lord Jesus, come!"

Even the birds making their way farther south seemed unusually quiet as Mother spoke. "Amen," Mother said at last.

Shirley loved the time in the prayer house, but she could not yell. Not the way Mother Johnson yelled. Not the way the old woman hollered outdoors—outdoors where people could hear her, hear her yelling praises and prayers at the top of her lungs.

"You hear me, Lord?" She would yell while she shook tambourines or beat on pans. "I love You, Lord. And I don't care who knows it!"

Shirley loved it, but she was sure that it was Mother Johnson alone who had been appointed to yell.

A car pulled into the driveway. "You wait here, Shirley." Mother walked to the drive and stood talking to a young man who had gotten out of the car. They were too far away for Shirley to hear. Suddenly, Mother Johnson threw her arms about the young man, and he hugged her back. Mother shouted then. She spoke so loudly that Shirley could hear her. "Glory!" she said. "Hallelujah! Troubles over!"

Mother waved Shirley over, and the three of them stepped up on the porch and went into the house.

Several weeks later—Shirley wasn't sure exactly how many, it could have been months—there was a knock at the door.

"Come on," Mother said. The screen door opened, and a young woman stepped inside. Her skin glowed like amber, and her eyes were large and dewy.

"How are you, Mother Johnson? Look what I brought you. Your favorite huckleberry pie."

Mother stretched to her tiptoes and kissed the young girl on the cheek. "Look at you, Naomi. You are just the sweetest child. Um, um, um, smell that pie, why don't you? And look at that glow on your face."

The girl beamed at Mother. "I had a little free time and thought I would come here and do your feet, Mother." The young woman smiled and nodded at Shirley. Then Naomi continued talking to Mother Johnson. "I figured we were about due for a session."

Following Mother's pointing finger, Shirley opened a cabinet door, sifted among the buckets and jars, then pulled out a yellow plastic tub that Mother Johnson used to soak the joints that ached in her feet. Shirley stood on her tiptoes, turned the water tap, and filled the foot tub with hot water.

"Thank you, baby." Mother turned back to the young woman and moved to sit in her favorite chair. "Ain't that nice of you, Naomi. You got a baby and all that you got to take care of, but here you come out here to worry with me."

"Mother, I love to come. It blesses me more that it blesses you. How could I not come after what you did for me?"

"Not me, baby. It was the Lord's good plan. No matter what it looks like, He's got a good plan for us all."

TWENTY-TWO

⚮

*M*other Johnson sat in the worn, unpainted, wooden porch swing. The rusted chain it hung from groaned as she moved back and forth. Shirley sat on the porch with her legs folded up under her while she leaned her head against one of Mother's knees. Mother's knotted hands, hands that had washed too many loads of other people's clothes to support her family, rubbed Shirley's hair. Sometimes she lifted a braid and toyed with it. A chilly but not uncomfortable fall breeze blew around them. It was a gray early afternoon, when it should have rained, but didn't.

"We're going to have to get out there and rake those leaves pretty soon, 'fore they take over."

Shirley snuggled closer.

"See those trees?" Mother lifted her hand for a moment and pointed. "The Lord gave me every one of them. Gave them to feed nine head of children. What me and Daddy couldn't earn, he hunted; and what he couldn't hunt grew in this backyard. Pecan trees, pears, apples. Over yonder is a peach tree, farther back is a cherry tree. We always had a little patch to grow tomatoes and collards and such. But these trees…"

Shirley turned her head so that she could see Mother Johnson's face. "Why do you love the trees so much, Mother?"

The old woman closed her eyes. "I worked hard all my life. Don't even know what a vacation is. And I'm a hard working woman; I ain't afraid of work. But sometimes…I lived through and seen some things I shouldn't have had to see. I worked for folks, washed their underwear, cooked for them, raised their kids, wiped their snot noses. They let their children treat me like I was a child, and those same grown folks talked in front of me about how people like us wasn't human and couldn't learn. But I was good enough to raise their kids and try to teach them right from wrong."

Mother Johnson opened her eyes and shook her head. "People cheated me, didn't pay me what I was due because they could get away with it. Those same people had big houses and cars and their chirren were taken care of. Seemed like me and my husband worked so hard and didn't have nothing except somebody's mean mouth calling us lazy." Mother gave Shirley a weary smile. "Sometimes it was hard to keep loving. And I wondered if me and Daddy wasn't working for nothing. We both had to smile a lot of times when we didn't feel like smiling."

Shirley remembered her cot, the doctors, the questions about the fire and about Sheri and the home. She remembered how the needle hurt going into her arm, and how she wondered what she had done to be locked away and to have lost everyone that she loved…

She didn't like the memory, so she turned from it back to Mother Johnson voice.

"Then we planted these trees." Mother's smile looked as

though *her* memories were sweet. "We were digging and laughing, like we had lost our minds. We tended to them like chirren, giving them water, feeding them, praying for them."

"Praying for *trees*. That sounds cr—doesn't sound right, Mother."

"Well, that's we what we did all right. We would drag home too tired to play with our own chirren, but all of us would come out and stare at these trees. Sometimes it seemed like they wasn't never going to get big enough and old enough to bear fruit."

"What do you mean, Mother? Does it take a long time?"

"Oh, my goodness, yes. Most folks don't have patience enough for a tree to grow and bear its fruit. They want quick things—tomatoes, green beans, squash. And that's good. We need those things too. But most folks don't have enough patience to be tree tenders. But those folks that do have the patience, they get to have what you see here, a crop that keeps on giving over and over.

"When these trees started bearing, it did my heart good. Still does. Looking at these trees makes me know all my work wasn't in vain, when these trees wasn't much more than twigs, didn't look like nothing. But here we come up with a gift good enough to feed our family and lots of other families around here." She nodded. "Still givin'."

Mother Johnson smiled at Shirley, who laid her head back against the old woman's knee while they watched the gray skies and gently rolling clouds.

"I think I hear somebody coming up the drive." Mother didn't move from her seat, did not turn her head. Shirley didn't hear anyone coming, but she had already learned that somehow Mother knew.

"I ain't fooling with you, Mavis Johnson. I declare, you going to have to get a shorter drive or a little cart that comes out to meet people at the road. If I wasn't your friend, I wouldn't be here. That's for sure."

Shirley leaned forward to see the woman huff and puff as she stepped up on the porch. "That road is too long, Mavis. That's enough to cause a body to leave this world."

Mother laughed. "The problem's got to be with the road, right Ma Dear? Couldn't be that something is wrong with you."

The hefty woman turned, pretending to leave. She looked back over her shoulder. Her face was pretty, like a young girl's. Her gray hair and stiff back gave her away. "You must not want company. You must just want to be left alone to yourself...to think a while."

"Oh, come on now, Ma Dear. You know I'm always happy to see you. Come sit a spell." Mother Johnson patted the seat next to her. "This swing loves it when you come to visit."

The woman's smile got bigger the whole time she walked to the swing. Ma Dear plopped herself into position and the swing groaned.

"Oh, don't mind that, Ma Dear. It's been groaning the whole morning. That's just the swing's way of saying hello."

Ma Dear looked at Mother Johnson over the top of her glasses, and the two women tittered like schoolgirls. "So who is that sitting on the floor by your legs, Mother Johnson? Is that a new friend of yourn? Mighty pretty."

"Well, yes, she is my new friend, but more like family. This is Miss Shirley. Miss Shirley, I want you to meet Miss Augusta Charles. Her loved ones call her Ma Dear, though. And since any friend of mine is a friend of hers, you can call her Ma Dear too."

Shirley stood and nodded, her eyes downcast. "Nice to meet you, Ma Dear."

Ma Dear spoke to Mother. "Look at all that hair. Look at them eyes and that pretty brown skin. Just like velvet."

"You can sit back down now."

Shirley nodded at Mother and walked to the edge of porch. She would be quiet. She would be invisible. *Little pitchers shouldn't have big ears.* She wasn't sure what it meant, but she knew for certain that if she was quiet and didn't interrupt, the adults would let her stay near. Sometimes she could take a peek, but for certain she would hear things normally not meant for children's ears.

"So, how's it going, Mother?"

"Oh, about as good as an old woman can expect, I reckon. And how about you, Ma Dear?"

"Well, last Friday I was up in Dallas."

"Do tell."

"Um-hmm. Family had a sick man. Very sick, and they ask me to come and pray for him. Even sent a car for me."

"That so?"

"Yes, was a well-to-do family. But they treated me real nice on the way down there. Sure enough, the man was good and sick. So sick that people was speaking in whispers, like they didn't want to alert the Death Angel where he was. When I walked in the room, you could hear the death rattle in his chest."

"Ain't that something, Ma Dear? I tell you I just don't have it in me…the way you go pray for those people and don't get discouraged by what you see. Whew-wee. I don't think I could sleep at night."

The swing continued groaning. "But look what you do,

Mother. People coming to see you all hours of the day and night. Same folks come see you by night that don't want you to sit next to 'em by day. And you don't say a mumbling word. I couldn't take it, that's for sure. You know me and my mouth."

"Yeah, it is a little spicy at that, Ma Dear." Mother gave Ma Dear a sideways glance. "But now go on and tell me the rest of the story. Did the man get well?"

"Mother, I laid my hands on the man and prayed. 'Fore I left there, he was sitting up in the bed. He even asked for some tea. You know me, Mother, I wanted to shout and dance all over the place. Every time it happens I can't believe it—my Mama said that I had healing hands. I get excited when I see the Lord move." Ma Dear's hands fluttered about her like butterflies while she talked. "Mother, I just wanted to do a little holy dance. But they wasn't that kind of people, you know—a little on the snooty side." Ma Dear pursed her lips. "In fact, they was a lot on the snooty side. Before I left there, I had cussed out one of the women there, one of the man's children. She was so rude, treating me like I was trash, like I was ignorant. But not so ignorant I couldn't pray for her daddy. I cussed her out so bad I was afraid they wasn't going to give me a ride back home."

Mother groaned softly. "Oh, Augusta."

"I know, Mavis. I know. I try so hard. You don't know how many times I been down on my knees praying to the Lord. Asking Him to clean out my filthy mouth just like He did for Jeremiah." She lowered her voice to a whisper. "And, my goodness, Mavis. I still got that other problem. Look at me. I'm an old woman, and you'd a thought by now my wandering eye would have dimmed. I ain't doing nothing but looking. And my old eyes can't hardly see, but when a young, good-lookin' man walks by. Mercy, there my eyes go. It's embarrassing, Mavis. And my wandering eye is bad enough, but the cussing is worse. I can keep my eye pretty well hid, but *everybody* knows about the cussing."

Mother Johnson shook her head. "Well. Well."

"And goodness knows I pray, Mother. At night, I fall down on these old, fat, stiff knees, and I just weep and pray." The woman's voice shook. "You know I love the Lord. And I try. And I do okay long as nobody makes me mad. You know how that is."

"Yes, I do know it's a hard thing to smile when somebody hurts you or makes you mad."

"That's right, Mother. And I intend not to say a mumbling word. Then—bam! The next thing you know I done laid somebody out. Next thing, I'm doing the very thing I intended not to do. Just like old apostle Paul."

Mother sighed. "I know what you mean, honey. But we just have to keep trying, keep praying, because one day we going to overcome this old sin, this old flesh that makes us do wrong."

"But when, Mother?" Ma Dear's whisper got even softer. "After I cussed that woman, I was so 'shamed. How does it look? Here I am trying to be a godly woman, and people saying I got healing hands. Then all that is just nullified by a cussing mouth. The Lord must be so 'shamed of me. It's a wonder He don't hate me."

Shirley was afraid to stir too much, but she wanted to see if the woman was crying.

"The Lord wants us to keep trying to do better, and He wants us to believe that through Him we have the power to change. But He doesn't hate you, Ma Dear. He hears you confessing your sins, and He is faithful and just; the Lord will forgive your sins.

And He is gone clean you up, Ma Dear." Mother patted her old friend's knee.

"But how long is He gone tarry with me, Mavis? How long until He is just too mad at me to put up with me anymore?"

"You know what I say, Ma Dear. God is a mercy God. And His mercy is new every day. The Lord is committed to us for the long haul. We stop loving people when they do wrong, but the Lord just keeps right on loving us and keeps working with us long as we'll let Him."

"I don't know, Mavis. Some things just seem so easy to overcome. Remember when we was young girls and used to drink a little too much? Well, I don't even think about drinking no more. Just one day I looked up and I wasn't drinking. Both of us got delivered of that. How come it all ain't like that? How come I got power to pray for healing, but I ain't got power to overcome my cussing?"

"I guess it's just like the apostle Paul and that thorn in his side—God's grace is going to have to be enough for you until it goes away. You just keep praying and confessing and weeping. Your change is coming."

"Hmph!" Ma Dear gave the swing a few hard back-and-forths. "Well, how come the Lord straighten you all out and not me? Seems like you overcome everything. You just perfect."

Mother Johnson patted Ma Dear's hand. "It just seems that way, Augusta. Just seems that way. I got my struggles too. You can't measure the row you got to hoe looking at mine."

She held her hands up. "Look at my hands. Old, knotted up. My feet the same way. Now look at your hands. They just flutter like angel wings. Look at your pretty face. Don't you think sometimes I would have liked to be the pretty one, Augusta? Don't you think I would have liked to be the one the boys fell all over themselves about? Why you get to be pretty, and I get to be plain? I try to be a good girl, so why can't I be pretty? I used to cry about it, Augusta."

"Why you cry, Mother? I always thought you were beautiful, Mavis. And you always had the most beautiful spirit of anyone I knew."

"Well, I cried and cried and prayed about it. Even after I got married."

"What you say, Mavis? Your husband was a good-looking man. And you *know* I know a good-looking man when I see one."

"Yes, Augusta, he was good-looking. And I spent the first three years of my marriage thanking God for John one minute, then wondering why he wanted to be with me the next minute. Then I would go back to asking God to make me beautiful."

"Well, if that don't beat all. I never would have thought such a thing."

"But one day I was praying and when I finished, I came out here to this very swing to sit next to my husband." She patted her hand on the swing next to her. "He was sitting near, 'bout where you are sitting now. I said something to him and looked into his eyes and realized that the answer to my prayers had been there all the time. I asked God to make me beautiful, and he sent me John—a man who looked at me and saw beauty. And when I realized John saw me as beautiful, then I realized how much God loved me. That God saw me as beautiful enough to have that handsome man. I was always beautiful in God's eyes. I always had what I was praying for. I was just too jealous and too selfish to see it."

"Do tell."

"Yes, indeed. And that man told me I was beautiful every day. And you know what? I started to believe it. The power of life and death is in the tongue, and John spoke my beauty right to life."

"I tell you, Mother. Every time I come to see you, I declare you make me feel better."

"So don't think, Augusta, that I don't have no struggles. It's been a long time, and now that John is gone, I have to fight with myself to remember that I'm beautiful, to not offend God by thinking I'm ugly and being jealous and selfish again. We all got our cross, Ma Dear. We all got our cross."

TWENTY-THREE

Mother Johnson watched Shirley slump into her room. "How was school, Shirley?"

She dropped her book satchel on the floor and then stuck her head around the corner so Mother Johnson could see her. She shrugged her shoulders. "It was fine."

"You sure?"

Shirley shrugged again.

"Well, you change your clothes and come on in here. I got something I need you to try out for me."

Shirley skinned out of her sweater and threw it across the bed. When she pulled off her other clothes, she hung them up. She took her play clothes off the hook in her closet and pulled them on. As she was leaving her room, she looked at the sweater on her bed. *I should hang it up.* She shrugged her shoulders again and started for the kitchen.

"Shirley! Don't you leave that room without hanging up that sweater. You know better than that."

Shirley stopped and stared in the direction of Mother Johnson's voice, then at the sweater on the bed, then back in Mother Johnson's direction, then back at the sweater. She shook her head, then picked up the sweater and hung it in the closet.

"Thank you," Mother Johnson called. "Now, come on so you can try this for me." Mother patted the back of a chair as Shirley came in the room. "Come on. Sit down and close your eyes." Shirley did as she was told. "Okay, now open your mouth," Mother said.

When Shirley opened her mouth, a metal spoon slid between her teeth, but what landed on her tongue was something warm and sweet, something tangy, something with a crust that tasted like butter.

"What you think?"

Shirley nodded her head. "Mmm."

"I was never much good at making cobbler. But I was looking at all those jars of peaches, and I thought I might as well try it again." Mother still held the spoon in her hand. "So, you think it was a good idea? Think I did a good job?"

"Yes, ma'am!"

"Well, I was going to wait until after dinner, but I think encouragement like that deserves a little something. I'm going to give you just a little in a bowl if you promise you'll eat your dinner."

Shirley nodded and watched while Mother Johnson got a bowl from the cabinet and a fresh spoon from the drawer. Mother dipped a small serving of cobbler and put it in front of Shirley. Then she sat down in a chair across the table from Shirley. Mother watched while Shirley opened her mouth wide to accommodate a juicy bite.

"Wait a minute, Shirley. First we have to remember to be grateful."

Shirley looked up toward the ceiling. "God, thank You for these good old peaches that got turned into a good old pie."

214

The spoon slid into her mouth. She had a crumb beard and mustache that circled her smile.

Mother leaned forward. "All right, now. Tell me about school." Shirley felt her smile disappear. "You might as well spit it out…you know I'll find out one way or another." Mother sat back and folded her arms. "Is the work too hard?" Shirley frowned, and Mother Johnson laughed. "I guess I was wrong about that. So what is it, then? The children?"

Shirley held up a finger. "One. A boy." The other kids, after a few weeks had tired of the new-girl, different-girl game.

"A boy? You think he's sweet on you? Boys act crazy when they're sweet on a girl."

Shirley made a funny face. "I don't think so. He's mean! And he follows me around bothering me."

"Did you tell the teacher?"

"Yes, but the boy doesn't care. He just keeps on bothering me, no matter what I do."

"Is he a smart boy?"

"I don't know. He stays to himself—except for when he's bothering me."

"What's his name? Maybe I know his people."

"Tony. Tony Taylor."

"Tony Taylor? He's new here too, I believe. Just moved here from Cuney." Shirley nodded. "You want me to come up to the school and see about it?"

Shirley's plaits flew when she shook her head. "No, please!"

"All right, baby. All right. We'll just see how it works out. He might just be hungry for fruit."

Shirley cocked her head and squinted one eye.

"Don't worry about it, baby. I'll explain some other time. Go on and eat your cobbler. Just maybe try talking to him with a prayer in your mind and a little honey on your tongue—speak to him nice. Be grateful when someone wants to love you, baby. Love is a gift. You know, Shirley, there are a lot of rules to friendship and love. Some people don't know the rules—how much to give, how much to care, how close to come—some people just don't get to learn the rules for one reason or another. Don't miss a jewel just because he needs to be polished up a little bit."

Shirley frowned at Mother Johnson, then turned her attention back to the dish in front of her.

Mother Johnson watched Shirley take three more bites. "So you ready to talk to me about everything that happened... about Sheri?"

The bite of cobbler became a lump in her throat, and she could feel tears in her eyes. Shirley shook her head, dropped her spoon, and closed her eyes. If only she could see Sheri.

Mother patted her hand. "All right, baby. All right. Not until you're ready. All right? It's still a little raw. But one day you're going to be able to talk about it, and it's going to be all right. Yes, it will. And you remember that I told you so."

The screen door creaked when Mother Johnson pushed it open. "Come on in here, Ma Dear. Girl, what are you doing out and about so late?"

Ma Dear puffed up the steps and smiled at her friend. Even at night, Ma Dear's face still glowed like a young girl's. "Oh, I know you know why I'm here. I put my foot in it again. That's why I'm here. What am I going to do with myself, Mavis? I don't understand my own self sometimes." She huffed to a chair at the table.

"Is this going to be a short one or a long one?"

Ma Dear's laugh was a whisper. "You better heat up the pot, girl."

"Oh, Lord!" Mother whispered. "I guess I might as well heat you up some cobbler while I'm at it."

"Cobbler? What kind is it?"

Mother lifted a single eyebrow.

"I'm trying to cut back, Mavis. Honest." Ma Dear waved her butterfly hands. "Oh, go ahead. I can't take care of but one weakness at a time." Ma Dear shook her head.

Mother wrapped her robe tighter about her and got things ready for a long conversation. "So what happened?" she asked when she finally sat down.

"Girl, I did it now. I really, really did it." Ma Dear pursed her lips as if she was disgusted with herself. "You know the Milton brothers? Remember them from when we were in school?" Mother nodded. "Remember the one brother, Ely?" Mother nodded and started dunking her tea bag. "Well, we've been talking…. Oh, I don't know what we've been doing…spending a little time together."

Mother stopped dunking. "Ma Dear, no, you didn't."

"No, Mavis! My goodness. Don't get me upset before I can even get the story out." Ma Dear put four spoons of sugar in her cup. "We've just been spending time, sort of. And okay, I'm kind of sweet on him…a little." Mother Johnson smiled, and Ma Dear blushed. "Don't make more out of it than it is, Mavis!"

Ma Dear pursed her lips, stirred, and then her hands started flying. "Well, Mavis, I really planned to do the right thing. I said, 'Okay, now, Lord. You know I'm a little weak—'"

Mother Johnson cleared her throat.

"Well, maybe more than a little, Mavis. But not a lot, either."

Sharon Ewell Foster

She waved her hand. "So anyway, I said, 'Lord, I'm going to try to do this the right way. I'm going to put my own natural desires second to doing Your kingdom's work.' Because, Mavis, the man is really hungry for the Lord. And I figured if I helped him, taught him about the Lord and all, the Lord might give me the inside track."

"Ma Dear! You are shameless!"

"All of us ain't able to be perfect like you, Mavis. The Lord knows I had good intentions. So anyway, everything is going along just fine. Then one day he asks me can he go along with me to one of my healings. And I'm thinking, *Oh, my goodness, this could be it!* Mavis, I just knew if a man could love God and could accept my healing gift and not be scared, that might be the man for me. You know what I mean?"

Mother nodded. "Go on. We're going to be here until daybreak at the rate you're going, Ma Dear. I might as well pull out the couch."

"Don't get sassy, Mavis. You keep interrupting me."

Mother waved a hand and Ma Dear resumed her story. "So, he went with me just as nice. He came and stood in the room while I prayed—he had his little Bible with him and everything. I looked at Ely out of the corner or my eye. And, Mavis, he wasn't even scared.

"When it was over, I kept thinking, *He is going to run now. It's over now.* But he didn't run, Mavis. He was just as sweet as punch." Ma Dear shook her head. "Then it happened."

"What? He left?" Ma Dear shook her head. "What then, Ma Dear? What happened?"

"The woman I went to pray for, her husband…"

"Oh no!"

"Yes, Mavis. I didn't mean for it to happen. He was all nice

218

to me when I was praying for his wife and when she sat up in the bed. But soon as we were out of that room, well, he got hisself a little attitude. And Mother, my tongue just started flying! I was cussing out everything that moved."

"No, Ma Dear!"

"Yes, Mavis. And Ely, sweet as he is, tried to take my arm to tell me, 'Let's go.' But you know how I am once I get going, Mavis."

"No!"

"Yes! I commenced to cussing poor Ely out. I cussed him up one side and down the other. And even while I was cussing, I was thinking, *Girl, you are messing up. You won't be linking arms eating wedding cake no time soon.*" Ma Dear dabbed her napkin to the corner of her eye. "I don't know whether to laugh or cry. And I really liked him—I more than liked him—now I don't know what to do."

Mother Johnson shook her head and sighed. "The Bible says, 'That that I would not do, that I do.' Lord, have mercy."

"Mavis, I just feel like a teenager. I just wanted him to see the good parts of me. I was worried about how he would feel about my healing, but the last thing I wanted him to see was me cussing like I had lost my mind."

"We always want them to see just the best. But ain't it funny how it always seems that at some point, just when we don't want them to, they get to see the weakness in us. I tell you, Ma Dear, I think it's the Lord. A man needs to see all of who you are. I know all of who you are and I love you, you know that. If a man can't accept all of who you are, weakness and all, then you need to know that way before you're eating wedding cake." Mother Johnson smiled. "But I tell you, Ma Dear, it's a joy when you meet the man that the Lord has for you, the man who looks beyond your faults, who has love enough to cover your faults. It makes you grateful to him, and it makes you just want to praise God even more. You know what, Ma Dear? I think the Lord was just giving you a little help."

"See, you can smile, Mavis, 'cause it's not you with the broken heart. And I can't even hardly eat. I ain't heard from the man in two days…I can't believe I cussed him like that. Why do I do that, Mavis? Why right after the healing?"

"Well, you know I ain't no preacher, Ma Dear. But I think it might be one of three things. Or it might be all three." Mother Johnson sipped her tea. "It might be that when you go in to pray for healing, you are under pressure. And when we get under pressure, like when you're really using your gift, your weakness just pops out cause you don't have any reserve strength left to control it."

Ma Dear held her head down. Mother took another sip of tea. "Or it could be spiritual. Maybe when you go in to pray—to heal—you are disturbing all the demons and dark angels. Maybe you are taking away whatever spiritual weakness or darkness they been feeding on in that person or in the room. Maybe those demons get mad; they feel themselves being starved. So maybe then they attack somebody else that's there, hoping to get that person to do something wrong or something that offends you."

Ma Dear looked up to watch Mother Johnson speaking.

"The powers of darkness are hoping that you will give them some strange and dark fruit, some deadly fruit—a fit of rage, hatred, discord, or the like—that they can feed off of and get their strength back. Because maybe when you're healing, your spiritual fruit is on display—love, joy, peace, patience, kindness, goodness, faithfulness, gentleness, and self-control—maybe it's good food that strengthens good and poisons those that are evil.

"Or it could be that the powers of darkness bother you cause they just want to get something on you so that after you do God's work, the devil will have something he can use to accuse you to God. But I keep telling you, Ma Dear, you keep working on it. Christ is interceding for you until you get your breakthrough. Or like I said, it could be all three." She smiled at her friend. "And if God wants that man to be in your life, to eat wedding cake with you, there's not a devil in hell that can prevent it. Greater is He that is in you—"

"—than he that is in the world."

The friends sat talking until Mother Johnson took her own advice and let out the foldout couch. "Don't count old Ely out, Ma Dear," she said as she tucked the corners of the sheet. "You hold on. The story ain't quite finished being told."

TWENTY-FOUR

ony Taylor sat on the wooden bench right next to Shirley. Right next to her, almost on top of her. She scooted over, careful not to let the splinters from the old wooden bench stick the back of her legs. The other children were playing and there was lots of school yard noise—kickball, hopscotch, jacks, war with little green plastic army men. Maybe if she stayed away from the fun, the fun would call him and he would leave her alone. Shirley was stuck on the bench, and Tony was stuck next to her.

Maybe if you talk to him with a prayer in your heart and a little honey on your tongue…

Shirley turned to look at Tony and frowned—he was just staring at her like she was from another planet. It was impossible. "What are you doing?"

Tony shrugged his shoulders.

"Why don't you leave me alone?" Tony shrugged again. Shirley's chest filled with air, and a sound more like a whistle, less like a sigh, escaped her mouth. "Are you trying to be *in love* with me? Because if you are, I am *way* too young to be in love." She gave him her most stern, most grown-up look. "You are barking up the *wrong* tree. That's all I've got to say." Tony shrugged. "Don't you talk?" He shrugged. "Are you going to keep sitting here?" He nodded.

Shirley shook her head and surrendered. "If you're going to sit here, you might as well talk." Tony said nothing. "I *said*, if you're going to sit here, you might as well talk." Tony said nothing. Shirley stood up. "All right, I'm going then. I'm going to—"

"Okay."

Shirley stared at the boy and froze. "Okay," he repeated, and Shirley sat down. Now what? She looked around her, then thought about her moon cookies. She bought them at least once a week from the Blind Man's Store on the way to school.

She pulled out her bag. "You want a cookie?"

Tony shrugged. Shirley jumped off the bench, ready to stomp away. "Okay," he said. "Yes." There was something about his voice that surprised her, something that was far different than what she would have imagined. She reached into her bag to break him off a piece of one of the hand-sized cookies. Instead, as though her hand had a mind of its own, she withdrew an entire cookie and gave it to Tony. "Here," she said, hoping to convey what a burden he was.

Tony stopped staring and opened his mouth to bite the cookie.

"Wait a minute, Tony. You have to be grateful first. Listen— 'Dear God, thank You for this delicious cookie that Tony is about to eat.'" She waved her hand. "Okay, now you can eat." Shirley looked at the nonexistent space between them. "Are you going to move over now?"

He shook his head.

"I told you—"

"No," he interrupted.

"Don't you have any friends?"

Tony shrugged. "Got a brother."

Maybe if you talk to him with a prayer in your heart and a little honey on your tongue… Maybe surrendering was the way to win the war. Things were so much easier with Sheri. If only she could see Sheri. "Tony? We will be much better friends if you give me some room!" She was exasperated by the end of the sentence and gave him a little shove. "I'll be your friend, okay? You just have to give me a little *room."*

Tony bumped over and then smiled. "Okay."

Shirley looked at the cookies and candy in her bag. *If only I could see Sheri.* She began to dig frantically in her pockets for her change. When she found it, she relaxed. "Tony, did you ever ride on the bus?"

"That's how I got here," he said between bites. "On the bus. All the way from Cuney." Crumbs hung on his lips.

"Do you know how much it costs to ride? To ride the bus?"

"It depends. Depends on where you're going."

"What about Illinois? What about like East St. Louis, Illinois?"

Tony shrugged. "Maybe five dollars. I don't know. Never been there."

"Five dollars!"

He shrugged again. Shirley looked at her change—fifteen cents. "Will you help me do something?" He shrugged. "And if you do it, it's got to be a secret." She held out her pinky. "Swear."

Tony held out his. "Swear," he said.

Sharon Ewell Foster

Mother Johnson and Ma Dear watched Shirley scoop up leaves with her hands and throw them in the air. They drifted down around her. Some of the orange and brown leaves fell down on her hair and rested there, as if unwilling to leave her and complete the lonely journey to the ground below. Other leaves, Shirley kicked. Then she stretched open her arms, laid her head back, and smiled.

"She has come a long way, Mother." Ma Dear sat next to Mother Johnson on the groaning swing on the back porch while they watched Shirley kick at the leaves. They watched Shirley spinning among the drifting leaves.

"Yes, she has, Ma Dear. But sometimes I can see it creep up on her. Like she is feeling joy, and sadness just comes creeping back...trying to take her back to the hospital or back to whatever the sad place is that she thinks about. It's almost like that sadness...that spirit of heaviness...that old spirit thinks that it owns her. It's almost like something makes her feel that she's not doing right, or not being loyal, if she doesn't keep those sad memories alive."

Mother patted her knee. "But the devil is a liar. That child is going to be set free. She's got a little secret, something the Lord told me not to let on that I know. Just trust Him is what He told me. He's going to work it out, and she's going to be all right."

"I believe you're right. She'll get set free."

"Oh, I know I'm right. You and I both know the Word of God says that when we—those of us who are God's children—when we pray in His will He hears us."

Ma Dear's hands started fluttering. "You know, it's funny,

girl. I was just telling somebody that the other day. That, you know, when I'm praying for healing, I just keep thinking that in my mind. I know the Word says He wants us well and healed. That's what I'm asking for, so I know that He hears me."

"That's right, Ma Dear. And I know He wants that child set free. I know He is hearing me when I pray for her. And when He hears, God says that He will do what we ask…and I believe Him. I don't care what anybody else says, what it looks like, or how it feels—I put my trust in what God says." She turned in the swing so that she was almost face-to-face with Ma Dear. "He don't want us walking around sad or depressed or angry."

"I know that's right."

"We are new creatures, and He wants us to walk in that newness. The devil keeps telling us it is hopeless—oh, I know it's the devil. I don't care what nobody says. The devil keeps saying, 'You'll never be free.' But you know what, Ma Dear?" Ma Dear cocked her head. "He's a liar."

"A big nasty liar, girl. Yes, he is."

"He is. But the Lord told us that he already saw Satan defeated, saw him fall from the sky like a burned-out falling star. The Lord tells us we already got the victory over Satan. But the nasty father of lies keeps on telling us lies. 'You'll never be free—might as well take a pill.'"

"'You'll always be fat—might as well eat some pie.'"

"'Might as well give up on loving again.'"

"'Might as well give up on being happy. Might as well give up on your family being happy.'"

"'Might as well give up on not cussing people out!' But he is a liar—a big, fat, nasty liar."

"I know that's right, Augusta!"

"So, I'm praying for that child. Shirley has got a lot on her. She doesn't know where her uncles are, we haven't heard a word of her mother, and her father is gone. I'm praying for her—and while I'm at it, I'm praying for every child that the nasty devil is trying to kill. And for everyone that he is trying to kill, everyone whose joy he is trying to steal, everyone he is trying to make depressed or angry or frightened or hopeless." Mother Johnson wagged her head, and the breeze lifted her head scarf. "I claim this child's life back and all the other children's lives. I claim them back in the name of the One who died on the cross."

"Well, *Jesus!*" Ma Dear clapped her hands.

"I claim this child and all the others—especially the ones who don't have anyone else to pray for them—I claim them for the kingdom of God, for the Light of the World."

Ma Dear lifted one hand in the air. "'Lift up your heads, O ye gates, and be ye lift up, ye everlasting doors; and the King of glory shall come in. Who is this King of glory? The LORD strong and mighty, the LORD mighty in battle. Lift up your heads, O ye gates; even lift them up, ye everlasting doors; and the King of glory shall come in. Who is this King of glory? The LORD of hosts, he is the King of glory.'" Ma Dear began to clap her hands.

Mother joined in. "Oh, Light of this world, shine in darkness everywhere. Since I'm praying in Your name, Lord, let me just call out this prayer for every single person that needs to be set free—I don't care where they live, what color, nothing. Everywhere Satan is, everywhere spiritual darkness is—Lord, just shine! Set this child free, Lord. Lift the heaviness from her. Take it away, Lord. Take it captive."

Ma Dear closed her eyes. "And Lord, You know we all got at

least a little bit of jealousy in us. So, Lord, take that away too. Bind it up, Lord Jesus. Only in Your name can it be done, but we believe you, Lord. We know it can and will be done—just like that old fig tree."

"That's right, Lord. And while You at it, get rid of that old lying spirit and that old familiar witching spirit. And Lord, we don't know what this child has been through, but we come against any perverse spirit, against the spirit of fear, and against that old spirit of antichrist." The two women held hands.

"In the name of Jesus."

"We know your tricks, Satan. We know you're trying to take this child and the lives of all of us. But you and your demons got to get out of here. You got to leave, in Jesus' name."

"In *Jesus'* name," Ma Dear echoed.

"And then while You at it, Lord Jesus, loose Your spirit in our lives—give us more love, more joy, more peace, more kindness."

"Lord, we need more of Your patience, more faith, more meekness, more self-control." Ma Dear nodded. "I know I got to have it."

"Lord, let light come in and take darkness captive."

"Hallelujah!"

"She's coming out! No matter what the devil says, Shirley's coming out. You might have planned to steal her joy, Satan, to kill her dreams. You might have planned to destroy her spirit. But this child is going to come running out of the shadows. Darkness can't hold her. She's going to coming riding out victorious—going to come riding right on through the shadows! Riding with no hands!" With her eyes closed, Mother Johnson began to laugh. In her mind's eye, she pictured Shirley riding on a bicycle, riding against the wind. Mother Johnson raised her hands high, as though she were riding a bicycle, riding freehand. "She's already free!"

"Hallelujah!" Ma Dear repeated.

The two women began to talk about past victories they had witnessed, great things they had seen the Lord do.

"Remember when?" one of them said.

"How about the time He…" the other one said.

Mother began to sing, and then Ma Dear joined in. "'Would you be free from the burden of sin? There's power in the blood, power in the blood. Would you o'er evil a victory win? There's power in the blood of the Lamb.'" They clapped like they were at a Saturday night revival. "'There is power, power, wonder-working power, in the blood of the Lamb. There is power, power, wonder-working power, in the precious blood of the Lamb!'"

"Oh! I know that God is able, and I know that He will do it," Ma Dear said.

"Oh, He's already done it! Don't matter what it looks like right now, that child is free. Children all over the place being set free! Thank You, Lord, for setting the captives free." She shook her head in a Sunday-go-to-meeting kind of way. "Shucks! I feel a little free myself. In fact—" Mother hopped to her feet—"in fact, I'm feeling *mighty* free!"

Ma Dear jumped to her feet. "Well, you know, Mother. I'm feeling free my own self. Greater is He that's in me than he that is in the world. I think I'll thank the Lord some myself." Ma Dear closed her eyes and began to dance. Mother joined her, lifted her elbows, and began to do a little holy dance. The two old women got so excited that they began to giggle.

Shirley stopped spinning and watched the two old women on the porch. Ma Dear was light on her feet—dancing and singing. Mother Johnson was all angles—elbows and fast moving feet. Shirley could not help laughing. She began to dance along with them, to mimic them, to shadow them. Something about how the women danced and laughed reminded her of Wednesdays in the prayer house with Mother Johnson. She loved being in the little screened hut with Mother. But there was something…something that would not let her speak, that would not let her pray. She was able to beat the pots, to shake the tambourines, but there was something…

For now, though, Shirley lifted her head and danced. And for a moment, she was free.

Ma Dear and Mother Johnson sat on the swing, trying to catch their breath in between bouts of laughter. "You know, it's getting good to me, Augusta. While we're praying, let's pray for our leadership—better yet, let's pray for the ones standing in the doorways trying to keep Negro children out of schools. Let's pray against pride, and for God to give them people understanding, and for God to turn their hearts."

"Let's pray for forgiveness…"

The two women began to call out ridiculous prayers, silly blessings. When they had danced themselves out and prayed themselves out, they sat back, held their heads forward, and fanned themselves using their dress hems.

Ma Dear spoke first. "Girl, that was fun! I never would have thought that praying could be so much fun—that I would take so much joy in it. It's like a new kind of prayer."

"You know, Ma Dear, I guess what makes it fun is knowing

in advance, knowing for certain, that the Lord is going to do just what He said He would."

Without warning, light cut into darkness like a sword, and demons began to howl. Child Killer Shirley cringed. It was the army of the Lord. The child killer smelled the burning even before he felt it. His beautiful, beautiful scales. He turned his one good eye toward the angels of light and hurled himself in different directions. If he could avoid them, he might survive.

The prayers, it was the prayers.

And now the old woman was praying beyond her borders, beyond her family, beyond the child—beyond her boundaries. That was especially dangerous. There was no telling where the old woman's prayers would hit. There was no way to predict where the Host would attack. There was no way to predict and protect themselves. It was what darkness feared most: unpredictable prayers—enemies praying for each other, individuals praying for people they did not know, countries they did not know, for leaders they did not vote for. Races and nations praying for each other, people praying for those who persecuted them, for those that had caused them harm or even just hurt their feelings. United prayers were dangerous—dangerous and confusing.

The angels of light could not move when there were no prayers. So the angels of darkness made sure there were disagreements between neighbors, divisions among ethnic groups, strife in families, and wars among nations. They ensured conflicts that hindered prayers, conflicts that kept the soft ones from praying delivering prayers—prayers that authorized the movement of the angels of the Most High God from the Third

Heaven to the Second Heaven, where darkness reigned. The dark angels were masters of confusion and strife, even of discouragement, so that the soft ones stopped praying just before they got answers, before they got breakthroughs, before they were healed.

But not today.

The two old women—especially the one they called Mother—had prayed unpredictable prayers. The women had prayed prayers that loosed the powers of light and bound the powers of darkness. Prayers that made him and those like him impotent.

Child Killer Shirley shuddered as he thought of the attack.

It had been impossible for the child killer to see the angels of light—the brightness hurt his one good eye; their illumination blinded him. Some of the shapeless things that normally clung to and hovered near the child killer had been taken captive; some just no longer existed. The angels of the Most High were relentless. Prayers had given them authority and direction; praise and joy had boosted their power and strength. The angels of light did not leave until they had done all, until their assignment was complete.

They had taken the territory of darkness by force.

The wounded child killer hid in a sour, dank place of darkness. He licked his tongue from his mouth, then allowed his mouth to collapse when his tongue went limp. He looked down at his singed body. Both arms were now gone.

The soft one would pay, and the old one with her. He might have to go before the powers, or even the rulers of darkness, to seek help.... But it was warfare—he would not have to fight alone.

Darkness would win. He was better than any angel of light!

He would make them all pay for keeping him from his rightful place. Especially the child—he would enjoy it when the child screamed. And the old woman would soon be dead—he and the others would see to it.

TWENTY-FIVE

Shirley could hear Ma Dear bustling around the kitchen helping Mother Johnson prepare dinner. Shirley sat near the doorway in her dimly lit room. Quiet, so quiet…so that she could hear the mysteries of women.

Shirley could imagine Mother shaking her head as she slid the biscuits into the oven. "You know, I thought about what you said earlier when we were praying. I want you to know that I repent of giving you that peach cobbler last time you were here."

"Oh, girl."

"No, really, Ma Dear. I know you are trying to do better, and what I did didn't say to you that I believe that you can— and you will overcome, Ma Dear. But you know, you're already coming out of it. It's all around you. I can see it; you are just blossoming."

"You know what, Mother? I feel it too." Shirley heard the faucet turn on and off, imagined Ma Dear drying her hands on a tea towel. Then the two women erupted in nervous giggles.

"Are you blushing, Ma Dear?"

SharonEwellFoster

"What are you talking about?"

"Are you thinking about that man, Augusta?"

Ma Dear sounded as though she was trying not to laugh, as though she was trying to sound sensible. "There you go, Mavis, being messy and causing trouble."

Mother Johnson sounded tickled. "No, I'm not. It's just good to see you smiling—smiling from the inside. You don't have to feel bad about the fact that you like—maybe it's getting to be a little *more* than like—"

"Mavis!"

"Come on now, Ma Dear."

Ma Dear's voice lowered. "I don't understand what's happening to me, Mother. You and I both know how I used to be. But the Lord has been keeping me. First I thought I could never live life without a man's arms around me. But when I really, truly came to know the Lord, I wanted to learn to live my life His way." Mother murmured her agreement. "It's been just me and the Lord for years. And to tell you the truth, I have kind of liked it that way. The Lord is always kind, always generous, always loving, always the same. I wasn't looking for anyone else. Honest!" She laughed. "And besides that, Mother, you know we're no spring chickens."

"You speak for yourself, Ma Dear. I still got quite a few good years left in *me*."

Both women laughed. "I hear you, Mother. It's just that I felt so comfortable, and now since this man has appeared…"

"Are you unhappy about it? Your eyes don't look unhappy."

"No, Mother, I'm not unhappy. When I see him or talk to him, I feel breathless. Like I'm a schoolgirl. I don't know whether to be embarrassed or to enjoy it or to run. Sometimes when I think running is the answer and I put on my P. F. Flyers to run, it's like I can hear the Lord telling me to stand still, to wait on Him." Ma Dear's voice sounded dreamy. "Other times I feel like I want to just rush right in, take over, and get the show on the road. Then I hear the Lord tell me to relax, to stop struggling, and to just allow Him to give me this good and perfect gift. Not that it will be perfect according to what the world thinks—but I am confident that it will be what the Lord knows is perfect for me."

"My, my, my."

"Mother, it feels like I'm on a roller coaster, riding with no hands. Like I'm coming out of the dark tunnel into a bright and glorious light. And I want to draw back, but then I think of all the other good things God has done in my life. How all His blessings have given me great joy—even though sometimes they've kind of scared me when He first started trying to give them to me." Ma Dear sounded excited. "All my past experiences with the Lord remind me to trust Him this time. This man, this boy I used to know, he takes my breath away. And I'm just giggling all the time like I've lost my mind, and I can't stop thinking about him…"

"I see!"

"Oh, Mother!" Ma Dear giggled and Shirley imagined Ma Dear clapping her hands over her face. "I feel like everyone I walk by can see it. Like I'm blushing all the time. And I feel like I'm too old and too sensible for all this."

"They can, you are, you are, and you are."

"Oh, my goodness, Mavis. I knew it. I'm making a fool of myself."

"Oh, I'm just teasing you. But God wants us to have that joy, doesn't He? He wants us to be happy. I think He just wants us to remember that He comes first and that our happiness comes from Him."

Ma Dear sighed. "When I think about all the years and all the time I spent trying to make myself happy. You know, Mother. I was the party girl—happy on the outside but just not feeling too much of nothing on the inside. I kept thinking, *That man will make me happy* or *If that man will marry me, I know I'll be happy.* Why does it take so long to realize that the poor man can't fix it? Why does it take so long to realize that what was keeping me from feeling good on the inside had everything to do with me and nothing at all to do with the man?"

"Well, don't beat up on yourself about it, Ma Dear. You're not the only one."

"I know, Mother. But I was going from pillar to post looking for a love to make me complete. And think about it. I got married four times and never had a clue. I just wanted someone to love me, to really love me. Here I am all these years later and I'm finally realizing that marriage is a spiritual union—it's ordained by God."

A pot lid was lifted and then closed. "You got that right, Ma Dear. Now how you going to have a marriage when you don't even have a relationship with God? How can God be in a relationship with you and a man when He doesn't even know who you are?" Shirley could imagine Mother shaking her head.

"That's just what I'm trying to say, Mother."

"Oh, honey, believe me…I've learned a thing or two my own self. In marriage the man is supposed to love the woman like Christ loves the church. Now how can a man copy that love when he doesn't know who Jesus Christ is? He ends up imitating his Uncle Joe Bob or something. If Joe Bob was a fool, that man will act like a fool because that's the only image he has of what a man is supposed to be like in marriage."

"I tell you, Mother, it just makes me tremble to think about all the folks getting married like I did, folks that don't have no idea."

"You know what, Ma Dear? The other thing I been thinking about is that Christ came as leader and servant to the church. Lots of men been taught about being boss in the marriage, but they haven't been taught about being servant, provider, counselor, healer—"

"Watch out there now, girl. We going to be having church here in a minute!" The two women laughed. "But, you know, while we're talking about the men, what about us women? What about all the foolishness we believe?"

Mother laughed. "What about us? Seems like we're doing all right."

"How many women go into marriage really ready to trust, honor, submit, and obey? I know I didn't."

"I think most women try not to think about it."

"Honey, hush! I thought I could pick and choose. You know, I'll have a little bit of trust, until he does something I think is wrong. Give me just a pinch of honor because I can't take too much of that. And obey…well, it just depends on how I'm feeling on any given day—but don't expect me to swallow it without frowning. Submission! Don't even put that on my plate. I don't do submission. And let's not even talk about reverence. I don't even know what that is, so don't bring it to me. If he wants *me,* he better take *me* like I am—of course, all the while I am looking for perfection in him."

"Ma Dear, you are just a pistol! I tell you. I think you missed your calling. With all those faces you are making and those gestures, you sure could have been an actress."

Ma Dear tittered a little more, stopped, and then sighed. "It's just so much to marriage and relationships that I never knew. All my life I was taught not to trust a man. Don't trust a nig— You know, that's what I was taught. Most women I know were taught that. I was taught to run if it looked like things might even possibly go bad. Mother, I'm sure I probably left a few perfectly good men behind me in the dust. Both of those things go totally against what God says about marriage. So here I am at this late age trying to learn a new way to think."

"Well, Ma Dear, it's just a blessing that we've even come to this point of understanding and that you've got a second chance—or a fifth chance." Mother laughed.

"Girl, I have learned so much about men and women, even about marriage. So now I'm at a point where I understand... but my body is old and tired. Stuff is sagging here and stretched out of place there—and I've been through so much, I just feel like damaged goods. My hair is getting thin... How can I offer a man damaged goods? What man would want that?"

"First of all, Ma Dear, if the man—a man that God sends— loves you, he loves you because God turned his heart. Girl, come on. Let's go on and get free in this kitchen. The man doesn't love you because of you or the blush you put on your cheeks. He will love you because he can't help himself— because God put that love for you in the man's heart. Don't let the enemy fool you."

"Well, I understand that, Mother. But still, you know...you know how it is. I look in the mirror and think, *Where is that young girl I used to know?* But there's nothing to do about it but accept it."

"Now, Ma Dear, it's funny to hear you of all people saying that. You lay your hands on the sick and you see right before your eyes that God can make them whole and well. If you can believe that He heals, if we really believe that He created the universe, how can we not believe that He can make all things new? God says that He can, and He will. He is a God of restoration. With what you've been through, Ma Dear, and the way you love Him and trust Him, if I were you I would be counting on Him to make things not only new, but also better."

"You sound like you think God is a fountain of youth."

"The Lord God Most High and Lifted Up renews eagles— He's even taught a bird how to go off alone and make himself brand new. Now why would He do it for a bird, and not do it for us? He loves the birds, but He loves us so much more."

"Well, I know that's right, Mother. But we just have to face it, girl. What's drooping ain't gone all of a sudden start rising again."

"I think that's because we become what we believe. We are fearfully and wonderfully made; we are precious to the Lord. Why would He do it for a bird and not for us? Why would He be able to restore life and not be able to restore hair? Why can he restore a soul and not be able to put a little life back in our steps?"

While the women talked, Shirley pulled back the edge of the quilt that covered her bed and reached underneath for her cigar box. It was covered with construction-paper leaves of red, yellow, orange, brown, and green. The veins of each leaf were drawn with glue covered by gold glitter. Shirley quietly counted the change she had been saving—a nickel here, a dime there. Her fingers poked over the silver.

The women's voices were an attendant to her counting.

"I guess I'm just foolish enough to believe Him, Ma Dear. You know, I love Psalm 103. It says to bless the Lord and to forget not *all* His benefits—I think that we just forget His benefits, and we give up good things He has promised us."

"Oh, Mother. You are just being silly."

"No, I'm not. I'm going to take Him at His word. You just shrivel on up if you want to, but I'm going to claim my benefits. Folks believe in Social Security benefits, but they don't believe in God benefits. The benefits are waiting for you, but if you don't go down to the office and claim them, you won't get them. Same thing with kingdom benefits. You believe what you believe, and we'll check back in a few years and see what's what. I'm going to claim my kingdom benefits."

"What benefits are you talking about, Mother?"

"The Psalm says bless the Lord and forget not all His benefits. Then it lists these benefits—most of them we believe. Like it says that the Lord will forgive our sins."

"I believe that. I know I'm saved."

"Then the Word says He will heal our diseases."

"Well, you know I believe that, Mother. That's why I have faith to pray and lay hands on the sick. I believe the Word of God—I know He is a healer."

"Next is says that He will redeem our lives from destruction."

"Of course He does. You know I know that He paid the price for me on Calvary. 'Behold the Lamb that takes away the sins of the world.' You know I know that He paid the price."

"Then the Psalm says that He will crown us with loving-kindness and tender mercies."

Shirley wondered what tender mercies were. She shrugged and went back to her counting. No one would believe how much money she had. And it was hard to believe that Mother Johnson, who always seemed to know everything, still had no idea about the secret stash. It had seemed to take forever for

Shirley to get her first dollar. The first dollar represented lots of missed cookies and candy. But it was worth it; Tony had even given her a few pennies and a few nickels. *Try a little honey…*

Maybe Mother was right about him after all. But he still sat too close.

Ma Dear's voice softened, and Shirley strained to hear her words. "No doubt about that, Mother. God knows that I wouldn't be here, that I wouldn't be sane right now, if it was not for His kindness and His mercy. I tell people all the time that if it had not been for His mercy…"

"Well, then, if you believe all that, Ma Dear, how can you not believe the last benefit? He satisfies your mouth with good things—"

"Oh, Mother, I know that's true. He will make your mouth satisfied with what's good for you. Some things I used to eat, I just don't have a taste for anymore. Matter of fact, some of it you couldn't pay me to eat. Matter of fact, He'll make all of your appetites so that you desire only good things. No doubt about it. It really hasn't been me. It's been God's grace. I just made a commitment to do one small act of daily obedience— maybe a walk or turning down a candy bar. The Lord is doing the rest."

"Well, Ma Dear, if you believe all that, then how can the last little bit be a lie? The Word says that He will satisfy your mouth with good things so that your *youth* is renewed like the eagle's.

When the eagle's feathers get old and worn out, God has told the bird what to do to get rid of the old ones and grow a whole new set. Pretty soon he is looking all new and flying around like he did when he was a young, stronger bird. Only he's probably better because he also has more wisdom than he did as a younger bird. So I'm claiming that kingdom benefit."

Sharon Ewell Foster

Ma Dear laughed. "Mavis! I swear, for a sensible woman you are just talking foolish!"

"Well, that's all right, Ma Dear. Just let me be foolish. When I was young, I didn't enjoy my youth and my beauty; I couldn't believe I was beautiful. Now I realize that the devil was just lying to me and I believed him. God is the one I believe now, and I know that He is the God of restoration. So I'm going to believe Him. Because I've been watching you, Ma Dear. You have been a testimony to me. Whoever would have thought that this man would come back into your life after all these years? Who would have thought that God could plan something like that and give you a second chance, bring you back to life and give you romance in a way that honors him? A love that puts God first."

"Oh, Mother, it's really something what has happened. I feel just like a schoolgirl. Sometimes I find myself almost skipping, and I giggle all the time. But you know what the most wonderful thing is? Instead of just thinking about myself, or worrying about the man and making him an idol, this time this man's love makes me love God even more. It makes me even more grateful. This love makes me more worshipful."

Mother Johnson's voice was almost a whisper. "Maybe I'm not too old, either, Ma Dear. And maybe I need to take a chance on love again. Maybe neither one of us is too old. Maybe someone old will come into my life, and God will make him new. Maybe God will make me new on the inside and on the outside, and maybe—before I leave here—He will give me new love. And what's the harm in taking God at His word? The worse thing that can happen is that we'll just feel young on the inside. But maybe, just maybe… And what I pray for us, Ma Dear, is that the new loves that God grants us will be like the

244

eagle made new—love full of old wisdom, patience, and gratitude. But also it will be high-flying, full of strong, young passion, new kisses, and newborn hope."

The two women began to giggle, and it was difficult for Shirley to make out their words without creeping farther into the doorway. She did not want to give herself away—especially not the money she had been saving.

Then she could hear the women setting plates on the table. "You know what, Mother? I think I just had so much love inside of me, I could never really give the man a chance to figure out that he loved me. I was so full of emotion—I could feel the man's heart—and I just figured that's that, and wanted to rush in, get married, get it done." Ma Dear laughed. "It would seem like the man was taking too long, so I would feel rejected and run. Like I said, I left some good ones in the dust. But this time, the Lord is telling me to wait on Him—and this time I'm listening."

"I can see the difference."

"This is a different kind of romance for me. It's more like me and the man are having a romance through God. The Lord is purifying and touching me physically, mentally, and spiritually. He's telling me to wait on Him—to be like Him. He has so much love for us, so much He wants to do for us, but He has to wait until we're ready. My love has to be like His—patient love—love to last a lifetime, everlasting love."

"The Lord is sweet. Yes, He is."

"You know, Mother, I'm learning patience. And while I'm learning patience waiting for this man's head to catch up with my heart, God is tenderly loving me...and while He's at it, He's teaching me to pray better and trust the outcome to Him."

"Wonderful Savior," Mother Johnson said. "He's sweeter than the honeycomb."

Shirley closed the cigar box and imagined the two women lifting more lids and stirring pots. She breathed deeply so she could smell the aromas that drifted in the air from the room next to her. The house was cozy, and warm light from the kitchen touched the shadows in her room. Shirley closed her eyes and pressed her back up against the wall. Soon she would have the bus fare, and Tony had promised to help…and not to tell.

She was sure that she would see Sheri any day now.

There was a soft rap at the side door that woke Shirley. She did not sit up; she didn't even open both of her eyes. She pulled the covers up to her chin and listened.

Shirley could hear Ma Dear snoring softly in the living room. The three of them had sat late at the dinner table, talking and laughing. In the end, Mother Johnson had persuaded her friend to stay the night, and the pullout couch had been pressed into service. But now Shirley could hear Mother's house slippers whisking over the floor as she made her way to the door.

"Well, Deacon, come on in here. This is quite a surprise…a pleasant surprise." Shirley could not make out the man's first few words, but she heard the screen door creak, and she could hear his footsteps in the kitchen. The sound of running water, of cabinet doors opening and closing, and the sound of the lid being removed from the percolator told Shirley that Mother Johnson was making coffee. "Now, Deacon, you just make yourself comfortable and just hold on a second while I get these few things together and get this coffee to percolating." Ma Dear still snored in the other room.

The man spoke, and Shirley was not sure if she recognized his voice or not. "I'm sorry to disturb you, Mother. I probably ought to go…this is no hour to be visiting."

"Oh, come on now. Sit down. Don't you be 'shamed with me. I've been knowing you since you were a young boy. Besides that, Deacon, you know God doesn't have office hours. And if He troubled you to come here, the least I can do is sit up with you. Besides, He might be sending a word to me through you. You just never know." A few early birds twittered.

The deacon sat down while Mother Johnson sat things in order. Shirley could hear rattling cups, and the smell of freshly brewed coffee stole quietly into her bedroom. The refrigerator door opened and closed.

"All right now, we've got coffee, sugar, and cream. Talk to me. I'm listening."

Their voices were hushed, and Shirley imagined that their voices matched the early morning shadows in the kitchen. "It's really nothing, Mother. The Lord has blessed me. I don't have any real reason to complain. A beautiful wife, son, and daughter—they make my life worth living. And my son has accepted the call to ministry."

"I heard that, Deacon. I know that must make your heart happy." Cups clicked and spoons stirred.

"You know it does, Mother. For him to be so young—lots of young men his age, teenagers, haven't accepted Christ, let alone made the commitment to preach the Word. I'm proud, very proud."

There was silence, and Shirley imagined that they must have been sipping the hot coffee. "Hold on a second, Deacon. It's a might chilly in here to me. Let me turn up the heat a bit." Mother moved in one direction. Then the whisking of her feet

came back to the table. "All right now, Deacon. Just let it out. I know you didn't come all this way just to tell me nothing."

Shirley reached one of her hands under the cover for the cigar box. She pulled it closer and closed her eyes.

The deacon cleared his throat. "It really is nothing, Mother. Nothing really." More silence. "I was just wondering, if demons can live in someone that's holy, someone that loves the Lord."

"Well, my goodness, Deacon! You know the Word. How can a demon live in a body where the Spirit of the Lord has taken up residence? A demon and the Spirit of the Lord can't live in the same house. Of course, you know darkness tries to talk to all of us—the devil tried to tempt the Lord. Too bad, but sometimes we listen to his foolishness. The Lord didn't, but sometimes we do. But Deacon, tell me, why you ask?"

"It's my son."

"Your son? The young minister?"

"Yes, Mother. It's this expression on his face—this anger. I've seen it before. But last Wednesday night at prayer meeting, I saw it again. And I thought to myself, *I'm going to come against this thing. It's not going to steal my joy or my peace, and it's not going to come and stir up things in the midst of my family.* And I just started calling down glory."

"Well, I don't blame you, Deacon."

"Because you know, Mother, I have to have peace. Peace and order. I just have to have it."

"Well, Deacon, doesn't seem to be anything wrong with that. But you're going to have to tell me a little more. What made you think you saw a demon?"

"Mother, we were at the meeting and everything was fine. Just before it ended I tapped my son on the shoulder and told him that we needed to go. I had some other business somewhere else that I had to attend to. I couldn't be late so I had to go—I know he hates to leave service before the benediction. So do I. But I had to go. I had things to do. When we turned to leave, I saw this expression on his face, this anger. He didn't say anything, but when we got home that night, I called him and his mother into the room.

"I don't believe in letting stuff fester, Mother. Not if you want peace and order in your home. You have to take authority over stuff like that. You can't let your children get out of control, have them thinking they're the parents and not the children. But what got me, Mother, was his expression as we talked. And finally, he just exploded. His mother was quiet, but he just…he had so much anger. And I thought to myself that I had seen this anger in him before. So that's when I started calling down glory. I went from room to room rebuking the devil, telling him he had no place in my home. I told him I was not going to put up with it. Because, like I said, Mother, I have to have order and peace. I have to have it. His mother—you know my wife is his stepmother—her family has a wildness and a mean streak in them. I always have to watch out for that in him."

The cups clicked in the midst of a silence in the kitchen. "You need a refill, Deacon?" Mother's chair made a scraping sound as she pushed back from the table. Then the sound reversed when she sat again. "Some things are the devil. There is no doubt about it, Deacon. But some things are life. Sometimes it's easier to point at things outside of us than it is to take a look inside." Mother cleared her throat. "So let's see if we can't ask the Lord to help us know the difference."

There was more silence, and then she spoke again. "How many times have you seen your son get angry like this?"

"Not many, Mother. Just a few, but I keep telling the family I have to have peace. I try to let things go along, but I can't let things get out of order."

"All right."

"I know he was upset because he didn't want to leave the service—"

"Doesn't sound like demon behavior to me."

"I know, Mother, but the anger. Once I started trying to get a handle on his behavior when we got back home—that's when I saw it on his face."

"Did you ask him about it?"

"Well, he just said he didn't want to leave the service. Then he brought up some foolishness that he was angry about. Something from before his stepmother and I got saved. That's what he said, but I know my child. I know it's something other than that. We love each other. We have good relationship, so I know this anger—it's got to be demonic."

Mother was quiet again. Her cup rattled. "You know, Deacon, one of the things I have learned in my life is to listen. I've learned to listen even when it gets hard. Even when I don't like what's being said. And sometimes when I'm getting reactions from people that I don't like, I've learned to look at myself first, before I go looking for fault or demons in them."

"Mother, you didn't see his face!"

"No, Deacon, I didn't. But let me tell you something. If God is allowing you to be troubled, don't look out at the ones that are causing you trouble first. Look to yourself first. God wouldn't let trouble in your space if it wasn't for your good— you don't have a demon, you got a little relationship trouble."

"No, Mother, I think you're wrong this time. Everybody trusts you, and I believe you hear from the Lord, but I believe

Riding Through Shadows

you're wrong about this one. Maybe it's too early in the morning. My son loves me, and he would not get this angry with me on his own...not unless the devil was involved."

"When he got angry before, did you ask him about it?"

"Yes, and he brought up the same foolishness."

"Well, I'll tell you something else I know. We don't see our own blind spots."

"What blind spot, Mother?"

"The blind spot that's making your son frustrated with you."

"Mother, I—"

"And the sad thing is, I bet everybody around you knows what it is. Everybody knows but you, and they won't tell you because they're trying to spare your feelings, because they're afraid of you, or because it's too much trouble trying to get the information through to you."

"Mother, if you could have seen the anger."

"Oh, I believe you. He's probably been angry for a long time. Has your family been trying to tell you anything—about something that's wrong?"

"Of course not, Mother. Why would they? We love each other. I provide for my family, and I keep a house of order and peace. I have to have order and peace. The only thing that they have said to me is that everything revolves around me. If I'm happy, everybody's happy. If I'm angry, then there are bad times for all of us. But Mother, it's just that I have to. It's fine if things are going along all right, but when I see something out of place or out of order, when something disturbs the peace, I will do whatever I have to do to get it back in order."

"You keep saying that."

The man's voice sounded annoyed and frustrated. "Saying what?"

"That you have to have order and peace."

"Mother, we are supposed to follow after peace, and everything should be done in decency and order."

"No doubt about that, Deacon. That's what the Word says."

His voice sounded strained. "That's what it says."

"Our God is the Lord of peace, but He is also God of the storms."

"Mother, I—"

"Wait just a minute and give me a chance to explain. It's important for us to know that God also works in storms, or we'll be running or fighting every time we see one coming. God's got some people that are always tidy, but He also uses people—like John the Baptist—that look a little crazy, folks that look like they were born in a storm. We need to know that or we'll always run from people who look a little different. He uses bent-over people. If we don't know that, we'll always be trying to straighten them out.

"God sent a storm to Paul when he was on a ship bound for Italy to blow the ship to the place He needed it to be. God used the storm so that someone that needed to see a sign of His wonder could see Him at work in the storm."

"But what about when the disciples were caught up in the storm? When they were crossing the Sea of Galilee?" The deacon's voice sounded anxious. "They could have been killed."

Shirley wrapped both her arms around the box and began to think of the words to the song that she had made. She felt frightened, and she did not know why.

"Well, I know you remember the Lord telling them that they didn't have faith. I think it was because they didn't trust God. They didn't know that He was also God of the storms. They forgot that storms bring the rain that's needed for new things to grow. They forgot that sometimes storms come before the Lord delivers someone. They were afraid they were going to die because they didn't trust the Lord—they didn't trust that the storm He created and sent wouldn't kill them.

"Sometimes we don't like the storms in our lives—people that the Lord sends, situations that we go through. Some of us run from storms and hide, but others of us try to take control of the storms. We're going to make sure no storms or disorder come in our lives—so we force an unnatural peace, an unnatural order.

"We think we are doing a good thing when we prevent the normal, natural storms of life. We don't realize that we're stunting creation, that we're stopping growth, stopping things from developing. We're killing things. And what we also don't understand is that when we do that, those storms that we have tried to control, well, they just keep on popping up over and over in our lives. You can't prevent storms that the Lord sends."

The man's voice was quieter. "There's got to be order, Mother. There's got to be peace."

"But there also have to be storms. Places with no storms dry up and die. Let the storms come, Deacon. You don't have to be afraid. God is with you in the storm. I think maybe your son is trying to tell you that you've been trying to control him, that you're hurting him. That you're trying so hard to keep him and the rest of your family in order, to keep peace, that you're making dry, dead places. Trust the Lord and let the storm come. Because out of His storm will come peace, His peace. And at the end will be order, and it will be Divine."

The room was quiet, and Shirley held her breath waiting for the Deacon to explode, to begin to yell. But he was quiet. Shirley tried to take a deep breath, but it hurt her stomach too much to breathe. She clutched the cigar box even closer. She was frightened, but she did not know why.

She could hear Mother Johnson and the man murmuring softly. He sighed, and then Shirley heard them get up from the table and walk to the door.

"Your family knows. The people around you know. Ask them what's wrong, what information the storm is trying to bring. Then stand, have faith in the Lord, and let the winds of the storm lift you higher."

TWENTY-SIX

⟨ornament⟩

*H*ow much money you got now?" Tony stared at Shirley, and his face was even more serious than usual.

"Sh-sh-sh! Not so loud, Tony," she stage-whispered. "Everybody in the whole auditorium is going to know if you keep talking so loud." They were surrounded by children who laughed, giggled, and argued. Very few of them sat perfectly still. All of them were in the school auditorium for a special announcement. They had no idea what the announcement was, but it had to be important because they were giving up the last ten minutes of the recess period to hear it. Maybe that was why the teachers were being so lenient and allowing them to talk. The auditorium was dark, except for patches of sunlight.

Shirley looked around, taking her time answering Tony. Nothing about this school reminded her of her home—no blond hair, no blue eyes, no Cooties. She thought of Ken and Barbara and Misty and wondered if they were thinking of her.

Finally, she answered Tony. "I have $4.24. Almost enough to catch the bus."

"I don't think you ought to do this, Shirley. What if it gets cold? I don't even think you know the way."

"I don't have to know the way, Tony. The bus knows the way. But I'm going. I'm going home even if I have to go by myself. You don't have to help me. I'll do it by myself."

Tony did a half turn in his seat so that he was facing Shirley. "I didn't say I wouldn't help you, Shirley. I just don't want you to get in trouble."

She held her hands down at her sides and clenched her fists. "I can take care of myself, Tony. I don't need you to help me."

"I told you I would help you," Tony whispered.

Shirley shook her head. Two seats behind her, a conversation caught her ear.

"When I grow up, I'm going to be a Black Panther like my big brother in Chicago," the first boy said. Shirley and Tony stopped talking to listen to the two boys.

"Your brother ain't no Black Panther," the second boy objected.

"Yes, he is!"

"No, he's not."

"Yes, he is, and if you don't be quiet, I'm going to have him throw a Molotov cocktail into your house and set it on fire."

"Uh-uh."

"Uh-huh!"

"Forget you, then."

"No, forget *you*. Forget you, forgot you, never thought about you."

"Well, you can be a Black Panther if you want to—get you a black hat and a black jacket and some black sunshades if you want to. Go around killing people if you want to."

"That's not what happens. The Black Panthers are not trying to kill everybody. They are trying to set us free. They give out free breakfast to little kids, and, and, and—" The first boy stopped to catch his breath, then started talking again. "They are trying to get us our forty acres and our mule. My brother said so."

The second boy laughed. "Forty acres and a mule? What you talking about, man?"

"It's not funny." The first boy stood up. "That's what they said they were going to give to us for slavery—for making us slaves. That's what the white people said." His chest heaved and he had to stop to catch a breath in his skinny little bantam-rooster chest. "The white people said, the government said, they were sorry for making us slaves and that they were going to give us forty acres and a mule to make up with us. All the Negro—I mean, *black* people are supposed to get forty acres and a mule."

The second boy waved his hand. "Forget that. What I want with forty acres? And especially what do I want with a mule! Your brother is crazy!"

"No, *you* crazy. And don't be talking about my brother."

"I ain't got no forty acres."

"I know that, dummy. They took it back. The white people took it back. President Andrew Jackson took it back. My brother told me."

"A mule! I don't believe that. A mule. What I'm gone do with a mule?" The second boy fell down in his seat laughing, then stood up again like a jack-in-the-box. "You can have my mule. A mule is not going to make me free. And the Black Panthers not going to make me free." He doubled over laughing. "Forty acres and a mule! What good is that?"

The first boy looked up at the auditorium ceiling, but kept talking, kept holding his ground. "Because if you don't own land, you don't own anything. That's what my big brother said."

"Well, my granddaddy said, 'Live by the sword, die by the sword.' That's why I'm nonviolent. That's how we going to be free."

"How you going to be free being nonviolent? They killing all the nonviolent people."

"Well, they killing all the Black Panthers too."

"No, they not. They not going to kill my brother." The first boy's chest was heaving.

"Leave that boy alone," someone hollered from across the auditorium. "You know he got asthma. You gone make him have a asthma attack." But the two boys argued on.

The second boy shook his finger in the first boy's face.

"Yes, they are. The nonviolent people are going to win."

The first boy gasped. "You say they going to kill my brother again, and I'm gone knock your head off like a rock-'em-sock-'em robot."

"No, first I'm going to knock the black off of you. Then I'm going to knock your block off!" the nonviolent boy yelled.

"No, neither one of you is going to be knocking anyone's block off. Both of you sit your scrawny selves down." It was Miss Sherman, the fourth grade teacher, and everyone knew she didn't play. "And I mean now. Right now." She walked toward the front of the auditorium still mumbling. "Knock somebody's block off...I declare." By the time she walked up on the stage, the lights were on.

She walked to the edge of the stage. "Now, I know you all know better than to make all this noise here in the auditorium.

I know that you know how to behave after all the time we spend trying to teach you manners and deportment." She shook her head. "But the way you all are acting right now, I don't know if I should even tell you all what the principal has planned. She has planned something special." She looked disgusted. "But I just don't know now. You all are really showing your color up in here."

"We'll be good, Miss Sherman," someone in the back hollered out, and the other kids nodded their heads.

"I just don't know," Miss Sherman reiterated.

"Please, please, please!" the children begged.

"Well, the principal has been getting stuff together so she can take all of you to the movies."

"The movies?" all the children whispered.

"Yes!" she said. "Now, look at you, acting like savages. How is this supposed to make me and the principal feel like you can behave? You know that the white folks don't want us in the movie theater with them—and you know if you go in there and cut up, it will reflect on all the Negroes—all the black people everywhere. You know that."

"We'll be good," someone said.

Miss Sherman shook her head. "She went to downtown Tyler and begged the white folks, begged them to let you all go to the movies to see *Lassie*. You know that they don't let Negro people in the theater. But she promised them that you all would be good, told them you had good home training and said that she would just thank the Lord if they would let you all see *Lassie* with the white children."

"*Lassie*," all the children whispered as one. Shirley looked at the children around her. They were all spellbound—over a movie. Over a movie?

"That's right. *Lassie.*" Miss Sherman put a hand on one of her hips. "*Lassie!* And you all are messing it up. When we go—*if* we go—you got to be on your best behavior, and show the white people that we know how to act. That we have some pride, because you know they think we are all ignorant." She looked back at the two little boys that had set her off in the first place. "And when we go—if we go—I don't want to hear any of you talking about Black Power or none of that stuff. We're all going to sit up in the balcony and behave. But none of that civil rights stuff…you know the white folks hate that."

In East St. Louis, there was no special behavior required for Shirley to go to the movies. She could go to the Fox Theater, to the Loews, and sit where she pleased. And she remembered holding her father's and mother's hands…walking down the aisle between the two of them. How could someone stop her from going to the movies because they were white and she was black? They may not have wanted her family in the Centerville area of East St. Louis, but nobody ever tried to keep her out of a movie!

Miss Sherman was tapping her foot. "If we go—and I still have to talk to the principal about it after what I saw and heard in here today—" she narrowed her eyes at the two boys—"you are going to be quiet as church mice, walk single file, and keep your hands to yourself. And I *promise* you, if I have to pull you out of line—first I'm going to take you outside and beat *your* tail, and then *everybody* is getting back on the bus and nobody's going to see *Lassie*. You hear me?"

Shirley slid low into her seat.

"Yes, Miss Sherman," the other children said.

Shirley sat in her quiet place at the end of the porch. The place where if she was very quiet she would not be shooed away. *"Go on, now. Go on. We're talking grown people's business."* She had gotten good at being quiet, at being invisible.

"Ma Dear, if your chin drops any farther, you're going to have to pick it up off the porch. What is wrong with you?"

Ma Dear sighed and spoke at the same time. "Nothing."

Mother Johnson shook her head. "Now, if I ever heard a nothing that didn't convince me, that would be the one. What is wrong with you, girl?" Ma Dear shrugged her shoulders. Mother Johnson leaned toward her. "Is it the man? Your man?"

Ma Dear pulled herself up into a ball. "I don't want to talk about him, Mother. I really don't."

"Now what is this all about?"

"I think it's over, Mother. Really, I guess it never began."

"What are you talking about, Ma Dear? You mean he's still upset about the healing, about you cussing? Well, I thought you said—"

Words gushed out of Ma Dear. "Oh no, it's not that, Mother. Why, in no time at all after that he was coming to call and telling me that he understood, not to worry about it. We could work on it together." She stopped talking and then frowned. "Then all of a sudden he just stopped and told me he was feeling pressure. What is that supposed to mean, Mother? He's feeling pressure."

"Pressure? Well, what happened?"

"Nothing, Mother. Everything was just fine. Just moving right along. Then—" Ma Dear held her hand palm down and made a straight horizontal line in the air—"nothing. Mother, I was just telling him one day how much I thought of him, how much I enjoyed his company, how much he meant to me, and he just clammed up." Ma Dear shook her head. "And you know I'm too old for this, Mother. This is why I just wanted to stick with me and the Lord. I know the Lord; His ways are always the same. But men are just sometime-y. That's when he told me that he was feeling pressure. What pressure, Mother? Just because I told him how I feel. Why would telling him how I feel put pressure on him."

"Well, Ma Dear, maybe he thinks that you want him to respond, and maybe he's not ready."

"Not *ready*. Mother, I know how he feels. I can read him like a book. He is just as swept away as I am, except now he's trying to act all…" Ma Dear waved her butterfly hands in the air. "All funny. And I don't like it. If he doesn't want to be with me, then good riddance." She mumbled and waved her hand as though she were fussing at someone invisible. "Acting like he thinks somebody needs him. I'm doing just fine by myself."

"Ma Dear, calm down now. Remember you told me you thought that the Lord was in this."

"I did, but—"

"And remember how you're always telling me that you have faith?"

"I do, but—"

"Well, why can't you trust the Lord now? Why can't you wait on the Lord?" Ma Dear started pouting. "You know, Ma Dear, we love them because they are men. Then we get mad at them because they act like men."

"I don't know what you mean, Mavis!"

"Well, let me explain it to you. I know you, Ma Dear. You have made a heart decision. You've used your heart and your intuition and already come to a conclusion. Now this man, his heart is telling him something, but he is determined to make a head decision—not to let his heart rule him—so he's dragging his feet. At least it seems that way to you."

"Well, Mother, neither one of us is getting any younger. I declare."

"So you figure you will help him along and just give him a little bit more information, touch those heartstrings just a little bit more."

"Well, he seems like he's confused, Mother. And I'm just trying to help."

"And the more you help, the more he seems like he's putting on the brakes."

Ma Dear turned her head away. "Well, like I said, good riddance. I don't need this in my life. I will be fine without him. I don't need any confusion. I got gray hair, for goodness' sakes!"

"You just don't want to wait. Why is it we have such a hard time waiting?"

"I don't know what you're talking about."

"You know what, Ma Dear? You just have to wait on the Lord and be of good courage. In your spirit you already know what the Lord has said, but you just have to wait on the Lord—let the Lord turn the man's heart, because you sure can't do it for him. If you haven't heard from the Lord, then wait to hear.

"A man's got a big decision to make. And you know that you don't want a man that hasn't decided. Just like the Lord left his home to come and marry us, the man has got to decide if he wants to do the same thing. He won't do you any good trying to be married to his family—to his mother and father's house—and then married to you. You can't make him decide. The more you push, the more he will dig in his heels."

Mother Johnson smiled and patted Ma Dear on the shoulder. "You know something I figured out from reading Genesis? It takes the man a while to realize that he's alone and that he wants to marry. He's got to be hearing the Lord's voice, and he's not ready until then. Until he knows he's alone and decides it's not good for him, he'll always feel like you've taken something precious from him—his freedom—and he'll resent you for it. Then he's got to decide if he wants to give you his name. He's not ready or fit to marry until then. He's got to decide within himself that he's ready to make that commitment, to give you his covering. Then he has to be willing to give up some piece of himself so that you can come to him and be the precious gift that God intended you to be in his life—so that you two can be one. And I believe that there are different things that different men have to give up. But it's something that, if he doesn't give it up, will keep you from fitting in close to him.

"You just have to trust the Lord and wait on Him. Don't run off and leave because you're scared or impatient. And don't try to give the man a gift that he's not ready for in the hopes that you'll sway him. Just wait on the Lord. And while you're waiting, you just enjoy your time with the Lord. Stop worrying about tomorrow. Enjoy the single time you're getting to spend with the Lord today. Spend your time letting the Lord know how you love Him and how grateful you are to Him. Spend your time learning how to pray, and draw near to the Lord, because you're going to need that when you marry.

"If you believe that you've heard the Lord's voice, then trust Him. You listened. Now just watch and wait. Let the Lord show Himself strong. You don't have to work for the gift, Ma Dear. Just let Him give it to you."

Ma Dear looked away and shook her head. "I don't think

I'm any good at this, Mother. I just want to run away and hide."

"Anything worth having is worth waiting for. The Lord doesn't want either one of you to have the other until you are both just right and ready—not until the cake is done baking." Mother put her arm around her friend's shoulder. "Oh, come on now, Ma Dear. We know all the ways to do things *wrong*. Sometimes it's hard to learn to wait and do them right. But God promises to help. 'Wait on the LORD: be of good courage, and he shall strengthen thine heart…'"

Ma Dear sighed and then finished the quote. "'Wait, I say, on the LORD.'" She patted her knee and then laid her head on Mother Johnson's shoulder.

A whole dollar. She had a whole dollar.

Shirley's head bobbed to match the bumping of the school bus. A chubby girl with long, thick braids sat next to her. The girl ignored Shirley and talked across the aisle to her brother. Shirley could see the back of Tony's head across the aisle, where the boys sat, and two rows up. They were going to the Tyler Theater, just down the hill from the smaller Liberty Theater—which had no balcony and sat right on the square. She fingered the money in her pocket.

She had a whole dollar.

"I want to make sure you have enough to get your popcorn and your soda and whatever candy you want. I don't want you to have to beg anybody for anything," Mother Johnson had said when she gave her the money.

"I know that's right. Nothing worse than begging." Ma Dear had cocked her head to the side. "Well, not much, anyway."

While the bus jiggled her, Shirley mentally counted the money at home under the bed in her cigar box. She would be able to buy whatever she wanted at the Tyler Theater with the money that Mother had given her. And she would still have enough leftover to make up the difference between the five dollars she needed and the four dollars and change that she already had. She would be seeing Sheri any day now.

Shirley looked out of the window, and as the bus traveled, they passed by buses parked along the side of the road. Buses that carried rose pickers to the fields where they bent laboring sunup to sundown in the fields, harvesting the last of the roses. Picking, pruning, and de-eyeing the beautiful roses that made Tyler, Texas, the rose capital of the world. The Negro pickers—who, like their cotton-picking, blueberry-picking, tobacco-planting, orange-harvesting counterparts around the world, owned no crop-bearing land—nodded at the school bus but did not miss a beat. In hats and bandannas they picked, for their lives did not allow time, or permission, to wave or stand.

The bus rounded the square, and the children craned their necks looking at the Tyler Theater marquee on the square—attached to Regan's Department Store—that pointed to the building below. By the time the school bus arrived at the theater, the backs of Shirley's thighs were stuck to the vinyl bus seat. It felt like someone was stripping her skin off when she stood up. But even that was not enough to stop her from wiggling into the aisle when Miss Sherman gave them all the go-ahead to get off the bus.

Shirley stood in a single file line with the other children and squinted her eyes against the sun. Miss Sherman stood over them, silhouetted against the light. "Now, you remember what I told you the other day in the auditorium. And I don't want to see you chewing any gum, either."

They walked into the theater, past the round ticket booth, to the left of the red entrance doors. The marquee, which was like a canopy over the sidewalk, displayed the movie title—*Lassie*—outlined by what looked to Shirley like millions of lightbulbs. They walked past the ticket cage and into the lobby, where they were greeted suddenly by the smell of hot buttered popcorn and by candy bars wrapped in red, or yellow, or blue paper. The clerks behind the counter against the wall—most of them still looked to be teenagers—wore white jackets and hats. Shirley felt in her pocket for her money and kept an eye on Miss Sherman for the signal that would let her and the other children know that they could go to the refreshment counter.

While they kept an eye on their teacher, they noticed white children running through the lobby, laughing, yelling, pulling hair—completely unaware that their individual behaviors reflected on their entire race. Shirley and the other children watched the white children chewing gum and saw that they were completely unaware that they were showing their color, that they had no concept that they might never be invited back to the theater again if they weren't as quiet as church mice. Shirley watched and waited for their teachers or parents to take them outside and beat their tails, but it did not happen. Instead, treats were bought for them and they were ushered to the seats on the main floor of the theater.

Shirley and the others waited until the white children were served; then they were given the nod—the nod that said they should walk quietly and demurely to the counter. Once their purchases were made, a clerk indicated with his thumb that they should hike the stairs to the balcony. Shirley wondered why black children sat crowded in the balcony in Tyler, why white children got better seats. Tony was in line behind her, and when she turned to sneak a peek at him, he was scowling.

Shirley turned and followed the silent, single file line up the carpeted steps. The red carpet with gold leaf pattern on the floor was dizzying. Small fingers—beige, tan, and brown— glided over black, wrought-iron rails. She wondered why black children were scolded for having thoughts of misbehaving while white children were rewarded for doing the same old thing. Shirley wondered why the white children were served first. Why white children were allowed to look adults in the eye and shake their heads "no." Why black children were expected to bow their heads, lower their heads, and always say "yes, ma'am." Were white children better? If they were, why were they better in Tyler and not in East St. Louis? And what did better mean? Smarter? Why were they smarter in Tyler and not in East St. Louis? Shirley thought of Ken, Misty, and Barbara—of the Cooties. How did it all fit together?

She walked past the mommies with ribbons and pin curls and bouffants and beehives and ponytails in their hair. The mommies were posted throughout the lobby—mommies who smiled and shined and wore powder—and she wondered why they did not recognize her. Why did they not call for her to come back down the stairs? They did not love her, but she could sit with them, couldn't she? Why did they not call for her to sit in the seats next to their children? What had changed? But the mommies did not see her. They did not reach out their hands to save her. They did not see any of the children like her. The mommies did not see the children that were not like theirs. They did not care. They cared only for pink and gold and blue. Just like in East St. Louis, the mommies were not concerned.

Shirley followed the line into the dark, stuffy balcony. She sat on the front row and, without bending, peered over the edge. The white children talked and smiled…smiled as she used to smile when she was at home. Smiled as she smiled when she had a father, two uncles, a mother, and a friend.

In the darkness, she reached her hand into the box on her lap. For some reason, the popcorn had no taste. Shirley closed her eyes in the dark and dreamed of her bicycle, dreamed that she would soon see Sheri.

Just before the feature started, she stood. "Bathroom, please." She bowed her head and nodded to Miss Sherman when the teacher looked her way. Miss Sherman nodded, and Shirley walked past her, out of the dark balcony, and down the steps. As if she were still in line, she marched through the lobby, then through the doors that opened into the main theater. She walked through the shadows, down the aisle, and sat in a seat next to some girls who appeared to be her age. She said nothing.

The blond-haired girls giggled, talking to each other. Two of them were turned around in their seats. One of the girls had one of her feet propped on the seat in front of her. They talked and whispered.

Until they saw Shirley. She stared straight ahead at the screen, but saw the girls staring at her. One of them stood and motioned toward Shirley with her finger. Other children turned to stare. Then Shirley heard a voice. "Miss Blunell! Miss Blunell, look!"

Shirley kept her eyes forward.

"What are you doing down here, gal?"

She pretended that she did not hear the woman speaking to her, that there was no one in the theater except her.

"I said, what are you doing down here, gal? You can't come down here."

Shirley took in every detail of the screen and drowned out the voices.

"I told you they shouldn't have let them come here."

"I knew there would be trouble. They just don't know how to act—they can't keep them under control."

"They *know* that they cannot come down here and sit with us. I'm going to get the manager."

Lassie. She wondered what it would be like to have such a special dog. One that followed her from place to place. One that kept her out of trouble. A dog that followed her to school and waited until she came home. What did it feel like to have a dog special enough that people paid to see him or her?

Shirley felt herself come up out of the seat, before she realized that there was a hand gripping the back of her collar. "I don't know who you think you are," the hand said. "But you are coming up out of here!" The hand dragged her down the aisle, and Shirley felt one of her shoes come off. The hand cursed at her, and Shirley felt her behind bumping up the aisle while her legs and arms flew in every which direction.

The hand and her body burst through the doors that led to the lobby, and Shirley was lit by the lobby lights. And then the hand jerked her through another set of doors; then she was rolling on the sidewalk—legs over head, side over side.

I hope no one can see my underwear. Mama was right about changing them, she thought as she went tumbling, tumbling, tumbling until she hit the curb.

TWENTY-SEVEN

"Well, how are you, baby?" Mother Johnson held the telephone up to her ear. "Of course I recognize your voice, Agnes. How could I not recognize your voice? I've been knowing you since you were an itty-bitty girl. Since I used to wash clothes for your mama. You were always a precious child."

She leaned forward and pressed a hand against her free ear. "You said what now?" Mother nodded. "Well, that's good. The Lord always loves it when we come home, when we start asking Him what He wants us to do instead of us trying to tell Him what we're going to do and where we're going to go. When we surrender, that's when He can use us." She flapped her apron to catch a little air. "Well, I'm proud of you too. Your mama's been telling me how good you were doing on your job. Now it sounds like you're going to be doing even better. You can't go wrong following the Lord. It always seems like the people with the most gifts, the most capable people, have the hardest time surrendering to His help and to His will. The rest of us know we need help. It seems like some of us suffer from don't-worry-about-me-Lord-itis. "

271

Mother Johnson looked out the window at the car pulling up in front of her house. She nodded again at the phone. "All right, I know you're busy. But I appreciate your calling. Oh, you know that. You know I'm always praying for you. Always have, always will." She leaned forward and pushed back the curtain so that she could see better. "All right. Bye-bye."

A man was walking up the sidewalk, and Shirley—hands, head, and feet dangling—was draped over his arms.

Mother Johnson was sitting on the edge of Shirley's bed when she woke up. Shirley's head hurt; her forehead felt as if someone were pounding it.

"Well, well. Look who's waking up?"

Shirley opened her mouth to explain, but Mother Johnson put a finger to her lips. "Not now. We'll talk later. You just rest now." She smiled and touched Shirley's cheek. "Don't you worry about anything. Not a thing. It's going to be all right. This story is going to have a happy ending." Mother nodded her head toward the door. "In the meantime, you got a little company. Somebody that's been waiting to see you." Mother left the room, and Tony Taylor walked in.

He stood near the doorway. "Hi," Shirley said. Tony waved his hand, but the rest of his body was rigid, except for his chest, which swelled and then deflated, swelled and then deflated. "I'm okay, Tony. For real," Shirley said. He nodded. "My head doesn't hurt much." He shrugged. "How was the movie?"

He looked around the room as though he were looking for something in particular. "We left."

"Because of me?"

Tony shrugged.

Shirley started to cry. "I'm sorry. I…"

Tony took two steps into the room, then stiffened again. He looked as though he was struggling to speak. He took a step backward, then shook his head. "I hate white people! They don't care about us. Just like my Grandpa Anthony…" Tears popped into his eyes, and he raked his hand across his face. "I do! I hate them!"

He stared at Shirley, looking like he was about to burst. Then he walked quickly and quietly out the door.

Shirley looked after him. She watched him stride down the sidewalk. Tony's whole body looked as though he were willing it to fold together lengthwise—his nine-year-old shoulders hunched and convulsed as he walked. Shirley put her hands over her face and cried herself to sleep.

Mother Johnson's hand, touching the tender place around the knot on her head, woke Shirley. "How you feeling, sugar?"

"Mother, I'm sorry. I—"

"Don't you even try to explain. It's not for you to explain away. It can be a mean, cruel old world sometimes. But it's not for you to explain; you're just a child."

"But they made us sit upstairs, and I—"

"I told you, don't try to figure it out. You'll go crazy trying to figure people out." Mother sighed. "You going to be all right, Shirley. I know you been through a lot…it just don't seem fair. But you going to be all right."

Shirley closed her eyes and tried to imagine herself back at home, back on her bicycle, riding freehand.

"Running away is not the answer, baby."

Shirley's eyes popped back open.

"No matter where you run, the same troubles will find and catch up with you. Running is not the answer."

Shirley searched Mother's face for a sign, a clue that she knew about the cigar box. Mother Johnson looked away.

Then Shirley felt herself breaking—breaking and cracking apart. "I want to go home!" She couldn't stop herself from crying.

Mother Johnson took Shirley into her arms, walked to her rocking chair, and drew her onto her lap. "Tell me the story," she said. And so Shirley buried her face in Mother's bosom and told her the story of her uncles, of her father, of her mother. She told her about Vietnam, about the Cooties, and about Martin Luther King. While she talked, there was a deep ache inside of her, an ache that was like a wound. Shirley told Mother Johnson about all the times she cried. And she told Mother about Sheri; she told Mother Johnson everything she knew.

For a while, Mother was silent. The only noise in the room was the creaking chair. "Shirley, I want to you to hear me now, and really, really listen. Mother may not be able to tell you all this some other time, so you need to listen right now. Maybe this is just for you, or maybe it might be for Sheri—you might have to carry the word to her someday, but I feel like I've just got to tell you." Mother rubbed her hand in circles on Shirley's back.

"You know what I hear in your story, baby? Heartbreak. A broken heart. And you know how I recognize it? Because I walked with heartbreak all the days of my young life. Everybody has a different story of how they got the heartbreak. But when you've had it, you recognize it—you know the symptoms."

Shirley felt like she could not breathe.

"In my house, my mother was a lovely woman, a beautiful woman. But somewhere along the way I do believe she got deeply hurt or got frightened. And I think that what she told herself was she was going to make sure that there was no more heartache or storms in her life. So she wouldn't let anything that even looked like a storm come into her life. Of course, that also meant that she couldn't love. Because everyone wise in love knows there ain't no such thing as love that doesn't have any storms.

"You're too young to understand all this now. But if you got love and you got no storms, you got a playact or a movie, but not real love. 'Course on the other hand, if all you got is storms, you don't have love—you got drama.

"Keeping the storms away means you can't love much of anybody. You can do what looks like love—smile, wash clothes, tidy house, go to church, bake cookies, sing Christmas carols—but you can't let anyone touch your heart, so it's not love. Trying to keep the storms out of your life will run you crazy, 'cause you can't fight God and He's the one that allows the storms to come."

Shirley squeezed her eyes shut and whimpered. And she imagined the trees outside her window. She could see and hear the tree limbs that brushed against her window when the rain and winds came.

Mother stroked Shirley's hair and hummed the chorus of a lullaby in her ear. "'Hush little baby, don't say a word. Mama's going to buy you a mockingbird...'" She rocked her—back and forth, back and forth, until Shirley quieted.

Then Mother Johnson began to tell her story again. "So because she was heartbroken, my mother gave us everything but her tender, wounded heart. And anybody wise in love knows that the one thing children—or people, for that matter—can't hardly live without is love. We all looked pretty on the outside—fed, clothed, and polished. But we were messed up on the inside. See, Mother didn't intend to harm us—she probably went to her grave not ever really knowing it—but trying to keep the storms away on the outside, trying to do what she thought would keep her and us safe, just kept storms brewing on the inside of us.

"One of my sisters was so sad she just almost pined away. One of my brothers was so angry he almost busted wide open. Me? I was just heartbroken. I had this broken heart that I went to bed with every night. I would cry myself to sleep every night. I was so lonesome for love I expected to die every night. And I had so much love inside me that I wanted to give away, that I felt like I was going to explode. But on the outside, we looked like perfect children, and I guess she thought we were."

Shirley could feel herself in her bed, feel how she'd curl into a ball, her pillow pulled over her head…

"It's sad what heartbreak will do. It made me 'shamed. I didn't want anyone to know that my mother wouldn't love me. I tried to figure out every day what it was I could do that would make her let me in her heart—I figured there must be something wrong with me. And I tried to keep people away so they couldn't come to my house and see that she didn't love me, because then they'd probably see that something was really wrong with me."

Mother cuddled Shirley closer to her and rubbed her chin along the top of Shirley's head. "So I know heartbreak when I see it, all right. I just wanted true love. I know the look of people starving for love, starving to give love. And I wanted it so badly that I was willing to let people treat me in ways that I shouldn't be treated. I was willing to let them be mean to me, to make fun of me. I was willing to hide who I was, to try not to be pretty. I was willing to sit in the back and hide. I was willing to go along with anything, let them control everything I thought and did, just hoping for a little bit of love, for a little belonging.

"And that's a sad way to be—to be willing to do anything for love. Because you go out in the world looking for love, and there are some mean, cruel people out there. 'Course they're probably people that have been walking with heartache all their lives too." Mother sighed and then continued talking.

"But you know, Shirley, that's what makes me love the Lord. When no one else loved me, I could feel Him holding me while I cried at night."

Shirley raised her head and looked into Mother's eyes. "Baby Jesus. You too?"

Mother nodded. "Me too. And Shirley, He did something special for me. He healed my broken heart. One day, even if no one else loved me or let me love them, I knew His love was enough." Mother touched her finger to the heart place on Shirley's chest. "And I never heard anybody preach about it in church, but one day I was reading the Bible and there it was. God will heal our broken hearts. He wants to heal our broken hearts. 'The Spirit of the Sovereign LORD is on me, because the LORD has anointed me to preach good news to the poor. He has sent me to bind up the brokenhearted, to proclaim freedom for the captives, and release from darkness for the prisoners, to proclaim the year of the Lord's favor and the day of vengeance of our God, to comfort all who mourn, and provide for those who grieve in Zion—to bestow on them a crown of beauty instead of ashes, the oil of gladness instead of mourning, and a garment of praise instead of a spirit of despair.'" She wagged her head. "It was beautiful medicine to my eyes, ears, and heart."

Shirley thought about the song she hummed at night.

Rock me, baby Jesus,
Hold me, baby Jesus,
Love me, baby Jesus,
So I won't be afraid.

Mother Johnson hugged Shirley closer. "So I started praying to Him about my broken heart. I cried to Him about all the hurt and shame and confusion in my life. I begged Him. And I don't know what happened or when it happened, but one day I didn't hurt anymore. The pain just went away." Mother snapped her fingers, then put her arms back around Shirley. "So when I'm crying to the Lord—you know, like at church— and people think I got troubles, what they don't know is that I'm crying because He took my broken heart away, rolled it away like a stone. And he gave me a new heart."

Mother Johnson toyed with Shirley's braids. "Shirley, somebody in your life, or Sheri's life, maybe both…somebody was afraid of storms. And they were trying too hard to keep control of their lives, to keep pains and storms out of their lives. Trying so hard that they left somebody else with a broken heart. What they didn't know is that God is still God in the storms. They didn't know that thunder comes when God is creating—be it peace, or love, or joy, or families. They didn't know that God's storms won't kill you and that out of the storm God brings deliverance and order—divine order."

She rocked Shirley. "You know, I can't make all the hurt go away. I can rock you and rub your back. I can tell you that everything will be all right. But I know Someone who can make it go away. He can heal broken hearts. I'm living testimony. And when He got through healing me, He sent my husband and my children into my life, and they brought me all the love I had been dreaming of. And that is a happy ending. If He healed my heart, Shirley, I know that He can heal yours. And you remember that I told you so."

Mother Johnson took one hand and lifted Shirley's chin. She looked deeply into Shirley's eyes, and Shirley felt something inside of her tremble.

"Now, I can't tell you that everything was perfect. I still never got the love from my mother that I wanted—I never got to touch the sore place in her so that I could help her. And sometimes I still have to fight to keep that old shame off of me. For a while I was scared of anything that even looked like order. I been through a lot, and I got scars to prove it. But God gave me more love than I could have ever imagined. The scars I have, I just use them now to prove to other people that they can be healed. God gave me joy. And nothing—He won't ever let *nothing* separate me from His love. 'Cause God is a *good* God. He is a mercy God."

"You been through a lot today, baby. You been through a lot in your short life. But Shirley, you need to know that this world is not a place for the fainthearted. And you need to know that the Lord is with you, Shirley, and He is going to make something beautiful out of all the turmoil you been through. You remember I told you so."

Shirley pulled her chin away, closed her eyes, and began to cry. Mother Johnson adjusted Shirley's position on her lap. "I don't understand it all, baby. Why anybody has to suffer. But I think that the minute we are born, the devil has our number. He already knows what plan God has for you. When God has a mighty work planned for a person, the devil is a mean man. He's not going to wait until you get grown and can fight back. He wants to kill you when you're young, maybe before you're even born. Shirley, you've made it this far. Farther than some. You're an overcomer. And what I see in you—and what the devil must see—is that you're one of those people that will go, even if you have to go alone, even if you have to do what you have to do crying and afraid. That makes you dangerous to Satan's kingdom. Mighty dangerous."

Mother nuzzled Shirley's head with her chin. "I know that all you can see around you now are shadows. And in the shadows it feels like you're all alone—like you're in a thick, dark fog and there are monsters lurking in the darkness waiting to do you harm. You can't see anyone or anything familiar. But you remember this if you don't remember anything else I say: God is walking with you in the shadows. You have to learn to find Him, to hear Him in the shadows. You have to learn to recognize His touch. When you're lost or frightened, don't be afraid to cry out to Him. He knows the voice of His sheep. He'll walk with you and He'll direct you. He'll correct your path. Believe me, I know. No matter what darkness He allows you to walk into, He intends for you to come out. And you remember that I told you so."

Shirley pulled away from Mother Johnson's hand and spoke between sobs. "But I don't know *how,* Mother. I don't know how to call Him. I don't know how to find my way."

"Always remember that you are stronger than you think you are. You're in a battle, Shirley. You're a little girl, but it's still a battle. And the Lord would not have let you enter the battle if He did not know that you are strong enough to win. You're a child, Shirley, but you need to know that your battle is not with the man at the movie theater, or the doctors, or anybody else that might have hurt you. Our enemy is the devil. Our war is with all those that dwell in darkness. That's who you're fighting, and you've got to fight for your life.

"You can't fight the way spiritual darkness fights. But you fight and win by keeping a pure and forgiving heart. Forgive and forget the hurts that you suffer, no matter who does it. You win by praying to God. You win by doing what you hear me and Ma Dear doing—praying just a little bit of God's Word. And if you don't know what else to do, you win by crying out His name. Cry it out loud as you can. Sing to Him. Shout to Him. Beat something. Tell Him you believe and beg Him to come near. Beg Him to walk you out. And you keep pulling at the chains, Shirley. You keep pulling and pulling. Keep pulling until they break!"

"But, Mother, I don't think I can. I don't think I know how. I'm just scared!"

"Shirley, someday…someday just when you need it, you're going to remember what I'm saying to you now. You remember, no matter what it looks like—no matter how much it looks like midnight, no matter what stirs in the shadows—you are never alone. You are never, never, *never* alone. Your mind may be too young, but I want your spirit to understand: You have forces at work for you—God's army, in a kingdom that you cannot see. There are forces that are just waiting for you to pray, for you to beg, so that they can—at the direction of the Lord—come to fight against things in your life that are too big for you to fight. They are willing to do whatever is necessary to bring you out, so don't give up. Pray. Don't ever give up. Pray. Don't you ever give up, Shirley. Pray!"

Child Killer Shirley pointed at the old woman beneath him and hissed. The old woman held the held the child that was his. His yellow eye glowed in the dark, and the white and silver gills around his sockets glinted in the dim light as drool slid from the corner of the thing that was his mouth to his chin. The child killer stomped around the hole that allowed him to view his charge on earth. He nodded at the ones assigned to help him. They would have to move quickly, before the old one taught the soft one to pray, before Shirley learned who she was.

They had been silent. They had been planning and biding their time until the attack. It was better to let things be calm— to give no warning so there would be no extra prayers. The old one prayed all the time, but he had been given reinforcements, and permission had been received. She would be quiet soon. Very quiet.

He stretched his arms above his head and belched a foul smelling, grayish vapor that swirled and choked. It would be over soon. The old one would be as nothing. Soon the child Shirley would be his.

TWENTY-EIGHT

⚜

his was the day.

Shirley felt her forehead. The lump was gone. Then she felt her pocket—all the change was there—all five dollars and forty-eight cents of it. She would have to be quiet so that it wouldn't jingle and give her plans away.

For weeks she had been sneaking things away. A pair of socks or a shirt—sticking them into her coat pocket and carrying them to Tony, who stuck them in his pocket and hid them away for her.

"I don't think you should do this, Shirley."

"Tony, are you going to help me or not?"

"I just don't think it's right. What if you get cold? What if something happens?"

"Tony?"

"All right. Okay."

Today was the day. And she could not help feeling that Mother Johnson knew but wasn't saying anything. She looked behind her at the place where Mother Johnson stood with Ma Dear and some of the other women from the community.

Shirley couldn't help feeling that Mother knew about the cigar box, that Mother had missed the sweater and the dresses that did not make it to the wash. But Mother said nothing. And this was the day. Shirley would slip away from the crowd when the band marched by. She would make her way to the bus station, buy her bus ticket, wait for Tony to bring the clothes, and then she would be home.

She would see Sheri again.

It was the Rose Festival Parade in Tyler, and the air was chilly—at least what Tyler thought was chilly, which was not the same as East St. Louis chilly. Shirley stood at the curb surrounded by people—people huddled together waiting for the parade. People waiting for the parade to pass the hill and under the overpass—the place where the train passed, the place where all the black people listened, watched, and waited.

The grass was brown and there were patches of ice scattered around. There were gray skies and heavy clouds. The crowd murmured, and there was an occasional burst of laugher.

No one remembered whether they had been directed there, ordered there, or whether there was just safety in numbers. But this was the place where they had been standing for years, and where they now stood.

Boom! Boom!

It was the sound of the bass drum. They heard it even before the first band came into sight.

"Here they come!" a small boy hollered. And in the distance they saw a small spot that grew larger until it finally became the Tyler Junior College band. The Apache Belles, dressed in gold and black, held a white banner decorated with roses while they marched in front of the Apache Band. The crowd smiled and waved, careful not to get too excited, careful not to look too closely at one of the Belles, careful not to let the happy time turn into an occasion for a burning or a fast ride out of town.

They clapped politely for other East Texas bands, then hooted for the John Tyler High School band. The Lions, dressed in blue and white, stopped in front of the crowd to play their theme song, "Big Bad John." They twirled, blew their horns, and beat their drums, but they did not look at the crowd. And after a few bars, they marched on.

A few rose-laden floats with pretty blond- and brown-haired waving girls passed by, followed by decorated cars and a few clowns on foot.

The Robert E. Lee High School band marched into view. The drill team and the blue brigade pep squad swirled around a large confederate flag. The strains of "Waiting on the Robert E. Lee" played while the Confederate Band—dressed in the appropriate uniform—passed by, smiling, gleaming, apparently unaware that the crowd they entertained had grown quiet, unaware that their young pleasure recalled centuries of pain—even recent pain—for those they entertained. Some of the crowd looked at the ground, some looked side to side, and some looked down the street as though they were enduring, waiting for something better to come.

Just as the Confederate song finished, a chip of ice flew in the midst of the band. Shirley looked in the direction the ice seemed to come from, but all the faces were expressionless, blank. All the hands appeared to be in pockets or on hips. Without missing a step, the Confederate band moved down the street.

People on horseback passed by, their saddles and horses decorated with roses. The horses snorted and pranced. They held their heads high and left behind them what horses leave behind.

"Here they come!" the same boy screamed after the horses passed.

The crowd came alive. Hats flew up in the air and women began to dance, stepping side to side to the music they heard.

"Oh, shuck it now!" one of the women said.

The children laughed and began to dart back and forth. "When I get big, I'm going to be one of them."

It was what the underpass crowd had been waiting for.

It was the Emmit Scott High School band! It was *their* band. It was the band of children who had to ride on school buses from locations all over the area to go to the Negro high school. It was the band they could shout for, the band they could whistle at, the band they could march beside. The Bulldogs were the band the crowd had held their breath for—the best band, the band that they knew would be behind the horses. Always behind the horses.

And the Emmit Scott Band stepped high, so high the crowd gasped and then erupted. Their white spats moved up and down like pistons, being careful for nothing, not even for the things that horses always left behind. Dressed in maroon and white, the Bulldogs—led by the daring drum major and the baton-twirling, high-stepping Rosettes—made the underpass crowd proud, drove them into a frenzy. Reminded them that they were overcomers, that they were heroes, that they were indeed a piece of glory.

And that is when Shirley slipped away.

She moved quietly to the back of the crowd, then, head down, hurried down the street. Shirley ducked behind walls and trees, following the path, the way of escape she had plotted for what felt like forever to her. She passed barking dogs on chains, staring adults, pointing children.

It was too far away for a child to walk alone, but Shirley moved with the speed that purpose gives.

Mother Johnson felt Shirley go before she saw that the child was gone.

"Shirley! Shirley! Where are you, baby?" She tried not to panic over what she already knew. A chill wrapped around her ribs, and she stumbled against the car she stood near.

"Mother? Mavis? Are you all right? What's the matter?"

Mother Johnson could feel herself slipping down the side of the car. *God, take care of my baby. My sweet baby.* Mother couldn't breathe, and she was losing focus. She could hear voices around her, but the only one she could understand was Ma Dear. Her friend was always there. *Ma Dear…*

"Mavis, child, what are you doing?"

"Take care of Shirley." Mother tried to speak again, but her throat closed around the words. She felt her left knee hit the ground, and her hand flew up to try to stop her fall by grabbing one of the car door mirrors. *I'm too old to be falling like this.*

And as she slipped away, she thought she heard a voice laughing.

The child killer's scales had turned to a sickening, sluggish gray color. He pointed at the old one beneath him and cackled. Child Killer Shirley waved the stumps where his arms once were and danced around the air above the fallen woman. He used one of his stumps to point to his comrades, who had all turned the same gray, the same color of death. Together, they had weakened the old woman's defenses. And hope above hope, no one was praying. He pointed upward, and the others joined him in mocking the angels of the Most High God. He and the others turned and looked back down on the old one. They began to spit, hiss, and drool—sending death, fear, and confusion into the air around her.

It had been easy. The master would be pleased; Satan would be able to make lots of accusations—prayers that were not prayed, doubts, disobedience. It was a haul that would keep him busy before the throne of the Most High God.

But what pleased the child killer most was the soft one. He turned his one good eye so that he could see her running. She was exposed. There was no cover for her—and their timing had been perfect—a quiet time when the ones below felt no urgency to teach her to pray. He crouched nearer to where she ran.

He was certain—soon she would be his.

Shirley handed the ticket man her money. She tried not to breathe heavy, tried not to remember that she almost did not make it to the station. "This is only enough to go to Dallas. What's a gal like you doin' travelin' alone anyway?" He frowned. "Where's your mama?"

"Dallas is good enough," she told him. "My mama's in Dallas. I forgot. I got it mixed up." She smiled at the man. "That's what she told me to do. Come home to Dallas so I can see my relatives. Then we're going to meet up there, and we're all going to go to East St. Louis." The man looked at her like he didn't believe her. "Thank you, sir." She kept smiling.

He shrugged his shoulders, took the money, and handed her the ticket to Dallas. "They'll call for your bus in about thirty minutes. You be listening, because I'm not going to come get you."

"Yes, sir," she said and sat on one of the metal benches in the Tyler bus station. Dallas was a start. It was one step closer to home. Maybe she could get a job there. Maybe she could find someone that would want to hire a girl like her—she would make money and earn her way home. Like in a book or a movie—she would make her way home like Lassie.

Shirley watched the clock and alternately hoped that time would slow or pass quickly. *Where are you, Tony?* She pulled at the tips of her braids. *What will I do if he doesn't come with my stuff?*

But she twisted and turned on the bench, hoping that Mother Johnson would not come through the door and stop her from leaving. She would miss Mother, but she had to get back to her life—back to her home. Shirley had left a note in the cigar box on top of her bed. The note explained everything because she did not want Mother to worry. She wanted Mother to know that she would be safe at home, safe at home with Sheri. And maybe someday they would both come back to Tyler and visit.

The loudspeaker crackled. "The three-fifteen to Dallas is now boarding, with stops in…"

Shirley looked around for Tony. Where *was* he? She looked at the ticket in her hand. It was all she had. It was now or never. She boarded the bus and did not look back.

She found a seat in the back. The toilet stank, but in the rear of the bus there was no one near her to ask questions or to pry. Soon they were on the highway, and the lines painted on the road disappeared under the bus as though they were being eaten. Shirley looked out the window and thought she saw a car pass by, a car like the Impala, a car that held her uncles—Big Uncle and Little Uncle. She thought she saw her mother in the front seat of the car. And in the back, Shirley was sure she saw a little girl who looked just like her. But in the car, she was sure she saw a fifth person—a father in a uniform. The car passed too quickly for her to be certain.

Shirley turned in her seat to try to see, but it was too late. The car was gone too soon.

She took a deep breath and scooted back against the seat. Shirley put a hand over her nose so she wouldn't have to smell the toilet. She thought about the car and quietly started to cry...

At least she would soon see Sheri.

The doctor shook his head and said he wasn't sure exactly what was wrong.

"It's got me stumped," he said. "We're going to have to get her to the hospital for whatever tests can be done." He shook his head. "I just don't know."

Mother Johnson looked frail and lifeless lying in her bed. Ma Dear could feel fear stealing up her spine. "Well, something's got to be done, doctor, and I don't have time to do it. I've got to find the child." Ma Dear's hands waved frantically in the air. "And what do I know about children? Nothing, that's what. But what I do know is that *you*—" she jabbed a finger in the doctor's direction—"better figure it out pretty doggone quick. If my friend here dies, you don't want to pay the price you're going to have to pay. That's what I *do* know. But I don't have time to talk. I've got to find the child! And only the Lord knows where to start or how to get there."

Ma Dear felt a hand on her elbow. "Come on, Augusta." It was her friend, Ely Milton. "We'd better get going so we can find the child and take advantage of the daylight we have left."

When Shirley stepped off the bus, it was dark. Dark and cold. And the Dallas bus station was much bigger than the one in Tyler. She entered through the open doors, walked until she saw a clock, and then stood looking around her. Shirley moved to sit on a bench, but then turned away when she saw a strange man looking at her.

She walked past a machine that sold sandwiches. Her stomach growled. Everything in the machine was more than the eight cents she had left in her pocket. Shirley walked to a window and stood looking outside. Tomorrow would be better, she told herself. She looked around for a quiet, safe place she might sleep, then turned back to the window.

Tomorrow, when daylight comes... Shirley thought of Mother Johnson and the warm house and kitchen. Her stomach grumbled again.

"Shirley! Shirley!" She spun to find Tony running toward her from the far side of the station.

Shirley smiled, ran toward him, then suddenly stopped. "Where is my bag, Tony? I was waiting on my bag. You weren't supposed to meet me *here.* You were supposed to meet me in Tyler." Shirley wagged her head, and she could feel her braids flopping. "Where were you?"

Tony frowned and didn't speak.

Shirley put a hand on her hip. "Tony! Don't start that not speaking stuff again. I *mean* it." She gestured at the surrounding Dallas bus station. "How did you find me?"

"The man at the bus station—the one selling the tickets—he said where you were heading." He reached out his hand and touched her arm. "But, Shirley. Shirley. Something happened. That's why I couldn't get there…" He shook his head. It was the most Shirley had ever heard him speak. "Something happened to your mother."

"My mother?" Shirley's heart clutched. "You don't even know my mother. How do you know something about my mother?"

"Not that mother. Your Mother Johnson, your mother that's taking care of you. Something happened to her at the parade. She's bad off."

The lingering, stale, bus-station smell of frustration, anxiety, and despair was in the air. People walked all around them, nudged past them, and bus arrival and departure announcements drifted overhead.

Shirley grabbed Tony's arm. "What you talking about, Tony?"

"She's in the hospital. Mother Johnson…" He shook his head. Shirley tried to look back at the window, but the room began to spin. "We've got to get back," Tony said.

She jammed her hands into her pockets, searching for something that was not there. "I don't have any more money. How can I get back?"

Tony pointed at a man standing near the far door. "My brother."

Shirley hardly said a word on the way back. The three-hour trip felt like it lasted three years. She could not think. She could not even cry. When they pulled in front of Mother's house, Tony opened his door and extended his right foot as though he intended to walk to the front door with her.

"No, Tony," Shirley said as she pushed the seat forward so that she could slide out of the backseat. "I don't want you to get in trouble." She looked at Mother Johnson's house. "I have to do this by myself."

Shirley pushed the door open as quietly as she could. Ma Dear was pacing back and forth, talking to herself. A man, a quiet man, sat in a chair near the door. Shirley stepped into the room. She might as well get it over with. She sighed.

Ma Dear turned at the sound. She raised both her hands in the air, dropped them to her side, then raised them again. "Shirley, where you *been,* girl?" Ma Dear pointed at the man. "We been looking all over for you." She stepped toward Shirley with an I'm-about-to-spank-you look on her face. Then that expression broke and sorrow showed instead. "And Mother Johnson...my friend's in the hospital." Ma Dear closed her eyes for moment, then opened them, focusing on Shirley. "Where you been, girl? Where you been?"

Shirley shrugged her shoulders.

"That's all you got to say? After all Mother has done for you? After she took you in and treated you like you were her own child? That's all you can do is shrug your little shoulders? When she went down, she wasn't thinking about herself...she was hollering out your name. And who even knows if she's going to live—then where will you be? Hollering out your name might have been her last words. But all you can say is a great, big, fat nothing?" Ma Dear took one step toward Shirley.

"Augusta?" The man sitting in the chair spoke. "I don't think this is the time to do this. She's a child, Augusta. Let's get her settled." He looked in Shirley's direction. "Shirley, right?" He stood up, motioned Shirley toward the table, then looked at Ma Dear. "Why don't we see if she's eaten yet, then let her get some sleep? It's too late for all this now. We're all feeling a little raw." It looked like the man was forcing a smile when he looked in Shirley's direction. "But I believe things are going to look better in the morning."

After Shirley had eaten some soup and half of a grilled cheese sandwich—she couldn't eat anymore—she went to her room. The cigar box was still on her bed, untouched.

What was going to happen to Mother? What was going to happen to her? Was she responsible? Had she killed Mother? Shirley crouched in the darkness and wrapped her arms around her legs while she pressed her forehead down on her knees. She began to sing to herself.

Rock me, baby Jesus
Hold me, baby Jesus
Love me, baby Jesus
So I won't be afraid.

Sometime just before dawn, Shirley crawled into bed and slept.

TWENTY-NINE

Mother Johnson's daughters had been called home.

"Just in case," someone had whispered.

"You never know what can happen or when," other people said.

And Shirley watched and wondered. She drifted through the house like a ghost, feeling something pressing on her chest—something she could not speak about, but something so real it hurt. She felt as though she were watching a movie being filmed.

Both of Mother's daughters were tall and looked like coffee with cream. They looked the same, walked the same, talked the same, and it was difficult for Shirley to tell them apart.

"I've got to go out." The youngest one, June, brushed past Shirley as though she did not know she was there. Shirley leaned her arms and then her chin against the back of chair to watch. It had been the same thing for weeks. "I've got to run to the market," the youngest sister spoke again.

The oldest sister, April, stepped back from the sink where she was washing dishes and turned her face toward her sister and raised an eyebrow. "You've always got to run," April said. "It's just real convenient for you to run, isn't it? I just wish Mama could see you now. I wish she could see how her favorite child is holding up under pressure."

April, the oldest one, took her hands from the sink, yanked down the dish towel that lay on her shoulder, and began to jerkily dry her hands. "It's not fair for you to leave all this on me, June. You've been doing this since we got here. Coming and going like you've got nothing to do."

"Well, April, it's not the same for me...I've got a job. I've got things I have to do. I can't just stop what I have to do. You know that."

"No, *Miss* June, I don't know that. I don't know that at all. What I think is that you are selfish. Everything is all about you. That's what I think." Shirley turned her head from side to side as the two women spoke. "You think because I don't work outside the home that you're better than me? You think I don't have things to do? Well, you're wrong. I've got a husband and a family. They need me. My little girl needs me."

June's eyes narrowed, and she looked as though she was about to cry. The younger sister always cried. "That was mean, April. You don't have to throw it in my face that I'm not married and that I don't have children. I don't know how you can be so mean."

"You know that's not what I meant, June."

"Well, that's what you said."

"Well, what about what *you* said to *me* the other day?"

"What? What did I say?"

"You know what you said..."

It was the same argument, the same words they had been speaking since they arrived. And the tone was always the same.

Kind of whispered, but just loud enough, as though they were on stage and wished that someone around them could hear. Maybe they hoped Mother Johnson, back home from the hospital in her bedroom, would hear them fighting. Maybe they thought their anger would wake her up, bring her back. Maybe they thought if they argued like children, she would awaken from where she slept and scold them—like when they were children—for whispering too loudly or fighting too long.

But when guests came to visit Mother—to sit near her bed, looking uncomfortable, looking at her frail, motionless body—the two sisters smiled at the company and at each other.

"So the doctors say they don't know what to do, huh?" the company always asked.

"That's what the doctor says, but we know Someone who does." The sisters would smile and even nod at each other, clinging to each other like best friends.

"You all must be tired," the company always said.

"Oh no, we're just fine," the sisters always responded. "We wouldn't have anyone care for Mother but us. That's just the way we want it. We love our mother."

"Well, you let me know if you need me," the company always said. "Your mother was good to everyone around here, and me and other folks like me would be more than happy to help out."

"Oh no! We have everything well in hand," the sisters always said. "It won't be long now. She'll be up and around any time now. You know Mother. Death might want her, but he's crazy if he thinks he's going to hold our mother down!"

The sisters would laugh as though they were at a party instead of standing at the bedside of their mother—a mother about whom the doctors did not give much hope.

That was who they were with company. But this, after the first two weeks, was who they had become when they were alone. And Shirley knew that she did not figure in, that they did not even notice her.

The youngest sister was crying now. "You know what, April? I have to get out of here." June began to move toward the door. She grabbed her car keys off the nail near the door.

"Don't you leave here, June. I mean it. Don't you leave me with all this to do. Mother needs to be bathed and changed. Don't you leave me to do this by myself. How am I supposed to keep her alive by myself?"

June choked on her tears, then turned back to her older sister. "Can't you see I can't do it, April? Can't you see that? She's my mother, but I can't stand to see her that way. I can't change her diaper. Can't you see that?" She turned as if she was going to place the keys back on the hook, then stopped and began to move quickly toward the door. "I've got to go, okay? I'll be back. I'll be back soon."

"So what gives you the right to run out?"

"I'm not good at it, April? Okay? I'm not good at it! I can't do what you do." With that, June was out the door.

April stormed to the door behind her. "That's a lousy excuse! You might as well not come back. What's the point? You're not helping anybody—you're sure not helping me. And you're sure not helping Mother!" She hollered out the door after her sister. "Just don't come back, Miss Career Woman, Miss I'm-in-Charge-of-Everything! I wish Mother could see you now. I wish she could just see how you really feel about her!"

April strode back to the sink and fought with the dishes and pans until they were all clean.

While the woman stayed in motion, Shirley moved to a corner—anything to stay out of firing range. April's face stayed tight and still—except for the constant movement of her lips—until she had swept the floor and mopped it.

Shirley's stomach betrayed her, and April's head popped up immediately. "I *told* you to eat this morning, didn't I? Instead of just picking and playing with your food—I *told* you that you were going to be hungry. Well, I don't have time to stop to fix anything. I have a million and one things to do and no help." April squeezed out the mop, poured the mopping water out, rinsed the bucket and mop, and then moved toward Mother's room while she continued to talk. "It's not as if I don't have enough to do…all by myself."

Shirley placed her hands over her stomach and willed it to be quiet. She walked to Mother's bedroom doorway so that she could watch April. April was silent, and in no time the woman seemed to have retrieved a basin of water, a washcloth, soap, and other toiletries. She bathed Mother from head to toe, gently turning her and lifting her. As she touched her mother, the look on her face said love, and she appeared to be at peace. When April was finished, she left the room as quickly as she came.

Hours later, Shirley lay in her bed and recognized the sound of June's footsteps walking in the door. June walked into Mother's bedroom, and Shirley could hear her speaking to Mother Johnson as though they were conversing. "Oh, that's all right, Mother. You'll be up, around, and talking in no time— I'm certain of it." June stopped speaking briefly, then suddenly resumed. "You won't believe what I found at the yard sale I went to, Mother. I found these wind chimes. Aren't they beautiful? Almost a beautiful as you." She paused as though waiting for her mother to respond. "Well, I know. It might be frivolous,

Mother. But I just thought you might like something pretty." Again, the silence. "Well, I'm glad you appreciate it, Mother. I thought they looked like your colors." More silence. "Of course, I'll sing to you, Mother. What would you like to hear?" June laughed softly. "Well, that always was one of your favorites. Just the third verse? All right. Let me clear my throat, Mother."

And then, in a soft, sweet soprano, just scratchy enough to add color, June began to sing.

Though Satan should buffet,
Though trials should come,
Let this blessed assurance control,
That Christ has considered my helpless estate,
And has shed His own blood for my soul.
It is well…with my soul.
It is well; it is well with my soul!

Shirley looked out the window at the stars. How much more? She turned on her stomach and pulled the covers over her head. When Mother died, where would she go? There'd been no word from her uncles or her mother, so it probably would be back to the hospital and the doctors and the needles and the prodding. Shirley could feel herself beginning to pant. Her stomach knotted. For comfort, she began to sing softly.

Rock me, baby Jesus,
Hold me, baby Jesus,
Love me, baby Jesus,
So I won't be afraid.

So Shirley fell asleep humming her own song.

Ma Dear's voice wakened Shirley.

"I *know* it's early in the morning. I know that! I've seen more mornings than you two have ever even thought about."

Wiping sleep from her eyes, Shirley stumbled from her bed to see what had Ma Dear so agitated.

"The Lord woke me up this morning. 'Somebody's got to pray.' That's what He told me. Loud and clear, I heard it, just like a bell. It's Wednesday, I should have known the Lord would show up on one of Mavis's praying days."

April protested. "We're not even up, Ma Dear. This is ridiculous! It's not as if a few hours one way or another is going to make any difference. It's been weeks now. And the doctors don't even know what to do. That's why they sent her home. This is ridiculous."

June stood behind April, silent and watching.

"You're going to have to come back later when we have gotten ourselves together." April looked over her shoulder at June. "This is absolutely ridiculous!"

Ma Dear shook her purse. "Girl, I took a brush to you before when you were a child, and I got one with me right now. Don't make me use it."

Shirley felt her mouth drop open. April turned gray and pulled her housecoat tighter around her body.

"I've been all over everywhere praying for people, healing them. And I mean, they get up too! And you mean to tell me I'm not going to do it for my friend? I should say so. And this man right here—" Ma Dear pointed at the man standing near the door—"has been with me when I went to heal. He has seen what the Lord can do through me." Ma Dear looked at her man friend. "Ain't that right?"

"Yes, it's so," Eli Milton said.

"It's been long enough. We been sitting around here moping while my best friend is wasting away. So not you and nobody else is going to stop me from going in there to pray for my friend, especially when the Lord has told me directly that somebody's got to pray." Ma Dear threw down her purse and started pulling her sweater off. "And guess that somebody is going to be me. Old Satan's got a fight coming—and if I have to fight you first, you know I will!"

April and June held on to each other and stared at Ma Dear wide-eyed.

Ma Dear nodded. "All right, then. It looks like things are falling into place." Her voice softened, and she turned to the man beside her. "Come on, honey. Will you go with me? I feel like I need you."

"I'll get the Bibles," he said.

"Come on, honey! We got work to do!"

THIRTY

The air tingled.

Shirley tore her nightgown over her head and grabbed the first top and pants she came across in her bureau drawer—a red plaid top and pink pedal-pusher pants. She stuck her feet into her unlaced brown P. F. Flyers and ran to stand outside the closed door to Mother Johnson's room. At first, all she could hear was murmuring. Then Ma Dear's voice got louder.

"I've seen You heal before, Lord. So I know You can do it." She could hear the man's voice praying softly in the background while Ma Dear continued. "You woke me up this morning, Lord. And I know You didn't do it for nothing. You said, 'Somebody's got to pray.' So here I am, Lord. So come on, Lord. Heal like You healed Abimelech when Abraham prayed. Heal like You healed the people when Hezekiah prayed. She's got more to do for You, Lord. That child still needs her, Lord. I still need her."

Something in the room bumped, and it felt like the air outside the door quivered. Shirley looked around to see if something had moved. Ma Dear's voice rose again.

"Lord, I'm pleading with You! Heal her like You healed the centurion's servant. You don't have to be present—just Your very word heals. Send us a healing word. Heal Mother Johnson like Jesus healed the crazy man and that little girl—and she was already dead, Lord. This ain't nothing big for You, Lord. The doctors may have given up, but this is a little bitty thing to You. I've seen You do bigger. Way bigger! And I know I heard Your voice. I know I heard You. Give her some more years, Lord. I'm begging You!"

Shirley looked behind her. The two sisters were whispering; April was gesturing frantically. "This is…it's old fashioned…it's antiquated… This is *not* the kind of thing…it's like voodoo." She shook her head and then pointed at the sky. "We're going to be landing a man on the moon soon, for goodness' sake! This is crazy, and I can't believe I'm allowing this to happen."

June shrugged her shoulders. "I don't know, April. What can it hurt? We can try, can't we? Mother believed in prayer… and I don't know. Anything at this point."

"No, not anything at this point. We are civilized people. You're a businesswoman, for goodness' sakes. Can you imagine what people at your job would say if they knew you had a crazy woman—and even if she is a family friend, she's *crazy*—praying and yelling. They'd say you were crazy too. And she threatened me. You heard her threaten me. She threatened you too!"

"I don't think Ma Dear threatened *me*. I think she was just talking to *you*, April."

April's eyes bucked wide open, and she put her hands on her hips. "I think everybody in this house has gone crazy. Just crazy."

Shirley turned back to watch the door and to listen. "What about the woman with the issue of blood, Lord? You healed

her, and she had been sick for years. Healed her just like that."
Shirley heard Ma Dear snap her fingers. "Mother's been here for
just a short time. Come on, Lord! And I seen You heal people a
lot less nice than Mother, and some of their families were nasty
people, if I do have to say so myself. So come on here, Lord. I
know You hear me calling!" Ma Dear began to shout out the
Scriptures that Shirley had heard her recite over and over
again.

"'Lift up your heads, O ye gates, and be ye lift up, ye everlasting doors; and the King of glory shall come in. Who is this
King of glory? The LORD strong and mighty, the LORD mighty
in battle. Lift up your heads, O ye gates; even lift them up, ye
everlasting doors; and the King of glory shall come in.'"

They had to work hard to keep the old one stilled. She was
powerful, and it had taken all they had to bind her. But she
was bound, at least for now—until the prayers started. The
child killer glared at the old one called Ma Dear. They should
have taken her too. They had kept a chill around her, speaking
to her that it was impossible to heal or deliver the old one. But
she was causing destruction now; the Holy Spirit must have
been afoot.

Child Killer Shirley ducked and tried to writhe away from
the light that had come cutting into the darkness around him.
The demons that had huddled with him before the attack on
the old one had scattered. He looked at his blue and green
scales. They had all lost their gray death pallor—the color that
signaled their strength, their victory—but this was no time to
think about beauty. It was a time to think about survival. And
the Host was on the attack.

Why? Just for a stupid child? All this, all these angels of light, for one child? The child killer wanted to breathe on her—perhaps some fear or some despair—but there wasn't time. He was fighting for his own life. And the attack had come suddenly—there was no warning, no time to plan, no time to regroup.

Run! His insides told him. *Run!*

The air crackled again, and Shirley wondered if April and June felt it.

"I told you this was foolishness! I'm going to put a stop to it!"

June grabbed April's arm. "No, April. No, we need to leave her alone. At least it's hope. What does it hurt to hope?"

Shirley thought she heard thunder, and she whipped her head toward the door. Suddenly it swung open, and Ma Dear stepped out crying. When she swept past Shirley, Shirley looked and kept watching for Mother Johnson to follow.

Ma Dear was alone. As the door swung shut, Shirley could hear the man continuing to pray. Ma Dear sat at the table, laid her head on her folded arms, and began to cry. "I don't know what's wrong," she sobbed. "God knows I'm sincere. He knows I got compassion in my heart." She looked toward heaven. "I'm not even doing the things I used to do. And I just don't feel nothing. Just nothing."

Shirley stayed near the door, watching.

April looked smug and jerked her neck back and forth. "I told you all this was foolish. A waste of time. And now look at us! We're all worked up, and our routine for the day is ruined. This is just ridiculous, and I say we call it quits."

Child Killer Shirley prepared to jump into the abyss—then he heard voices of defeat.

Suddenly he felt himself growing stronger. He turned toward the Third Heaven angel that was opposing him and spit death into his eyes. Blinded, the angel continued swinging his weapon, but the child killer laughed and stole away. He could always count on the soft ones—they were always judging by their feelings.

No feeling, no prayer—he looked at the blinded angel still flailing with his blade—no prayer, no power. The light was dimming around him, so he turned his good eye to see the soft one named April. She didn't know the power of her negative words—power that was strengthening the attack against her mother. He nodded at her. He loved the unknowing allies—the doubting people—best.

June stepped around April and laid her hand on Ma Dear's shoulder.

"Don't give up, Ma Dear." April gasped, but June continued. "Mother believed in you, and she wouldn't want you to give up. You *can't* give up. And I don't know much about praying, but I'll go back in with you if you want me to."

Ma Dear shot up as though she had been hit by a bolt of lightening. "Say *what?*"

The telephone rang, and April fussed all the way to answer it. "Hello. Who? Yes, she's here." She nodded at Ma Dear. "It's for you." She whispered. "It's that white girl that calls Mother sometimes. The one whose mother our mother used to work for—I don't know what she wants at a time like this."

Ma Dear took the phone. "Yes, I know who you are. Agnes, right? You say what? You say the Lord told you to pray?" Ma Dear nodded and started smiling, even though her face was still wet with tears. "All right, honey. Well, you just keep praying. Oh, you're right. She's been good to all kinds of people. We're not going to give up this fight. I believe the cavalry is about to ride again!" Ma Dear hung up the phone and crooked a finger at June. "Come on, honey. We got work to do!"

The two women opened the bedroom door and stepped inside. April stamped her feet and grumbled to herself. Shirley turned back to watch the door.

"God, You're sending reinforcements!" Ma Dear sounded like she had her second wind. "So I know You're in this with us. You're not about to let us down. You said if we would ask anything in Jesus' name, You said we would receive and our joy would be complete. Well, we ain't received yet, Lord. But we believe You. We know all Your promises are yes and amen. We know that You're not a man; You can't lie to us."

Shirley could hear hands clapping in the room.

"Lord, You healed the man at Lystra when Paul prayed. You healed the man on the steps of the Temple Beautiful when John and Peter prayed. And Your arm is no shorter than Your Word. You're not a respecter of persons, so if You did it for Peter, John, and Paul—we believe You're going to do it for us. Heal her now, Lord. Let her open her eyes."

Shirley was sure she felt the room shaking, but April didn't seem to notice.

The prayer in the room ebbed and flowed, and the clock seemed to alternately speed up and slow down. Shirley shifted from foot to foot, too anxious to even accept the food that April tried to offer her.

"All right, Miss Prayer Warrior," April grumbled. "Man might not live by bread alone, but we'll see how you're feeling when your stomach is growling. And I promise you I won't be fixing you anything else." April wrapped the tuna fish sandwich in wax paper and stuck it in the refrigerator. "You know where it is when you get hungry." She looked at the room, seemed to be listening to the prayers, then turned up her nose and walked away.

In what seemed to be a few hours, the door opened and Ma Dear, her friend, and June came out. They sat at the table looking tired and confused. They shook their heads, and Ma Dear looked drained. Finally she spoke. "Maybe it's just not His will. Sometimes I felt like something was about to happen. But then, just nothing—like we were blocked, like we couldn't get a breakthrough."

They looked worn.

April walked back into the room. "I've had enough. I want this to stop. This is primitive and ignorant...it's embarrassing! We might as well be swinging from trees. I forbid this. It's got to stop now. June, I want you to cut this out now."

The child killer had been deeply wounded, and he could not stop howling. But he could see darkness falling. He turned his one good eye to try to see what was bringing the sweet darkness. He fell to his knees. It was the prince—his territorial master. And the prince had reinforcements.

The Third Heaven angels, the servants of the Most High God, would not take this one easily. The prince was strong; he was vain and not to be outdone. This battle was not worthy of his power, but Child Killer Shirley was sure he had come because the prince would not see his territory be taken. The child killer rose and threw himself into the battle.

Ma Dear reached out her hands to June and Ely. "Lord, if You want us to continue, we need a sign. We need some help."

April stood off to the side, watching and shaking her head. "Ridiculous. We might as well call for the leeches and the witch doctors."

There was a knock at the door, and April went to answer. It was the man from the grocery store. "I'm sorry to trouble you folks." He was carrying a peach cobbler. "I've been busy at the store and all." He shook his head. "That's just an excuse. I-I-I just felt funny coming, is all. But I just felt like I wasn't going to be able to rest if I didn't come out here and just look at Mother Johnson or maybe offer a word of prayer. I know it probably seems foolish and all, but I just felt like I had to come."

Ma Dear looked up toward heaven. "Well, that's sign enough for me, Lord. A white man out here in this part of Tyler, *and* You sent him with a peach cobbler. That's *most definitely* sign enough for me!" She nodded toward the bedroom. "Come on, you all. We're back on the case." The troupe walked back toward the room.

It was like that for the rest of morning—a woman with a young child and man came by, then a deacon from Mother Johnson's church and his family. They all prayed, inside the house and outside. Some just came for brief moments. Most felt uncertain about why they had come. The phone rang—callers sending messages of prayer.

Each time Ma Dear was spent, someone new would arrive, and she would go back into battle. Until finally, just before noon, Shirley could hear her laughing while she prayed inside Mother Johnson's bedroom. "Lord, You've got to be in this. How could all this happen without You, Lord? We're believing You. We're counting on You, Lord!"

Child Killer Shirley cringed. There was white light around him—and red light, and yellow, and green, and blue, and violet. The unthinkable, the unpredictable, was happening: united prayers. The Second Heaven forces were winning—at least they were not being defeated. True, many of his kind, some that had worked with him in this battle, were no more. But the Host, the angels of the Third Heaven, had also suffered great injury.

And so the forces fought, holding each other to the ground that each had already taken. A standstill, a block…what felt to the soft ones like defeat.

But the multi-colored lights were something different. They foretold worse things to come.

Child Killer Shirley battled on, but he began to look, with his one good eye, for a way of escape.

Shirley began to jump up and down. There seemed to be an electric pulse around her that grew stronger and stronger. She had forgotten about April until she heard her voice. "You better cut that out, young lady! There's enough foolishness going on around here as it is. And after all this, I don't see that anything has changed."

Shirley stood still on the outside, but jumped on the inside.

She jumped inside until Ma Dear and the others came dragging from the room. They were drenched with sweat. Ma Dear

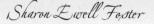

just fell into a chair. "I never had to fight this hard before. We been praying all day. All of us. I just don't understand it. I thought the Lord told me to pray. I thought He told me to come here, that somebody had to pray."

April smirked and rolled her neck. "Well, I *told* you that this was foolishness. I told you that. If anything, you've probably made things worse. You've probably *weakened* my mother with all of this." She pointed at her sister. "And you, of all people, June, should know better. But I tell you what. This little séance is over. Do you understand me? And I want all of you people out of my mother's house. I'm going to call the doctor, and then I'm going to call the police and tell them what's been going on in here." She slammed her hand down on the table in front of Ma Dear. "And especially you! Don't you ever threaten me again. I want you out of here now!"

Ma Dear's head dropped lower. She looked at Ely. "I don't understand. I know I heard the Lord…I thought I heard the Lord." She shook her head and sighed.

Shirley wanted to scream. *Get up! Don't stop now! Don't stop now! Keep pulling against the chains!* But she said nothing.

April pointed her finger at Ma Dear and then at the others. "Didn't I tell you I wanted you to leave? And I didn't say *later,* did I? I said *now.*"

Ma Dear stood up. "Don't you yell at me!" She pointed back in April's face. "I've got something for you."

The others stood up and joined in the fray. There was yelling and stomping.

Shirley walked to the cabinet and took out a large saucepan. She opened the flatware drawer and grabbed a large metal spoon. She walked past the adults and out the door. Shirley walked with her head held high, taking careful steps

312

until she reached the prayer house. She sat on the old, worn pillow where Mother Johnson used to sit, and she began to sing.

"Do Lord, do Lord,
Lord, remember me.
Do Lord, do Lord,
Lord, remember me.
Do Lord, do Lord,
Lord, remember me.
Do Lord, remember me.
When I'm sick and can't get well,
Lord, remember me.
When I'm sick and can't get well,
Lord, remember me.
When I'm sick and can't get well,
Lord, remember me.
Do Lord, remember me."

Shirley sang as loud as she could. *I can't pray, but I can sing. I'm going to sing until she's well.* Then she danced around in the prayer house while she beat the pot. She hollered the song. And then she cried. Cried because there was something stuck in her throat that made it hurt, something that would not come out.

She continued beating the pot so that God would hear her, but she cried. *You can't let her die, Lord. You can't let her die, Lord. Please.* But she was afraid to pray—something made her afraid to pray out loud. Shirley thought of Mother Johnson on the bed. She could see Mother, and it was almost as though she was being held down. Her lips began to move.

And then Shirley heard her own voice. "Don't leave me alone again, Lord!" She yelled the words out between gasps. "Don't let her die! I love her. Please, God. Please." It was like fire in her throat. Shirley beat the pot while she prayed. "Please, God. Please. Mother! Mother! I don't want you to die! Please, God."

She fought for more words...until she began to yell, "'Lift up your heads, O ye gates, and be ye lift up, ye everlasting doors; and the King of glory shall come in. Who is this King of glory? The LORD strong and mighty, the LORD mighty in battle. Lift up your heads, O ye gates; even lift them up, ye everlasting doors; and the King of glory shall come in!'" She gasped for air. "Come in, Lord! Come in, Lord! Please come in!"

Ma Dear ran from the house, the others on her heels, when she heard the child. It was the strangest thing.

Shirley was crying and praying!

"Look at her! Looking and acting more like Mother than Mother does herself," someone in the group said.

The child shouted and danced.

"Not like a young child at all," someone else said. "More like an old woman."

"I didn't even know she could pray," another voice said.

Men, who appeared to be of all nations and all tongues, advanced into the Second Heaven. But they were not normal men; they were illuminated by a glow from within—a glow almost like a flame that changed from green to blue to red to gold. They were taller than normal men, and they swung

314

blades that gleamed with multicolored lights—lights that darkness could not quench. The forces of the Second Heaven began to fall as the Host began to quickly take ground, to defend the children of the Most High God.

The Third Heaven angels fought until they loosed the bands of wickedness. They struggled until they had undone the heavy burdens. The angels of light clashed with the forces of darkness until the oppressed were set free. They continued marching into the enemy's camp until every yoke was broken.

The child killer watched them advance and saw that it was too late. And Child Killer Shirley knew that he was gone just before he was no more.

"You all come quick!"

Ma Dear turned her head toward the house when she heard the call. A woman standing in the doorway waved to them.

"Great God from Zion! Come see it for yourself!"

Ma Dear started running, but Shirley ran past them all.

When Ma Dear reached the house, Shirley was crying and cradled in Mother Johnson's arms. Mother was laying back on the pillow, but her eyes were open and alive. As she sobbed, Shirley cried out over and over again, "Thank You, God! I believe! Thank You, God! I believe!"

THIRTY-ONE

eeks later, when Mother Johnson was feeling better, when her daughters were gone home, when Ma Dear only visited twice a day, Mother patted the bed next to her and told Shirley to come close.

Shirley climbed onto the bed and did what she had been doing for days—she cried. Mother kissed the top of her head and held her close. "You've just been pouring out a fountain, day and night, these past days. What's wrong?"

Shirley shook her head. She didn't want the words to come out of her throat.

"Well, I guess we're just going to be sitting here till kingdom come, because we're not moving from here until you talk to me."

Her tears stopped, but her voice was just a whisper. "I almost killed you. I ran away and I almost killed you."

"Is that what you think? Is that why you're wasting all that water?"

Mother pulled her even closer, and the smell of her dusting powder comforted Shirley.

"I don't know if someone told you that, or if you just came

317

up with that bright idea on your own." One of her hands stroked Shirley's cheek. "But I've been meaning for us to talk about this. I waited because I wanted for us to talk about it when it was just the two of us. I'm not sure if you're going to understand all this, but I need you to promise me that you are going to remember what I say to you here today."

Shirley didn't want to talk. She didn't want to remember.

"I need you to promise me, Shirley." She nodded and Mother Johnson patted her side. "God knew us and all places on the earth before we were even formed. And as long as we are here, there will always be a struggle between good and evil. But there's going to come a time when God says, 'That's it. This battle is about to end.' God already chose the place for the final battle between good and evil. He chose the place because it was perfect—a perfect place for the final battle, for the final war. God chose the place even before the world began."

Shirley tried to bury her face in Mother Johnson's side. She did not want to hear about wars or battles, about people dying.

"When good and evil meet at that place—a place called Armageddon—the ground there is going to be torn and scorched. Some people are going to shake their heads and wonder what did Armageddon ever do to be torn and shaken so. But God will know that the place was chosen because it was the perfect place for a heavenly battle to be fought here on earth. God knows it is a chosen place of honor."

Shirley didn't understand it all, but something about what Mother Johnson said disturbed her, and she closed her eyes.

Mother laid her hand gently on Shirley's hair. "You know, Shirley, God's angels and the devil's angels are fighting battles in heaven all the time. Mostly God's angels are fighting to defend us, to redeem us and deliver us after we've got ourselves in trouble because of wrong we've done down here. They've got to fight in heaven to free us when we're in trouble because we've been lying too much, drinking too much, when we fearing too much. God has mercy on us and sends the Heavenly Host to fight and free us from chains in the heavens that keep us bound down here. That's why we got to pray all the time—our prayers keep things moving, keep the angels fighting on our behalf.

"Sometimes they are defending us from something that someone else has done to us that has caused us to be oppressed or bound up. Angels are fighting all the time to deliver us."

Mother squeezed her, kissed her, then went on talking. "But sometimes, there are battles that begin in the heavens—heavenly battles between good and evil. Battles between God and the devil—between the biggest good and the biggest evil—can't be fought in heaven. Not now; it's not the appointed time. If they fight the big battle too soon, it would tear the world apart before time. So God and the devil have to find a perfect place down here—an earthly place to have those heavenly battles. And sometimes a man is that perfect place.

"There was a man in the Bible named Job, and Job was a perfect place. Job suffered and lost everything he had. He got torn and scorched, just like Armageddon. And his friends gathered round and shook their heads, wondering what Job had done wrong. But I believe that God chose Job as a battleground way before the world began. Mother Johnson ain't no preacher, but you hear what I say now: Job was a chosen place, a perfect place for good and evil to face off. What Job suffered was a battle between good and evil fought right where he lived, right in his body, right in his heart and mind. And when he yielded up himself and said, 'God, I'm Yours. Use me how You want to; do with me what You want to. I'll do what You tell me to do,' Job did what the Lord knew he would do way before time began. That's why he was a perfect place. And the Lord honored Job, made him better than he was at the first. Just like I believe the Lord is going to do Armageddon, because God is a God of justice and restoration."

Shirley shook her head. "I don't understand, Mother. Don't tell me any more."

"I know you might not understand now, but Mother is not always going to be with you. And I need to tell you this now because you're going to need it later. Sometime when I might not be around."

Shirley wiggled her body until she was up under the covers with Mother.

"Sometimes we are the perfect place for a battle. When you are the chosen place—and you were chosen before the world began—you friends won't understand what's happening to you. No matter how you search and pray, the battle won't be because of something you've done wrong. You'll be a Job battlefield, an Armageddon battlefield, a person already trying to walk godly and righteous before the Lord. That's why you'll be so confused by the battle when it comes. But you just remember Job and that you must *stand*.

"You will find yourself pulled and tossed, and you will feel like you've been abandoned. You'll cry, and it will seem like the Lord just won't come—because you are the perfect place, the strong place, and the Lord cannot yield the battle because it is about something greater than you. And you won't feel like it, but remember that you are a person chosen and honored. The Lord chose you because He knows your will is His and that you will love Him and stand, even when you want to fall. Yield to the Lord quickly. Let Him have His way. Remember that you are chosen and that you will endure.

"Because in the end, when you feel as if you have died, the Lord will come to give you life again. And the battle fought in your perfect place will have delivered others—maybe some folks you don't even know. And then God will make your latter days better than your first, just like He did for Job."

Mother rocked her back and forth. "So, no, baby. You didn't almost kill me. What happened to me, what happened to all of us, was bigger than we can explain. But God is all-powerful. He is sovereign, and what we don't understand now we have to lay at His feet, knowing that He is all good and He loves us. We will understand it better by and by."

Shirley held tightly to Mother Johnson, who rocked her until she fell asleep. In her sleep she thought she heard Mother singing.

"Hallelujah, troubles over…"

THIRTY-TWO

May 1977

Shirley looked in the mirror as she pushed the back of her earring into place. She reached on the dresser, lifted her pick to her hair, and shaped her Afro until it crowned her face.

"Shirley! Come on here, girl!"

Shirley smiled. Mother Johnson's voice sounded as strong and as deep as ever. The sickness she had suffered almost ten years ago seemed like a dream, as if it had never really happened. Shirley could hear Mother moving toward the front door.

"Shake a leg, girl. You're going to miss the prom—and here comes that boy up the sidewalk, looking like he's afraid his creases are going to crack if he steps too hard."

Ma Dear and her husband were laughing in the background. "You know that child is slow as molasses!" Ma Dear giggled. "And that boy is just as worried as he ever was. They make quite a pair, if I do say so myself."

Shirley dropped the pick and walked to her bedroom window, lifting the curtain so she could see Tony. A gold medallion swung from a chain around his neck and bobbed with each step he took. *Good!* The bell-bottom pants to his powder blue tuxedo ended just before the toe of his shoe. "Make sure your pants aren't high-waters," she had told him when they had discussed what they were going to wear. The blue he wore matched the ribbon that trimmed her white gown.

Turning away from the window, she walked back to the mirror and smiled at her image. Shirley thought she heard the front door open and close.

Mother Johnson was so excited about the prom. *"I never thought I would see the day when Negro children—I mean black children—would be going to John Tyler high school, let alone to the prom."* Mother had clapped her hands together.

If only Mama could see her...and Daddy. If only there had been no Vietnam. Then they all would have been there with her. She could imagine Big Uncle lifting her into the air so that her gown drifted around them...and she could see Little Uncle smiling at her while he tried to sneak peeks at the TV news. And, for just a moment, she thought about Sheri...

The doorbell rang, and Shirley reached for her shawl. There was no point in worrying about them—not tonight anyway. She hadn't heard anything about any of them in years, and wishing and crying would not bring them back. Some things you just had to let go.

"Shirley! Shirley!"

She shook her head. There was no need for Mother to get excited. It was just Tony, and prom or not, Mother knew Shirley was on the way. Mother always knew everything.

"Come to the door. It's for you."

She checked her hair one last time. "I'm coming, Mother. Tell Tony to hold his horses. I'm coming." When she stepped into the living room, Mother Johnson stood facing the doorway with the strangest expression on her face. Mother motioned for Shirley to come closer until she could see.

The man in the doorway—Shirley turned her head slightly and noticed Tony sitting on the couch—wore a uniform. "The delivery on this is restricted," the man said. "I can only release it to Shirley Ferris. It's from East St. Louis, Illinois"

Shirley looked at Mother Johnson. The letter could change the whole evening—could make it brighter or turn it to gray. No…not the evening. Her life. It could change her life. She hesitated. *Do I want to open it?* Maybe she could refuse it and leave things as they were, leave things safe. Shirley swallowed. Mother Johnson nodded at her, then toward the deliveryman.

Shirley turned to the man, oddly aware that her future had come to call, and held out her hand.

Multnomah Publishers
The publisher and author would love to hear your comments about this book. *Please contact us at:*
www.multnomah.net/sharonfoster

Watch for the dramatic conclusion of
Shirley's story in the upcoming *Passing into Light*,
due out 2002.

ONE

Huntsville, Alabama, 1986

The silver Toyota Corolla clipped down the road. Shirley was making good time and had long since kissed Highway 55 good-bye. Mika and Lex were curled up in each other's arms—at least as much as the seat belts would allow—sleeping and drooling.

They would cross through Texarcana, and Shirley's plan was to drive straight through.

That was the plan before the police car stopped her.

"Where're you on your way to so fast, lady?" The policeman leaned into the window and looked closely at her, then at the children lying in the back. Shirley could see the other policeman in the patrol car and assumed he was running her plates. "You were going pretty fast. This one's going to cost you."

Her heart was thumping as though she had committed a crime—a greater crime than speeding. "We're on our way to California."

"California?" She heard the inquiry in the state trooper's

voice but wasn't sure how to respond, so she just nodded.

A voice from the other side of the car startled her. It was the other trooper. "Well, it looks like your trip is going to be delayed a little. You're going to have to come with us."

"What's wrong? What did I do? What about my kids? What about my car?" She could feel her cool exterior falling apart.

"Just calm down, lady. The kids will come with us," the second officer said from behind his dark shades. "We'll just go to the station, check out what needs to be checked out, and we'll take it from there. We'll leave your car here." He tipped his glasses so that he could see over the rim. "We should be putting you in cuffs, ma'am—" Shirley's heart jumped—"but we won't, out of respect for the children and until we can get this cleared up. But if I were you, I would be thinking about who I could call to bail me out and to come and get my kids."

As they rode, Shirley thought of every story she had heard about criminals masquerading as cops. How stupid she had been to go along with these men! She was too scared to even ask what she was being taken in for—to even ask why she was being taken to the station, why she would need to be bailed out, or why she would need someone to get her kids. How did she even know who they were? They might not be troopers— but imposters. She looked around the backseat. It was too late now. She and Mika and Lex were locked in.

Mika and Lex looked frightened. Their clothes and their faces were wrinkled with sleep. Shirley forced herself to smile at them. "Isn't this neat? I always wondered what the inside of a police car looked like," she lied. "Don't worry. Mommy's got everything under control. There's just some paperwork to complete. That's all." She hugged them until they pulled into town.

The police station was small. Somehow it reminded her of

Tyler. Everything outside was brown. A battered brown pickup truck pulled up beside them—it looked like a utility truck. A girl with dirty hair hopped out of the passenger's side. She looked dazed. There was a long, bleeding cut on her face. The man that got out of the driver's side door was also young, but he looked angry. His hair was almost the same color as the girl's, but he was balding prematurely on top. He stomped around the side of the car, his stomach pulling against his pizza delivery shirt, grabbed the girl's arm, and almost dragged her into the station.

"She's a thief!" He cursed at the two policemen. The girl said nothing in her own defense. She just stumbled along while the angry young man jerked at her arm. "I caught her red-handed. Stealing tips and money from the cash register. Hard-earned money—money *I* earned." He spit on the ground. "And she's stealing."

The inside of the station was another shade, a lighter shade, of the brown exterior. "It always happens this way." The first trooper nodded at the young man. "We're quiet and nothing is going on—" he shook his hands in the air—"then it's a three-ring circus." He motioned to Shirley to sit on a bench, then motioned for the pale-haired girl to sit on a bench across from her. The girl's lip was starting to swell.

The three men walked to a desk and stood talking, looking occasionally in the direction of Shirley and the girl. The trooper with the shades had them perched on top of his head. He sat down and started making phone calls. In between murmurings, sometimes the three of them would explode with laughter as though they were old friends.

Shirley kept her arms around Mika and Lex. She made small talk about where they were going tonight, what they would do when they got there.

After what seemed to be an hour, the first trooper approached them. "Well, ladies. We're having trouble getting through to folks we need to talk to to get things squared up. So we're just going to let the two of you cool off in the holding cell until we can get things cleared up."

The girl protested. "Well, if you put me in, you need to put *him* in. Maybe I stole a few lousy bucks—I ain't sayin' I did and I ain't sayin' I didn't—but he beat me up. What about that? You see this blood running down my face, don'tcha?"

The young man stepped toward them, raging. "She's a lyin' thief! I never laid a hand on her. She ran into a wall trying to get away."

"Right! And you're John Travolta!" The girl stuck her chin out.

"All right, miss," the cop with the shades called from the chair where he sat with his ear to the phone. "You just calm down!"

"She's the thief, and now she's trying to ruin my reputation." The young man shrugged at the trooper on the phone, as though to show he had calmed down and it was no big deal.

Shirley wasn't sure if she should speak or not, if her talking might make things worse. "What about my kids?" she whispered to the trooper who held her arm to pull her to her feet.

"They'll be okay. If we have to detain you much longer, we'll call social services. For right now, they'll be okay where they are."

"What am I being detained for? Why can't I just pay the fine and go?"

He narrowed his eyes. "Don't get cute, lady. There's a car missing just like the one you're driving. We just need to get

confirmation on the license plate number. So don't play inno-
cent. Things will go better if you just stay quiet."

The cell was dark, with bars, just like the ones on television.
The trooper unlocked the door. "You two girls play nice in
here." He chuckled as he walked away.

Shirley felt as though she were running out of air, as though
she were in *The Twilight Zone,* as though she were behind the
great rock at the end of her street. She looked at every corner
trying to find meaning, to explain what was happening. Panic
was overtaking her, and she wanted to scream. She closed her
eyes, and it was as if she could see Mika and Lex huddled
together on the police station bench.

Shirley looked at the girl. The girl reminded her of someone. Some of her hair had fallen on to her face, and she seemed
to be playing a game, blowing it off. Shirley felt overwhelmed.
"O God, help me." She closed her eyes.

She must have fallen asleep, because she suddenly saw a
light and heard a voice that spoke to her, but not in words.
And in that light was what seemed to a presence…like a
woman, but Shirley was not sure.

"It's going to be all right," the light said. "There is a great
journey before you—a great work for you to do. And you will
not be alone where you go. Come, let me show you." The light
took her hand, and Shirley could feel herself being lifted higher
and higher. "And we will go higher, still." The light held her
hand, and they drifted high over the treetops until it was
almost as though they could see the earth bend. "We're going
higher than we've ever been. And you will not be alone. Don't
be afraid."

Someone shook her shoulder, and Shirley realized her head had been nodding. "Come on, lady. You need to get out of here before your car gets towed from out front. We won't be responsible if you're car gets towed. We had it brought down here, but we're not responsible beyond that."

It was the policeman who had locked them in the cell, and he was holding the girl by the arm. "Everything checked out. We got a call about a robbery not far from here. You fit the description, but…" He shrugged his shoulders. "And we've got work to do, so the two of you need to get out of here."

"That's it?" Shirley frowned.

He cocked his head. "You got something else you want to tell me, lady?"

She stood up quickly and walked out the door and into her children's arms. The left the station. Together they walked past the girl who stood on the sidewalk, looking lost and confused.

"Just get out of town," Shirley had heard the policemen tell the girl. *"If we see you here at daylight, we've got the perfect apartment just waiting for you."*

Shirley, Mika, and Lex quickly packed themselves into the car. Shirley couldn't wait to leave Texas behind her. Mother Johnson would have to wait until another time. Shirley and her children had had about all of Texas that they could bear.

"Miss?"

Shirley turned at the voice and the hand that tapped her on the shoulder.

"Miss, can you give me a lift out of town? I need—if I can just get back home. I never should have come here in the first place." The girl's eyes were a clear, almost crystal blue. And Shirley felt again that there was something familiar about her. "Please," the girl begged. "I won't give you no trouble."

"Where is home?" *Why are you even talking to her? She's a thief. And you've got two kids in the car.* "How far away is your home?" Her mouth was speaking on its own, as though she had lost control.

"Tyler," the girl said. "I'm from Tyler, Texas. The rose capital of the world."

Shirley closed her eyes briefly and sighed. She motioned to the passenger's side. "Get in."

Something foul sat in the top of the trees and grinned at Shirley, at the four of them riding in the car. It was not over. She might have defeated the child killer. She might even have been able to free the old one. But it was not over. There was still a plan, and he had been sent to carry it out. He was stronger and more clever than the child killer.

He was prepared to battle. And in the end, he would not lose.

Dear Readers,

My prayer is that this book will reach you just in time, just when you need it—or just when someone you know and love (or someone you're having difficulty loving) needs it.

Most of my life I have lived with a profound sadness on the inside of me, a sadness that was most times a physical ache. Not only was I sad, but sometimes I was also insecure, angry, lonely, and confused, and I didn't know why. I don't remember ever not feeling heartbroken. I felt unloved. But as a child I learned that it was unacceptable to express my sorrow or my rage, so I hid it behind masks of perpetual joy, confidence, pride, and perfectionism.

As I grew older I searched for cures that would ease the *dis-ease* I felt on the inside. I thought romance—a man's love—would fix me and make me feel better, but it didn't. (Broken people attract other broken people, but lack the power to deliver each other.) I tried counselors, a little alcohol, a little sex, a little bit of drugs, a lot of food, withdrawal, children, education, a career, promotions, and money. I tried looking perfect and/or not looking perfect…but none of it really worked. Some things I tried didn't work at all, and I let go of them right away. Some dulled the pain a little, so I held on to them a little tighter. Some things I tried made me feel a little better, so I sucked the life out of them because I had very little to offer in return.

Ultimately, I learned that none of the solutions I tried helped permanently. I even tried going to church. I don't remember a time in my life when I didn't know the Lord—I've always been in a pew somewhere. But just going to church didn't seem to fix what ailed me.

What helped me was intimacy with God through His Son,

Jesus Christ...intimacy, where I learned to speak openly with the Creator about my fears, about my pains, about my longings. And that intimacy is about more than just sitting in a pew in church. It was being able to sit in my Father's lap and show Him my wounds that healed me. It was believing that He loved me and that He could and would heal me that allowed Him to work a miracle in my life. It was intimate conversation with God, prayer—conversation with God where I let down my walls and opened my heart so that God could speak back to me—that delivered me. It was learning to trust and obey His voice that lit the pathway...trusting that He would lead me out, no matter how long it took...that led me out of the shadows.

That's why I write what I write. No pew, no pill, no drug, no therapist, no job, no lover, ever really made it better. I write because I am grateful for a love that is strong enough to heal. When you see me smiling now, it comes from way down deep on the inside of me. When you feel peace around me, it comes from a spring far too deep for me to describe.

If beer had healed me, had delivered me, I'd be writing about beer. But beer couldn't do it. If Mary Magdalene was healed from seven demons, I can be too...and I know their names—Fear, Anger, and Depression are among them. And like Mary, I am so grateful that I have come to lay my best gift at the Master's feet, to cry tears of joy and rub them in with my hair.

I don't write to attempt to FORCE anyone to believe what I believe. I write to show my scars, so that people will know that I was once wounded, but now I am healed...so that others will know, even while they are being entertained by the reading, that there is a cure that works. My broken heart is healed, and I have something to give to others, something that has the power to heal and restore. I have great love.

Not even my family knows how sad, angry, and confused I was. So this book and the one that will follow are my testimony to my mother, my father, and my brothers so they will know that I have been made whole. This book is for others who are tormented so they will know that there is a way out of darkness. This book is for those who have the responsibility to lead others out of darkness through prayer, art, preaching, and other callings.

This book is to remind all of us not to give up hope…not to give up the battle. There is a Heavenly Host fighting on our behalf, and, if we don't faint, they will deliver us—we will win. There is a marvelous light.

I am living proof.